I0822525

BLACK BART

A STORY FROM
"A FEW BRAVE MEN"

—A NOVEL

iBooks
Manhanset House
Shelter Island Hts., New York 11965
Tel: 212-427-7139
bricktower@aol.com • www.ibooksinc.com

Library of Congress Cataloging-in-Publication Data

Taylor, John R.
Black Bart, A Novel
p. cm.

1. Fiction—General 2. Fiction—Thriller 3. Fiction—Military
3. Fiction—Vietnamese War
Fiction, I. Title.

ISBN: 978-1-59687-978-2, Hardcover
978-1-59687-985-0 Trade Paper

December 2021

BLACK BART

A STORY FROM "A FEW BRAVE MEN"

—A NOVEL

John R. "Rick" Taylor

iBooks
Habent Sua Fata Libelli

AUTHOR OF *GRUNT AIR*
A FEW BRAVE MEN
THE CAVES

Author's Website:

http://www.afbm-blackbart.com/

Dedication

This book is dedicated to my business partner and very good friend Bill Merritt also referred to as The Professor (ala *Shoe*). He has been working with me for over a quarter of a century during the good, the bad and the ugly of times. Lord knows there has been a lot of ugly! We yell and scream at each other like we are brothers, but in the end, we usually have created something exceptionally good. I could not ask for a better friend than Bill.

Now onward in search for the *good*. It must be out there somewhere.

Thanks Bill

Acknowledgments

I want to thank Jim Darnell for his support in all the Grunt Air books. His assistance and moral support have meant a lot to me and this effort. Many thanks to Terri Hamilton and Mark McGreevey for your efforts in making this book a reality.

Prologue

In the two decades that separated World Wars One and Two, America felt insulated from the troubled world outside by the vast Pacific Ocean lying beyond her Western reaches and the cold, gray Atlantic on the East. Friendly nations blocked her Northern and Southern approaches.

But even while airplanes were still being built from spruce and canvas, pioneer airmen like America's General Billy Mitchell and Italy's General Giulio Douhet began to catch visionary glimpses of the airplane's emerging potential to traverse oceans … and continents. Their subsequent theories of strategic bombardment and aerial supremacy were strange to the average American who still equated aviation with the single engine biplanes that landed in local cow pastures and took him for death defying rides - all for one dollar! How could these strange contraptions carry tons of bombs thousands of miles deep into an enemy's homeland, destroy his industrial capacity to supply his military forces in far flung fields of battle … and along with it, even destroy the enemy's will to make war?

Both Mitchell and Douhet were highly vocal in their prophecies that the airplane would change the entire structure of conventional warfare. They reasoned that since air supremacy was obviously becoming vital to a nation's successful conduct of war, then air power ought to be placed on an equal and independent parity with that nation's land and sea power. The impact the Mitchell-Douhet theories had on old line Army generals and Navy admirals was cataclysmic! They immediately saw everything, from their politically authorized operating and procurement budgets to their century's old methods of waging wars, threatened by the radical and unproven thrust of air power.

They fought to subordinate the emerging aviation technology to a mere supporting role, to contain it within the framework of their existing, conventional military operations. Mitchell was soon court marshaled. The battle was on!

Not even a global war would still the raging tempest of political and inter-service debate stirred by that early advent of air power. A few brave men, sixteen hundred more or less, made up the commissioned officers' ranks of the United States Army Air Corps in its early days. A relatively insignificant division of the United States Army, the Air Corps was dominated by Army Ground Commanders who had little, if any, expertise in the evolving art of aviation.

But ... that little handful of officers and men worked courageously toward the day when their beloved Air Corps would become an independent branch of the nation's armed forces, commanded by professional airmen who understood the advancing technology of air power and could develop an Air Force which would successfully meet the challenges that the inexorable forces of history and technology were shaping for it.

This is one of very many stories of individual and collective excellence and courage during this troubled period in history.

A Funny Thing Happened To Me On The Way To War

Major John C. Kennedy and a stocky First Lieutenant stood on the tarmac of Brooks Field in Texas watching the repeated flawless landings of a Thomas-Morse O-19 observation plane. After a full stop landing, the plane taxied over to the two officers and turned off the engine. The pilot, Samuel Barton Coltrane, an athletic built black-haired Second Lieutenant, approached the two men and saluted. "Pardon me, Major," he said with true military protocol, "have you given any thought to my request for reassignment to Bombers?"

The major looked into the hazel eyes of the nearly 6-foot aviator. "Bart, you really want to go from this agile 134 miles an hour observation aircraft to that lumbering LB7 Keystone Bomber? You know that damned thing is like flying an outhouse at a max speed of 95 miles an hour."

"Yes sir, I do. When the war comes, that monster and the new B-17 will be in the thick of things. That's where the action will be and that's where I want to be."

The First Lieutenant took the stubby unlit cigar out of his mouth and said, "So you think a lot of the role bombers will play in combat."

Before Bart Coltrane could reply, Major Kennedy interrupted, "Bart, let me introduce you to First Lieutenant Curtis Lemay. Curt is here to get a checkout in the O-19 before he goes to the Second Bomber Group."

Kennedy resumed, "Lemay here is a great pilot and an even better navigator but has the control touch of a gorilla when it comes to the O-19. Think you could help him?" Again, before Coltrane could reply, he added "Make you a deal. If you can get that control grip problem resolved within two days, I'll get you transferred to Bombers."

"Deal!" exclaimed Bart, who was more commonly referred to by his peers as Black Bart. "Lieutenant Lemay, give me ten minutes for a pit stop and to get my training aid, and we will go make smooth holes in the sky."

Bart took off at a run to the operations office latrine and came back on a slow trot to his aircraft. A couple of minutes later, he went to the two aviators and said, "Sir, we are ready when you are, this shouldn't take more than an hour."

Lemay looked at Major Kennedy without expression or comment, then started walking to the observation plane. As he got in, Coltrane came up to him and took away the flight gloves normally used by Army Air Corps pilots. This didn't faze Lemay until he started to reach for the control stick, his hand stopped when he saw that it had been wrapped with Texas barbed wire. "What the hell is this, Lieutenant?" Lemay said in a loud and gruff voice.

"Sir, that's my control touch training aid and every time you squeeze or jerk the control stick, you're gonna know it," Coltrane said with a positive tone. "It won't hurt if you are gentle, sir."

The aircraft took off and flew a series of maneuvers, turns and normal combat tactics before returning to the airfield. After five touch and go landings and takeoffs that got better with each succeeding attempt, the plane turned off the runway and went back to the waiting Major Kennedy. Coltrane and Lemay went over to Kennedy. Lemay had a slightly blood-soaked rag in his right hand.

Kennedy looked at Lemay and said, "Was that you or Bart making those landings?"

Bart interjected, "Those were all his landings, sir."

Lemay took the cigar out of his mouth and said, "If the 7th Bomb Group doesn't have a position for him, I will find one for him in the 2nd Bomb Group. He knows his aircraft and can fly it very well. He sure taught me a lot in a short period. Thanks to both of you for helping me on this transition. I'll be headed for home base." He saluted the Major then extended his left hand to shake Bart's. "Thanks, I meant it. If you want to fly for me in the 2nd Bomb Group, let me know." He turned and started walking away.

Bart and Major Kennedy stood there watching the departing Lemay. Kennedy then commented, "There is a man that will someday make aviation history."

Bart then quipped, "Not before his hand heals."

Chapter One

It was a hot and humid early morning in August 1937. Six B-17's gracefully pulled up to park at Oakland Airfield, and the pilots applied the brakes as their noses came even with each other. The engines ran up, and then the switches were cut. Several Army mechanics approached the fortress with wheel chocks, and one, an engineering officer, stood waiting expectantly as the crew members began dropping from the nose hatches of the aircraft. Lieutenant Colonel Olds approached the engineering officer, followed by three officers. Among the crew members dropping out of the B-17 hatch was First Lieutenant Curtis Lemay, the navigator.

"You got here from Phoenix earlier than we expected," the engineer officer said.

"How long to gas up and get our training bombs loaded?" Olds asked in a hurried tone.

"Maybe an hour." Colonel Olds turned to a crew member. "Lieutenant Jinkins, stay on the radio."

By this time, the rest of the crew members from the six ships had gathered around. Colonel Olds looked at them and nodded.

"The rest of you grab breakfast." He looked at his watch "I want everybody back here at ten hundred hours. I'm gonna check in with the Navy and see if they are ready to do this war game exercise." Concern was visible on his face.

Colonel Olds walked away, and the crew members began to do the same. A gas truck approached the aircraft, and several mechanics pushed a cart loaded with practice bombs. They passed the crew from the lead aircraft. Lieutenant Kilpatrick, the bombardier, and Lieutenant Lemay, the navigator, passed by and looked at the type of bombs on the cart. Both men immediately became perplexed. Lieutenant Kilpatrick turned to a Corporal, one of the men pushing the cart.

"Where the hell did you get those?"

The Corporal stopped in his tracks. "Navy sent them over, sir!"

"The Navy? Where are the practice bombs, we sent out?" Lieutenant Kilpatrick asked.

The Corporal shrugged. "We were told that we gotta use these, sir."

Lieutenant Kilpatrick shook his head in disbelief as the mechanic moved away with the cart. He and Lemay followed the other crew members to get breakfast and go over the war game rules.

Lieutenant Lemay gazed up at the overcast sky. "We'll be lucky if we have a five-hundred-foot ceiling out there."

A crew member entered the aircraft through the fuselage hatch that led to the radio operations area. He was carrying a paper coffee cup and a doughnut, which he gave to Lieutenant Jinkins who was still monitoring the radio.

"Colonel Olds wants you down there."

The Lieutenant took the coffee and stood up to leave. "Thanks."

The six crew members of the lead bomber Flagship 1 assembled in front of the lead B-17 as the Lieutenant joined them, sipping his coffee.

"Gentlemen," Olds said in a strong voice, "I just want to remind you how important our mission here is." He looked at each crew member. "You all know your jobs."

"What about those bombs the Navy sent over?" Lieutenant Kilpatrick asked.

"What about them?"

"Well, they have a different trajectory than the type we've been using in practice."

Colonel Olds grinned. "Well, Kilpatrick, the Navy holds all the cards in this game. They have stacked the deck in every way against us. However," he looked at the overcast sky. "Maybe we'll be too close to miss!"

The crew members laughed.

"Here's the plan," Colonel Olds said. "Sometime this morning, before the exercise begins at twelve hundred hours, the Navy will radio the fleet location, heading and speed to us here. We'll take off immediately." Colonel Olds turned to Lemay. "Lieutenant Lemay will calculate our heading to intercept the fleet, probably three or four hundred miles out to sea."

"What about formations, radio frequencies and search patterns?" Lemay asked.

"They'll all be exactly as rehearsed and as briefed this morning in Phoenix," Colonel Olds said. "The battleship Utah is our target. It will be flying the international preparatory pennant as a means of positive identification. It's been especially rigged for this exercise. Personnel will have been notified of our approach and will have taken appropriate cover."

The crew members began to smile.

"*Do not bomb any other vessels in the fleet,*" Colonel Olds said with emphasis.

A Navy Lieutenant came to stand beside him, and Colonel Olds gestured to him.

"Lieutenant Michaels, on loan from the Navy, will be on my ship to assist with identification. I want every man in his aircraft ready for immediate take off the minute we receive the fleet location. The exercise begins as twelve noon today and ends at twelve noon tomorrow."

The crew members listened closely to Colonel Olds' words and their facial expression registered their reactions.

"If we fail to locate the Utah and successfully bomb it in that time frame, we'll have forfeited the exercise." Olds frowned, "that would be a severe disappointment to me … and to General Andrews. The credibility of aerial bombardment and our future funding depends on our success. "He looked at his watch. "My time is ... five minutes past the hour of ten. Good hunting, gentlemen."

The crew sauntered out to their ships. Lemay settled down at the navigator's table and began to arrange the instruments for ready use. The clock on the navigator's panel read ten minutes past ten. When the clock read twelve noon, Colonel Olds put his arm out the window and tapped the side glass, impatiently. The pilot's head was resting against the back rest, his eyes closed in an attempt to catch a short nap before the mission. Olds pulled the side glass closed and turned to the co-pilot.

"Let's get airborne," Colonel Olds said. "We can get the Navy radio message on our way out. I don't trust the Navy to pull some trick on us."

"Stand by to start engines," the co-pilot said.

The engines of the three aircraft began belching smoke and flame then roaring to life. Lemay's head emerges into the cockpit.

"What's the heading, Colonel?' Lemay asked.

"West," Colonel Olds said.

The lead B-17 lifted off with the other two B-17's following close by. While the pilot did his best to stay out of the low hanging clouds, Lemay studied his navigation chart and looked at the course steered by the squadron of B-17's, turning here and there in various headings that extended out from the take off point, altogether an obvious dead reckoning plot problem. All at once the pilot took the formation through the overcast and above the cloud tops. After a little over an hour the crew started to look for a break in the overcast to descend through so they could start a search pattern for the Utah.

The co-pilot pointed to his right. "There's a hole over there."

Colonel Olds nodded "Yeah."

Olds' B-17 turned towards the hole in the cloud layer and the Colonel looked out the window and looked at the large hole in the cloud layer and the ocean far below. He turned to the co-pilot but did not speak. The radio crackled to life and the radio operator scrawled the Morse Code message which read as follows: *Flagship 1 from Navy station six-five. Fleet position to follow.*" The radio operator flipped a switch. "They're transmitting fleet position now, Colonel."

He glanced at his watch. "I got it," Colonel Olds said. He glanced at his co-pilot. "Four hours late!"

After Lieutenant Lemay finished his calculations, he spoke over the intercom. "Our heading will be two-one-zero degrees, three-zero minutes to intercept. Execute turn to heading two-one-zero in one minute."

"Tempest Flight … this is Flagship 1," Colonel Olds said. "Come left to a heading of two-one-zero degrees, for three-zero minutes. Stand by … execute!"

The B-17 moved away in a sweeping turn.

"Lemay, how far to the target?" Colonel Olds asked.

"About one hundred seventy-five miles, sir."

"How much daylight left when we get there?"

Lemay spoke into the intercom. "Half hour or so."

The Navy observer was silent and stayed as far back as he could.

The sun began to descend into the heavy cloud layer stretched out toward the distant horizon and the sound of the B-17's engine filled the sky. Colonel Olds' eyes searched the horizon, and then he spoke into the intercom.

"Tempest Flight … this is Flagship 1. We're gonna have to look down there. Hold your altitude until we break out."

The front section of Olds' B-17 began to plow through the cloud layer. The distant gray cloud layer hovered four or five hundred feet over the ocean surface. The B-17 emerged eerily through the bottom of the cloud layer in the distance. Colonel Olds watched as the clouds began to disappear, and then he spoke into the intercom again.

"Tempest Flight … this is Flagship 1. Come on down … EASY! Only four hundred feet to play with down here."

In the navigator's compartment of Colonel Olds' B-17 Lieutenant Lemay continued to plot the heading, the dead reckoning plot looking like a jig saw puzzle. The clock read seventeen hundred hours and twenty minutes later … and then the clock read eighteen hundred hours. Anger began to show on Colonel Olds' face as he gazed out the cockpit, ahead and to the side.

"Where are they, Lemay?" Olds asked sarcastically.

Lemay worriedly rechecked his dead reckoning line "We ought to be right over them."

Colonel Olds raised his voice. "Nothing down there but white caps and a couple of lovesick whales, Lieutenant!"

Lemay was determined to remain in control of his emotions. "We can set up a search square. We've got a half an hour of daylight left."

"Set it up!"

On the flight deck of Flagship 4, both pilots scanned the ocean surface intently. The pilot gazed out at the ocean which stretched out cold and gray below, white caps breaking across its surface in turbulent troughs.

In Colonel Olds' B-17 he scanned the surface below and Lemay leaned back from his chart, glanced at his watch, then out at the gathering dusk.

"We better break off, Colonel," Lemay said. "It's getting too dark."

Olds spoke wearily into the microphone. "What's the heading back to Oakland, Lemay?"

"Zero-nine-six degrees, for three-seven minutes," Lemay said.

Colonel Olds spoke again, his voice filled with disappointment. "Flagship One, break off! Turn zero-nine-six degrees, form up on me ... going home."

Lemay took out the bubble sextant and stood it up to take a celestial reading. At that moment Colonel Olds entered the compartment. Lemay knew how disappointed the Colonel was and understood how he felt and would be patient with him.

"Lemay, why didn't we find the fleet? Something smells rotten in this exercise and the stink floats!"

Lemay turned to Olds, the sextant still in his hand. "Well, they weren't where they said they'd be, Colonel. I'm gonna double check our position. But if I was right … the course I gave you … we should be seeing the lights of San Francisco any minute now." Lemay pointed to that position on the chart with his forefinger, indicating San Francisco.

Colonel Olds looked him in the eye, "You better be right, Lieutenant."

Olds left the Navigator's compartment and Lemay continued with his celestial shots. When Olds entered the cockpit, he found the co-pilot pointing off to his right at San Francisco and the California coastline ahead and below.

"San Francisco," the co-pilot said.

Colonel Olds smiled broadly. The co-pilot, having been instructed to proceed to Sacramento, glanced at Olds, who still had a big smile on his face.

* * *

The early morning sunlight was starting to light up the airfield in Sacramento. The crew members were spread out on the concrete floor, of the hanger, sleeping on blankets and life jackets. Colonel Olds entered the hangar, found Lemay, and roused him with his foot. Lemay rose up sleepily.

"How about breakfast, Lieutenant?"

Lemay shook his head to clear the sleep away and stifled a yawn as he stood up. They began to walk away.

"You were right, you know," Colonel Olds said.

Lemay looked at Olds, a grin playing at his lips.

"I've been up all night talking to Navy people," Olds said. "The position they gave us was one degree off. That put us sixty miles from the position they gave us," Olds clapped Lemay on the shoulder in a gesture of trust. "We're gonna resume the exercise. We've got until noon today."

Cumulus clouds filled the blue sky and the engines of six B-17's, in formation, roared loudly, the ocean floor far below them. In Olds' aircraft, the radio operator's voice came over the intercom. "… Stand by for fleet position," the radio operator said.

Lieutenant Lemay, inside the navigator's compartment was once again plotting the course. He leaned forward, intent on completing the task at hand. A few moments later, he walked into the cockpit.

"Colonel, we can't reach their position before twelve o'clock noon! Too far …."

Colonel Olds groaned. "Damn!" He paused for a moment. "We'll try anyway." He began to transmit over the radio. "Tempest Flight, Flagship 1. Form up abreast … half mile separation … four hundred feet altitude."

As the hour of noon approached Colonel Olds spoke to the pilots over the radio. "Keep your eyes peeled," he said.

The B-17's, six abreast, raced across the ocean. In the bombardier's compartment of Olds' B-17, Lieutenant Kilpatrick pointed excitedly out the window. "There they are!"

Colonel Olds glanced at his watch and kept grinning. "Five minutes to twelve." He looked out at the fleet steaming leisurely below.

"Which one's the Utah?" Lieutenant Kilpatrick asked the Navy lieutenant who was crouched beside him looking out the greenhouse.

"Can't make it out," The Navy lieutenant said.

Lieutenant Kilpatrick beamed. "Gotta do better than that, Mister!" He adjusted his bomb sight. "Something down there is about to get hit!"

Lemay, who has come up to the front of the cockpit, began to gaze through his binoculars. He pointed to one of the ships below. "There it is!"

"Let's go!" Colonel Olds said "Single file!"

The bomb bay doors opened, and the bombs began to fall away.

Both pilots began to yell "Bull's eye!" at the same time.

Several sailors were sitting casually on the deck, gazing upward at the oncoming B-17's. Suddenly, a dummy bomb struck the deck nearby, showering rubble everywhere. The sailors literally dove for cover.

One sailor looked up at the sky. "What the hell!! What do you bastards think you're doing?!"

The ship's general quarter's siren shrieked.

Olds' B-17 turned after the bomb run while the second B-17 released its bomb on the Utah.

Colonel Olds peered down at the Utah. "Look at them run for cover. They damned sure weren't expecting us."

At the Admiral's bridge, the Admiral was looking towards the Utah when a junior officer approached him.

"Sir, you want me to call off the exercise?" The junior officer asked. They have won sir! And ... they're reporting some damage over on the Utah."

The Admiral stood up and remained silent. His facial featured seemed carved in stone as he left the Bridge.

Colonel Olds entered the navigator's compartment and found Lemay and Kilpatrick grinning and laughing, much in the same way he was doing.

"Well Lemay ...."

Lemay interrupted "Remember I told you we couldn't get there in time?"

"Yeah," Colonel Olds said.

Lemay pointed to his chart. "They weren't where they were supposed to be.

Olds glanced at the chart, then at Lemay, puzzled. "Well?"

"The position they radioed us was one degree off just like yesterday," Lemay said.

"If you're right, Lemay, they were giving us bad information intentionally! We stumbled on them by sheer accident!"

Lemay nodded, and then turned to the chart. "Our heading to March Field will be zero-nine-six degrees based on my dead reckoning calculations here." He tapped the chart with his divider. "If I'm right we'll pass twenty-two miles north of Point Conception when we hit land fall about sixty-two minutes from now. That will prove my point. The Navy is not playing within the rules. They are going to discredit our entire concept of strategic bombardment like they did to Billy Mitchell if they can. We had to bomb the Utah during this war game if Army Aviation was to remain a credible concept even though they cheated."

Olds nodded and then left. A moment later he entered the cockpit, seated himself in the co-pilot's seat, glanced at the compass and as he did so he saw that the compass heading read, zero-nine-six degrees. Colonel Olds spoke into the microphone.

"Pilot to radioman: inform March Field mission successful. Tell 'em to notify General Andrews the mission was successful."

Colonel Olds turned and looked back at Lemay who was now standing behind the pilot looking out the cockpit window into the distance. "Okay, Lemay, I assume that you still want to quietly add some key people for future expansion in case of war?"

"Yes sir, I feel that we will need key people on board if we have to expand rapidly due to the war in Europe," Lemay said dryly.

"What war in Europe?" Olds said mockingly. "Okay, I agree. Get me your list of the four and only four people. I don't know anything at all about this Coltrane fella. Who is he?"

"He is a true believer, sir. He believes in strategic bombing and the value of Army Aviation. He is an excellent pilot and knows aviation engineering from the landing gear to the rudder top," Lemay said with a slight excitement in his voice.

Olds looked at Lemay and knew that this must be an exceptional officer to get that type of endorsement from Lemay. He looked at Lemay and said, "OK, bring Coltrane on board immediately!"

General Andrews, the March Field Commandant and Colonel "Hap" Arnold were seated in the Control Tower, obviously awaiting word from Colonel Olds. The tower radio man transcribed an incoming Morse code message, finished, walked to General Andrews, and handed him the message. General Andrews read the brief statement and his features broke into a broad smile as he handed the message to Colonel Arnold.

Colonel Olds and the co-pilot searched the horizon ahead for first sight of landfall. The co-pilot pointed to his right.

"There's Point Conception," The co-pilot said.

"How far?" Colonel Olds asked.

"About twenty or so miles I'd say."

"That proves it," Colonel Olds said. "They never intended for us to find that damned fleet."

"Hell of a way to run an exercise," The co-pilot said, "We're supposed to be testing our National Defense Systems and the Navy is playing silly games with us."

Olds nodded as disgruntled as the co-pilot. "General Andrews was right. Battleships are as obsolete as the horse cavalry."

The co-pilot glanced at Olds, puzzled by his remark.

"They are going to fight like hell to keep battle ships as our first line of defense. It doesn't matter a damn that they're totally vulnerable to air power." He gazed ahead, deep in thought. "And as long as they've got a strangle hold on the War Department, it's going to be damned hard to change that. However, the German Luftwaffe is proving my point in Spain. They bombed a couple fortifications successfully back in April. They have secretly developed their air force and now that Hitler has seen how effective the Luftwaffe is, he won't stop there. War in Europe is just about to start, and we are not ready if attacked."

The co-pilot looked at Olds, then he turned away, pondering the words he'd just heard. Then he looked back out the front of the B-17 and spotted March Field. He reduced the power setting and started the descent to land.

The three B-17's landed at March Field and Colonel Olds dropped from the lead ship and walked to where General Andrews stood waiting for him.

"Well done, Bob," General Andrews said.

Other members of the crew gathered around, laughing, and talking.

"You should have seen those sea jocks dive for cover," One crewman said.

"Yeah, they were scrambling like cats when the bombs hit," another said.

"All six of our ships scored hits," Lieutenant Kilpatrick said. "We could have sunk the whole fleet."

Colonel Olds began to walk off to one side and General Andrews followed him.

"I've got a call in to the San Francisco Examiner. They're going to break the story in the evening edition."

Even as the General spoke, he saw a junior staff officer walking towards him, his face a study in disappointment.

"What's wrong, Lieutenant?" General Andrews asked.

"The story, sir … it was killed."

The general threw his arms up in disgust. "Why?"

"War department request," The lieutenant said.

The crew began to walk toward General Andrews and Colonel Olds, each one of them sensing that something had gone wrong!

Chapter Two

There was a perfunctory knock on the door jamb as Missy LeHand, FDR's personal secretary of over 17 years entered the Oval Office and said with a tired business-like tone, "Mr. President, that attorney from Buffalo you sent for is here."

Roosevelt smiled at her tired reference to a World War I hero and a well-respected international attorney. "Please show Colonel Donovan in."

Seconds later William J. "Wild Bill" Donovan entered the room and walked over to the side of the President's desk where he grabbed the President's hand with both of his. The greeting was very warm, and Donovan said with emotion, "Franklin, I mean Mr. President, I was delighted to get your invitation to come meet with you again. It's been over three years since we last met at Campobello. What can an old, battered Buffalo attorney do for you?"

"Wild Bill, you and I go way back together, and I have always trusted your judgment and advice. My intelligence people have been reporting to me about the deteriorating situation in Europe and what I see gives me a cold shiver down my back. That fella Hitler appears to be preparing for another war. What is your read of things over there and how scared should we be here in the States? Bill, am I looking for the Boogy Man under the bed when he doesn't exist or is Hitler a real threat to Europe, England and perhaps our country?"

Donovan knew Roosevelt well enough to know this was not an idle question for two old friends just talking about the weather. He thought for a moment then replied, "Franklin, we have known each other for over two decades and I will tell you what I see. I am in contact with my overseas law clients regularly and from what I can determine is that Hitler is the Boogy Man and we must quickly become prepared to do serious battle with this crazy man!" Donovan paused to see Roosevelt's reaction and he was comforted to see the President take a serious demeanor and nod. "Let's look at the situation as it is today. Since he became Chancellor in 1933 with dictatorial powers, he has created the Berlin-Rome Axis treaty with the Italians who have a small but respectable army controlled by another crazy sociopath Benito Mussolini. Hitler has also included Japan into their Axis of Power. Now Japan has invaded China with overwhelming force. The initial reports that I am getting from my clients in Japan and Hong Kong are horrifying. The carnage and brutality against the unarmed Chinese civilians are sickening. Japan has invaded China for the sole purpose to build an industry capable of supporting a powerful war machine. My contacts in Tokyo boasts about them planning to go south into Malaysia and Indochina for oil and more resources. He claims that this general Tojo who is rapidly gaining political as well as military power boasts about forcing the US influence out of the western Pacific. You had better not lose focus on this situation as you prepare for war in Europe," Donovan said in a serious toned voice. "Recently, Hitler quietly annexed Austria without a shot being fired and he has spies running all over Czechoslovakia and Poland. He has big plans and Austria is not the last country on his Christmas list. Hell, if you read Mein Kampf, he will take the western part of Russia. This guy is charismatic and a megalomaniac that must be taken seriously."

After being stunned by the bluntness of his friend's analysis Roosevelt responded. "Then you feel certain that the United States will become involved in a full-blown land war in Europe with Hitler."

"Of course, we will, and don't forget Germany's submarine fleet. That will be a factor in supporting England and our own forces over there," he concluded. "Franklin, have you started beefing up your war industry yet?"

"Yes, I have but not to the extent that will be required to support the type of war you suggest," responded the president in a tone of resignation. "That is a sensitive political matter given that the country favors isolationism over helping England or another war in Europe. Obviously, I must do more and soon."

"Absolutely!" responded Donovan. "Especially your air force."

"My friend, you have been invaluable in helping get a better perspective on the deteriorating global situation. Would you consider coming and helping me here at the White House on intelligence matters? Your country needs you once again."

"Thank you for the offer but I can be of more use as far as intelligence matters working at my law firm in Buffalo. My clients will talk to their lawyer more easily than an official of the government. My job takes me overseas frequently. If you let it be known unofficially overseas that I have your ear and you have charged me with some diplomatic tasks, then I can be of more use to you. In the future I will make a special effort to be more observant and meet with as many key players before the balloon goes up. When we go to war, we can revisit the job offer."

"As you wish my friend," responded the President.

Donovan got up and shook the President's hand warmly as he left the office.

Chapter Three

There were six loud knocks on a second-floor apartment in Moreno, California. Then two knocks. Then door was opened in impatience by the anxious visitor who entered the apartment of James Barton Coltrane, better known as Bart.

"Bart, Bart, you son-of-a-bitch, wake up, it's almost 8 o'clock and you have orders," said Tom Dillon, a fellow pilot with the 7th Bombardment Group stationed at March Field, California. "Wake up! You have transfer orders," Dillon said as he opened the bedroom door to find Coltrane in bed with a long-haired woman. The woman by this time had awoken and had pulled the sheets up to her eyes in fear and embarrassment.

Dillon started shaking Coltrane as he looked around at the three empty bottles of cheap champagne from a northern California vineyard.

"Dillon, I'm going to kill you if I can get out of this bed," Coltrane said in an angry voice. "That could take some time and a medic. My head is blowing up," Coltrane looked at his bed mate and asked, "What kind of rotgut were we drinking?"

"Forget it," he said as he turned his attention towards Dillon who had taken a couple of steps back as a precautionary measure knowing of Coltrane's often belligerent attitude when awakened with a hangover. It was an event that had become a more frequent event in recent months. Coltrane was bored with the lack of emphasis being put on war training. He had found temporary relief in the volume of booze that he consumed and the never-ending sexual conquests.

Coltrane, now sitting bare-assed on the side of the bed with his feet on the floor and his head in his hands, asked, "Now what is this shit about transfer orders?"

"You are being transferred to the Second Bomb Group. That guy Lemay got you transferred to that B-17 Squadron."

Coltrane's head snapped up despite pain and almost said something but didn't.

He looked over at the gorgeous blonde who was silently observing the whole event. He then turned back to Dillon.

"Pardon my manners, Amy this is Tom Dillon my ...."

"It's Ann," the blonde said interrupting.

"Oh yeah, Ann. It was a rough night and you damned near killed me," he said, then turned his head towards her and smiled saying "Thanks, you made life worth living!"

She smiled and pulled the sheet back up to her eyes trying to hide her embarrassment. Then asked shyly, "Do I get another chance at giving you a heart attack?"

Coltrane laid back over on her hugging her and biting her ear.

"Excuse me," Dillon said loudly, "I'm still here and you have to report to Colonel Olds at thirteen hundred today."

Ignoring Dillon, Coltrane asked "Okay, when does your husband fly off into the wild blue yonder again?" Quickly looking at Dillon, "He's a pilot with Western Airlines."

He's on the Friday afternoon flight to San Francisco - Salt Lake and back on Sunday," she said.

"Perfect, Coltrane said, same bar stool at 7:30 Friday?"

"Absolutely, better take your vitamins," she said in a deep sexy voice while rubbing her hand on the inside of Coltrane's thigh. "I'll do my best to do you in next time."

"Okay, okay, Bart. I've done my job to let you know. Here are the orders, you are on your own," a frustrated Dillon said, throwing the orders on the bed as he left the room.

Precisely at 1300 hours, Bart Coltrane entered the office of Colonel Olds. He advised the Master Sergeant of his name and instructions to report to Colonel Robert Olds Commander 2nd Bombardment Group. The tough looking NCO knocked twice on the door and went in. Moments later, he came out leaving the door open.

The Colonel will see you now, sir," barked the Sergeant.

Coltrane marched into the office and stopped less than two feet from the desk and saluted. "Sir, Lieutenant James Barton Coltrane reports as ordered, sir."

"At ease, Lieutenant," said the Colonel as he got up and extended his hand. "Welcome to the Second Bomb Group. Have a seat," he said pointing to a chair just to the right of the desk. He then noticed Lieutenant Lemay sitting in the other chair. "I understand that you already know Curt Lemay."

"Yes sir," stated Coltrane.

"Good, you will get your B-17 transition from him and will become his co-pilot for now" the Colonel said in a matter-of-fact tone. "Curt tells me that you share the same two fundamental beliefs that we do. First, you believe in the bomber as a strategic weapon of the future and second, the world will once again be at war. I assume that you expect that the United States will be drawn into the fight."

"Yes sir, if Britain is attacked, we have no choice but to come to her assistance," responded Coltrane. "It's going to be a bomber and fighter war. You can see what Hitler has done in Spain with his Condor Legion bombers and dive bombers. He is training his pilots for a bigger operation that he has planned. You can hear the Fat Lady tuning up for the big show now.

Olds nodded and then walked over to a wall map of the world and pointed to March Field. "Currently, we have six B-17's at March Field. More will be arriving soon. We must take what we have and accomplish a long list of tasks. Mission deployment plan, tactics, operating procedures, maintenance procedures, crew training, war preparations, and lastly convince a 'battleship-minded Congress and War Department of the importance of strategic bombing in a new type of warfare. Europe will be won or lost in the air. Hitler has already proven his new emphasis on aviation in his Luftwaffe attacks in Spain. Intelligence has been getting some very disturbing rumors on the size of the new Luftwaffe, especially in its bomber fleet. If the rumors are true the, Germans have an air force over twenty times the size that we thought … and he plans to use them in any invasion or assault as a front-line force. Our little Army Air Corps is massively outnumbered and outgunned. We must prove that the Air Corps can be a major force in any future combat in Europe and that we must start building thousands of fighters and B-17's. What you and the others here in the Second Bomb Group are will be the nucleus of that future force. Europe will depend upon our ability to support them with air power and more importantly, the fate of the United States may also depend upon us," Olds said as he sat back down.

"You will work for Curt, but you will also work with others on the staff in the development of tactics, operations and maintenance. I understand you are quite knowledgeable in aviation maintenance. That is a critical area for us," Olds said as he leaned forward. "Are you ready to take on this assignment?"

"Sir, I've dreamed of this assignment. I am ready, willing, and able to do this job for you," Coltrane said in a confident tone as he stood up to salute.

"Carry on, Lieutenant," Olds said as he returned his salute.

Coltrane did an about face to leave then paused long enough to say to Lemay, "Thanks, I owe you. How is your hand?" he smiled then left.

Lemay broke out laughing as he held up his right hand.

Chapter Four

With the telephone receiver to his ear, the sergeant receptionist at the office of the Chief of the Air Corps office, flipped a switch on the intercom.

"General Arnold, the radio room is on the line, sir," the sergeant said. "They've got a radio message coming in from the Queen Elizabeth. She's docking in New York in a few hours."

General Arnold was working at his desk and lifted the telephone receiver from its cradle. "General Arnold here." He listened for a moment. "Lindbergh! Tomorrow?" He paused for a moment. "Well, I don't know. Mrs. Arnold and I are leaving for West Point tonight. Going to the Army-Navy game. Look … tell him we'll be at the Thayer Hotel up there. It's a good place to meet. Private … no reporters. Maybe he'll want to see the game too."

A passenger ship docked at New York Waterfront Pier and people began to disembark. Crowds of relatives, and friends waited anxiously, happily at the foot of the gang plank. Among those who started down the gang plank were Charles and Anne Lindbergh who were met by several reporters as they stepped onto the pier.

"Colonel Lindbergh … Colonel Lindbergh!" shouted one reporter.

Lindbergh frowned, unhappy with the reporter and the crowd that had begun to gather around him and his wife.

"Why do you think Field Marshall Goering gave you such a complete look at the Luftwaffe?"

"Look, gentlemen, I've just finished a two-hour press conference on board the ship there. Why didn't you fellows attend that?"

The reporters completely disregarded Lindbergh's position and continued to clamor over the crowd noise with their questions. Every few minutes a photographer's flash bulb popped.

"Do you think your report to the British Parliament was responsible for Chamberlain's giving in to Hitler at Munich?" another reporter asked.

"As I told your colleagues earlier, I only told the British what I had seen in Germany," Lindbergh said.

The first reporter asked: "Colonel, do you really think Hitler could whip England and the United States?"

"They're presently superior in air power," Lindbergh said.

"You were treated pretty royally by the Germans over there. They even decorated you, didn't they?" A third reporter asked.

"I'd rather not respond to that," Lindbergh said.

"Are you returning to the U.S. to live, or just to visit?"

"We've come home to stay."

"Have you and Mrs. Lindbergh gotten over the kidnap-murder of your son, Colonel?' The reporter glared at Lindbergh. "Is that why you've come home?"

Suddenly, Lindbergh, repulsed by the line of questioning, pushed his way through the crowd, propelling his wife ahead of him.

* * *

In the main dining room of the Thayer Hotel near West Point, New York, a waiter dressed in a white waist coat and a black bow tie brought coffee to a table where Colonel Lindbergh and General and Mrs. Arnold were seated. The waiter refilled their coffee cups and then walked away. The dining room was empty, having been cleared in deference to the meeting taking place there.

"Well … I guess that's about it," Lindbergh said thoughtfully. "I'll submit a comprehensive report just as soon as I can get my notes in order."

"I'd appreciate it," General Arnold said. He paused. "I find it difficult to believe that Germany could have amassed such air power without our Intelligence people having more detailed knowledge of it."

"They'll continue to use the Luftwaffe as a black mail capability," Lindbergh said. "Of course, I was selected for their premier unveiling because they felt the world would listen to what I had to say about air power … no matter whose power it was!" "They have a new dive bomber called the Ju 87 Stuka which is very accurate and has a siren sound in the dive that will scare you to death. Besides being an incredible terror weapon it is the finest dive bombing platform that I have ever seen." He continued, "General, they're preparing for a major war, and I believe the Luftwaffe will lead the way. Lindbergh drew closer to Arnold and said in a soft but commanding voice, "But that may not be all of the story. At a cocktail party, Göring was boasting about his Luftwaffe when a young general with a few too many said it would not be the Luftwaffe that would scare the world but his unstoppable Panzers. I thought Goering was going to have the officer taken out and shot on the spot. Goering told me that was a proud Panzer officer with too much to drink as an attempt to brush off the incident. At another meeting with General Joachim Peiper, I asked about the development of their tank force, and he said that it was staggering in size and much better prepared for war than the Luftwaffe. Now that scares me, and I think you should pass this on to the President and the War Department." Lindy looked into Arnold's eyes and said in a stone-cold tone, "While I passionately believe that we should stay out of war, regrettably we must get prepared for a global war because we will get dragged into it! If not with the Germans, it will be with the Japanese or worse … both!"

Arnold was stunned by Lindbergh's revelation and paused momentarily to comprehend what he had been told, before he replied, "I spoke with General Marshall before I left Washington, yesterday afternoon, Colonel Lindbergh," General Arnold said. "He's appointed a board to develop a five-year plan for the Air Corps. It'll be headed by General Kilner. The President and General Marshall would like to have you serve on it."

"Well … I see a need to do what I can, General," Lindbergh said, "Especially after what I have told you."

Chapter Five

A White House aide hurried along hallway, and then turned into the doorway leading into the old Cabinet Room. He entered the room quietly and then stood waiting for a break in the discussion around the large conference table. President Roosevelt was seated at the head position with Secretary of State Cornell Hull and two aides to the right and Harry Hopkins on the President's left. Hopkins had been speaking when the aide entered the room.

"I respect Secretary Hull's opinion, Mr. President," Hopkins said. "But as Secretary of State, I'm concerned about the broader consequences that could arise from our failure to support further negotiations."

The aide approached the Secretary of State, leaning towards him and speaking softly. "Excuse me Mr. Secretary ... it's Ambassador Joseph Kennedy, he's on the line from London, sir," the aide said. "You can take it right here, sir."

The aide turned to a bank of telephones along the back wall, lifted a receiver from the hook.

Hull got up and went to the phone. "Hello, Joe?" He said, "Yeah, the President's here now." Hull paused and listened. "Well, we're trying to reach a decision on that matter right now, Joe."

Roosevelt spoke softly to Harry Hopkins. "I agree with Cordell, Harry. I believe the United States ought to evidence some final leadership in the matter. After all, England and France both have consistently sought our opinion ever since the crisis began."

Hull was still on the phone. "Right down the middle, eh?" He listened. "Lindbergh? When?"

Roosevelt paused, looked at Secretary Hull, and then turned back to Hopkins. "If war does break out, I want it clear to the rest of the world that it was Hitler's ...."

Harry Hopkins interrupted the President. "But Mr. President! The American press is already accusing both England and France of selling Czechoslovakia down the river. They're saying the Czechs are being raped! If you send still another last-minute message urging the participants to further negotiations, you're opening yourself to ...."

"Damn!" Cordell Hull said, still on the phone. "All the frontiers? That serious, eh?"

"Harry, we can't sit by idly and let another world war engulf Europe and us without at least *trying* to do something to forestall it ... anything," Roosevelt said. "I certainly don't agree with Chamberlain's course of action so far, but we're at the eleventh hour now!"

Cordell Hull ended the telephone conversation with Ambassador Kennedy. "All right, Joe. Yes, we will keep working on it and, I'll be in touch tonight."

"Secretary Hull briskly walked back to the conference table and sat down.

"Mr. President, Ambassador Kennedy sends his regards."

"Joe is in a pretty tough position over there tonight!" the President said.

Secretary Hull nodded affirmatively. "Chamberlain and Daladier both hope that you'll send one more message to Hitler ... urge him to meet with them. The British Parliament is split right down the middle on Chamberlain's appeasement issue. If Hitler crosses the Polish border October first as rumored, Chamberlain's opposition wants an immediate declaration of war. I think Chamberlain will resign if there are any hostilities. I get the feeling that the real powers are waiting for the inevitable and will then bring Churchill in. They have already established wartime military and clandestine intelligence operations. J. P. C. Holland has a workable plan and has put it into operation."

"And Chamberlain's for peace at *any price!* You can bet on that," Roosevelt said.

"Seems that way, Mr. President," Hull said.

"What's Germany doing?" Roosevelt asked.

"Joe said Hitler has got massive troop concentrations pulled up along the Polish border."

President Roosevelt slammed his palm down on the table. "Any fool can see Hitler's overall plan, and it goes a great deal further than the Sudetenland! Germany's armed to the teeth! Colonel Donovan predicted this over a year ago."

"Some of the top British politicians had Lindbergh apprise them of the strength of Hitler's air arm," Hull said.

"What did he tell them?" the President asked.

"That Hitler's Luftwaffe could defeat all of the air forces of Europe combined," Secretary Hull said.

"I'm sure Lindbergh made quite an impression on Chamberlain, if no one else," Roosevelt said. "However, Hitler's air power seems to be what everybody is afraid of, but the top Panzer general told Lindberg that his Panzers forces were larger and better prepared for war that the Luftwaffe."

"My god!" gasped Harry Hopkins.

"The French must be aware of Hitler's war machine as they began evacuating all of the art objects from the Louvre this morning, getting them out from the threat of German bombs," Hull said. "England, France ... the Polish... they're in the process of full mobilization."

Roosevelt thought pensively for a moment. "Cord, I want you and Harry to go ahead with options two and three that you've outlined here." He pointed to brief sheets sitting on the table before him. "tell Hitler he'll achieve a greater place in history by preventing a world war than he would by starting one. Urge him to abandon the October ultimatum ... and ... instead ... strive to reach a negotiated solution to the problem. We'll send it out to all the parties concerned tonight."

"Yes, Mr. President," Cordell Hull said.

"And Harry, I want you to set up a meeting tomorrow with the Secretaries of War, the Treasury, and the Navy," Roosevelt said. "I want to meet with General Malin Craig, George Marshall, Admiral Stark and Hap Arnold too, and, of course, I definitely want you there too, Harry."

Hopkins nodded. "Yes, Mr. President."

Chapter Six

Two well-dressed middle-aged gentlemen got out of a government car at the historic Reform Club situated in the Pall Mall suburb of London. They were met by a tall, slim man of the same age who extended his hand in welcome. "Welcome back to the Club, Winston," said the man as he walked into the main salon on the first floor.

Churchill looked around briefly and said "It's the same bloody place as it was in 1913 when I resigned. Some things just don't change. Now where are we going to meet, Holland?"

"I have arranged for us to use the library. I have asked that we are not disturbed," Sir J. P. C. Holland said in a matter-of-fact tone. They entered a large room with beautiful cherry wood paneling surrounding walls of books, paintings and other important documents encased in ornate picture frames. Churchill took a seat at the end of a long mahogany table with twenty Louis XVI chairs.

"Okay, where are we with our as yet unapproved clandestine intelligence service?" Churchill asked.

"A quick question, Winston. Have the King and Parliament set a date for you to become the Prime Minister?" asked Holland.

The future British Prime Minister leaned back lighting his cigar and looked at the group seated around the table. "Yes, we are looking at mid-May. He has got to let Chamberlain try one last time for a deal with that mad man … a fool's errand! He feels that the appropriate political posture and maneuverings can be done by then. In the meantime, he fully expects this group to develop a viable and operational clandestine intelligence service. We should be able to officially authorize it in the Commons and Lords in July. The political problems should be resolved by then. Until then, we must proceed without legal authorization and completely hush hush. We must not be exposed as it would embarrass the King and cause a great deal of political problems. Yes, his majesty has given us clear direction, but it must be done totally behind the veil of secrecy."

"Grubbins," said Churchill, "how is Dalton doing across the Channel?"

"Sir, it is difficult to find capable people in the countries who we can rely on. The locals often don't have a clue on how to organize the locals and maintain secrecy. The Gestapo is finding and interrogating them as fast as they get started. Supply is another problem along with communications. We have developed a radio called a Type A Mark III transceiver to send in with our people to get into the hands of Resistance leaders who have some basic knowledge of how the radio works. We must send in more trained and qualified people. We are identifying and recruiting and training agents to insert. This is a far bigger challenge than we originally projected. Supply and resupply are another major problem. We have set up a unit down at Tangmere, flying Lysanders. They're great for this type of mission, but they are limited on range and payload. They can only carry one passenger and about 250 kilos of supplies. We have some excellent operations in the early stages of organization in Norway, Denmark, Spain, Holland, and France. We just can't service them by air due to the short range and limitations of the Lysander. We tried using Whitney and Wellington bombers. They have the range and payload capability but are extremely vulnerable to anti-aircraft fire. So far, we've lost 4 out of 5 missions. We really need a medium range aircraft that can fly at very low altitude and has the maneuverability and fire power to provide ground support and if necessary, take on the Luftwaffe fighters."

Churchill turned his head back to the map slowly smoking his cigar. He remained silent for almost a minute contemplating the situation. "What is Dalton's position on the aviation requirement and ability to develop the number of agents capable of working behind the lines?"

"Let's first cover the recruiting and training," said Grubbins. "We've found that it is extremely important that selected agents be very knowledgeable on the specific area being assigned to or be arrested by the Gestapo. They must already speak the specific language of the area. Book or school language education will not really work. Dalton is encouraged by qualified volunteers and has begun to acquire facilities."

"Most of our facilities are being requisitioned in the Milton Keynes area. Chicheley Hall is recently opened, and training commenced. Poundon House is due to be operational in 45 days. There are many Volunteers in the respective countries that we can use if we can deploy them by air. The Lysander is the only aircraft that can work for us as long as it isn't further than 400 air miles away. Dalton has learned of a possible aircraft that is being developed in the United States that could solve the problem for us."

"What would that aircraft be?" Churchill queried with increased interest.

"The U.S. has a plane being built known as the NA-62. It is still classified as secret, but we got word about it from the U.S. Air attaché in London. They are going to give it a designation of B-25. It is maneuverable, good firepower, has a 1,200-mile range and can carry a payload of 3,000 pounds. It is perfect for low altitude resupply missions. Do you think we could get the Yanks to lend us one?" Grubbins asked in conclusion.

Churchill pointed his cigar at Grubbins and said in contemplation of the many ramifications of the issue, "That will be a real sticky one for sure. I'll make a call to Harry Hopkins and see what can be worked out. We might get lucky and get one or two with experienced crews. Tell Dalton to be ready to go over to Washington in a couple of weeks. Is there anything else? If not, I will leave you gentlemen to your cloaks and daggers."

Chapter Seven

A newsboy riding a bicycle approached the Lemay residence at March Field and tossed the morning newspaper against the door. Presently, Helen Lemay opened the door, retrieved the paper and a bottle of milk, and then closed the door behind her. She unrolled the newspaper and gazed at the headlines. *Hitler Invades Poland.* Underneath that in smaller, but still bold column headline: *General George Catlett Marshall succeeds Malin Craig.*

Helen walked from the door into the dinette area where Curt Lemay and Janie were sitting at the table eating breakfast. Lemay playfully fed Janie some baby food. Helen passed the newspaper to Lemay as she sat down at the table. "What does it all mean, Curt?" She asked.

Lemay glanced at the newspaper. "That we're in a hell of a lot of trouble!"

"At least they had the good sense to appoint George Marshall to succeed General Craig," Helen said.

"Thanks to that old fuddy-duddy Craig, and the others up there on General Staff like him, we're four or five years away from an adequate Air Force ... and the damned War *started yesterday*," exclaimed Curt Lemay!

"You shouldn't speak so gruffly around Janie, darling." Helen said.

Lemay gazed at Janie and then smiled at her.

"Guess I shouldn't at that."

Lemay folded his napkin, placed it in his plate, brushed Janie's cheek with a kiss, and then kissed Helen tenderly. He went to a coat rack by the front entrance, put his garrison cap on, then, waved goodbye to Helen and Janie.

Helen rose, went to the kitchen window, looked out at Lemay as he started the family car, began to back out of the driveway, then caught sight of Helen gazing out at him, and blew her a kiss. Helen gazed after Lemay pensively.

When Lemay got to the flight line, there was a lot of unscheduled activity. The news from Europe had made everyone very conscious of what could happen here and its effect on their lives. They had been training for this situation, but in training it was always just an exercise. It was just play and not the real thing. When they were finished, they went home and had supper and sat down in an easy chair and listened to Amos and Andy on the radio while drinking a beer. This changed things for everyone. In a war people die, especially if they are not properly trained as a combat unit. Now they eagerly looked forward to training and what it could do to keep them alive when the U.S. ultimately got into the war.

Lemay saw Bart Coltrane looking at the left main landing gear of his newly assigned B-17.

"What's the problem, Bart?" asked Lemay.

Without looking at Lemay he pointed to a hose and explained, "It eventually fails after three or four hundred hours of flight. I got the boys in maintenance to put high-pressure connectors on the ends of a grease gun hose. I just installed it in this plane to see if giving it an additional four inches so it could go further back in the wheel well during flight would stop the chafing problem. I just don't think the boys at Boeing had enough test time to detect this problem. I put a new hose on the other side, so we had a good comparison."

Lemay took off his hat and stuck his head in the wheel well to see the unauthorized installation. He noted the path and projected movement of the new test hose. He came out and looked at Coltrane.

"While you're right about the problem, this is unauthorized," Lemay said, then looked up at it again. "Okay, write a memo to me covering your thoughts and anticipated results. We'll call this a "field test."

"I think you have a good idea and a practical solution. Keep it up. This is what we need to really make these birds ready for combat," Lemay said as he walked away.

Chapter Eight

The weather was clear but unusually hot and humid for mid-October 1940 when Colonel Olds walked up to Lieutenant Lemay at the March Field Transit Terminal. Lemay stiffened up to attention and salutes Olds and asks, "What's this all about, sir?"

"Curt, I don't have a clue." I got a call from General Andrews who said to meet these VIPs and give them our absolute cooperation. They are here at the specific direction of the President."

"Wow, that's real horsepower," he said expressing his being impressed with the situation. "That must be their C-47 landing on runway three-two."

The C-47 transport pulled up in front of the transit terminal and shut down the engines. The door opened and General Andrew's aide-de-camp deplaned ahead of three men in civilian clothes and General Andrews himself. The delegation came over to Colonel Olds and Lemay.

General Andrews returned Olds and Lemay's salutes and introduced the civilians. "Colonel Olds, this is Mr. Roberts, the Deputy Under-Secretary of State, and this gentleman is Major Sir Hugh Dalton and Squadron Leader Colin Howarth, our special visitors who have the full backing of the President. Major Dalton works as a special representative of General Sir J. P. C. Holland of the British government. He needs some highly specialized personnel of ours for an extremely important mission. Squadron Leader Howarth is our liaison to the RAF Special Operations Executive and will be training our people for a special mission. Let's go find a place we can talk besides this hot ramp."

"This way, sir," Olds said pointing to the two staff cars standing by.

Ten minutes later they were in a conference room at the base headquarters building. After all were seated and the door closed with a guard posted outside, General Andrews continued. "Major Dalton and I are looking for an experienced and exceptional bomber pilot who has a keen understanding of aircraft maintenance and has the intelligence and leadership to be a project manager."

"Our second requirement is for a highly skilled navigator that has the ability to fly over water missions," he said looking directly at Olds.

"Third is for a crew chief that is an exceptional aircraft maintenance man. This man should know all aspects of aircraft operations and maintenance. Plus be able to work independently in a clandestine environment."

"Four is two junior maintenance personnel that have at least three years in either military or civilian aircraft maintenance."

"Fifth is a co-pilot that has above average potential and won't freeze upon in a combat situation."

"Now Colonel Olds and Lieutenant Lemay, who do you know and recommend for this mission?" the General said with confidence.

Lemay raised his hand and asked, "Sir, you didn't mention a bombardier."

"Not necessary Curt," Andrews replied.

Olds and Lemay turned to each other and discussed various names for about 30 seconds, then turned back to Andrews, "Sir," Olds said, "Lieutenant Lemay has some names for your consideration."

"Question, sir," Lemay asked, 'can I assume that the crew will be working with a new aircraft at the factory level and taking it to a combat situation?"

A big smile came over Major Dalton's face and he said, "That is correct."

"That narrows the possibilities to a very few. Sir, we would recommend the following, sir," Lemay said taking a breath.

Pilot – First Lieutenant Bart Coltrane
Navigator – Second Lieutenant Kelly Sharp
Co-pilot – Second Lieutenant Robby West
Crew Chief – Technical Sergeant Rupert Royston
Chief Mechanic – Sergeant Jack Martin
A&P Mechanic – Corporal Andy Lightfoot

"These are the very best men we have at March that meet your requirements," Lemay finished.

"Colonel Olds have these men in this briefing room at 1330 hours today," the General commanded. Then he turned and left the room.

Lemay and Olds stood to attention as the General and Major Dalton left.

"That just gives us 45 minutes to round them up," said Olds. "If you can get the pilot and navigator, I will get the others here, okay?"

Lemay nodded and left the room in an almost run.

Lieutenant Coltrane came into a drab conference room with only an aeronautical map on the side wall. He quickly noted that there were five others already there. He knew all of them even if most were from other units. As he took his seat, everyone looked at him and silently asked the question, *why am I here?* Coltrane looked around at the stares and said, "I haven't a clue." Everyone smiled or chuckled at the comment. Coltrane thought to himself *It is never good to be in a room of excellent people without knowing why you were there*!

Just then the door opened, and General Andres came in as Curt Lemay called the room to attention. Then he was followed by Colonel Olds and a bunch of men in civilian clothes.

Seeing a four-star General everyone got nervous and weak in the knees.

"At ease, gentlemen, take your seats," commanded the General.

Colonel Olds stood at the end of the table next to the blackboard. He lifted a clipboard and looked at the paper on it then looked up. He stated a roll call of sorts. “Lieutenant Coltrane, please stand.” General, this is First Lieutenant Bart Coltrane who is an excellent pilot and is our Group Maintenance Officer. Okay, “Bart, sit down.” “Lieutenant Kelly Sharp”, he said as Sharp stood without being told, “is an outstanding navigator. He flew for Pan Am on the Miami to Buenos Aires-Rio run.” Olds nodded and Sharp sat down. He continued, “Technical Sergeant Rupert Royston, is a 1922 British immigrant who worked for North American Aviation and Boeing before joining the Army Air Corps in 1933. He knows every nut, bolt, and rivet in our bomber aircraft. Sit, please. Next is Sergeant Jack Martin, who worked in the Curtis Wright Engine Plant prior to joining the service. Our other aircraft mechanic is Corporal Andy Lightfoot, who was an assembly line supervisor at Douglas Aircraft.”

Robby West looked around to see why he had not been introduced. This attracted Olds attention who smiled and said, “lastly, General, we have Second Lieutenant Robby West, the selected co-pilot who has volunteered.”

West blurted out, “Volunteered?” Everyone laughed.

Olds smiling ear to ear continued, “Just pulling your leg, Robby. Lieutenant West is considered by his commander to be an exceptional aviator dispute his youth and limited experience. General Andrews, these are the best we have here at March Field that match your request.” Then he sat down next to Coltrane.

General Andrews moved forward to where Olds had been standing and put his hat on the table. He looked at the six men at the table silently then said, “Gentlemen, from this point on everything said in this room is top secret. He paused then continued, “The two gentlemen at the end of the table are special visitors from England who have a special situation that requires some support from us. The President has sent them here for us to provide a solution to their problem. It will require volunteers, I repeat volunteers, who can undertake an exceedingly difficult and extremely dangerous mission in Europe. If you volunteer, you will be reassigned overseas and will be working with our dearest allies in their struggle against the Axis

Powers. Again, I must warn you that the mission is extremely dangerous, but of utmost importance. If anyone wants to volunteer, remain seated. Others, who are not interested, may now leave. Remember you are not to divulge anything said in this room should you not volunteer." Silence came over the room. Nobody moved or even looked around. Andrews looked over at Dalton and smiled. "Very good! Now let me introduce our visitors," the General said with a calm air and easy demeanor. "The gentleman in the corner is Mr. Roberts who is the Deputy Undersecretary of State here as the personal representative of President Roosevelt. The gentleman at the end of the table is Major Hugh Dalton, who is a special representative of General Sir J.P.C. Holland, head of Section D, Sabotage and Subversion Section, of the British Intelligence Service. Across from him is Squadron Leader Colin Howarth, who is the British Liaison to this mission from the RAF Special Operations Executive, or better known as the SOE. His section flies a Lysander over hostile territory supplying Resistance fighters and deploying British agents. He will be assisting in the modifications of your aircraft for the mission. Later he will train you in the type of flying to be performed out of England. He will also teach you the important policies and procedures for flying in and out of England and not get shot down by friendly fire. When you and your plane are ready, you will deploy to England. Once there, you will conduct extremely sensitive clandestine flights into Occupied Europe in support of Resistance movements operating throughout the area of conflict. You will report directly to Major Dalton who directs their entire operation. Lieutenant Coltrane is the project manager for the aircraft development portion of the U.S. side and is Squadron Commander of the unit. Bart, your squadron consists of one aircraft…for now."

"Mr. Roberts from the State Department has some information. Mr. Roberts," the general said as he sat down, and the bureaucrat came forward.

"Afternoon gentlemen," Roberts said in a soft voice. Coltrane could see this was another limp-wristed bureaucrat who was as worthless as teats on a bore hog. He took an immediate dislike towards him.

"As you know, the United States is not at war and is maintaining a position of neutrality at this time. Officially, you are members of the U.S. Army Training Command in England to train British pilots on the characteristics and deployment of U.S. aircraft as a part of the proposed Lend-Lease program to the British government. This is your cover story for everyone on both sides of the Atlantic. Unless told otherwise by Major Dalton, you must assume that nobody has been cleared to know about your mission. This program and your operations are classified Top Secret Sensitive Information. Very few people in State, War, Army Air Corps and the White House know of the mission."

"The President has decided to show his appreciation for accepting this important and dangerous mission by promoting each of you one rank. That will help as you will need the extra money living on the British economy instead of a military base. Since you will be living near the remote base or in London, you will be given an additional allowance. You will be paid a $5 per day food allowance and a $10 per day housing allowance. Officers living in London next to the headquarters will also get a $20 per month train and taxi allowance. This is to cover your travels back and forth from the headquarters and the remote airfield at Tempsford. Lastly, your mail will be sent through a special Armed Forced Postal Office in Washington. You will write your mail and put it into another envelope and send it to the APO where it will be mailed from there. Return mail addressed to you at the same APO. This will show a Washington address instead of a British posting. This is an important security matter. You are to tell your family and friends that you are training pilots at various bases in the U.S., so you don't have a permanent base assignment. That will avoid the desire for people to come see you. For all intents and purposes, you are to disappear here in the states. Any questions?"

Major Dalton stood up and went over to the map. "Gentlemen! First, congratulations on your courage to volunteer and your new promotions. You will certainly earn them and quickly. As you know, we are in a nasty conflict in Europe. Mr. Hitler has attacked Poland last October and is gobbling up all of Western Europe in his so-called Blitzkrieg. Currently, we are engaged in what the press has called the "Battle of Britain," and so it is. Our chaps are fighting off the bloody Bosch aircraft by day and night and I might say in a bloody good fashion."

"One of the problems Mr. Hitler has that the population of the countries that he has occupied and those that he obviously intends to conquer has some basic objections to his plan. They either are trying to form or are in the process of forming, local Resistance groups to timely fight the Bosch in guerrilla type operation. They also gather critical intelligence for us which is critical to the war effort."

"Since the outbreak of hostilities, we have been trying to make contact with these Resistance groups and others within Europe that will fight the Germans once they have completed their land grab. Communication is difficult at best. Knowing who will fight and who will report the Resistance group activities to the Gestapo is even more difficult. We have sent in a half dozen agents who all were killed or captured within a fortnight. We learned a lot from their sacrifices and have changed our tactics and procedures. We are getting footholds in France, Spain, Holland, Netherlands, Denmark, Belgium, and Norway. And yes, we even have a couple of resources in Germany and Italy. All of these are in the exceedingly early stages of development and training. Most of the people are just farmers, shop keepers and the average bloke. They do not know a bloody thing about sabotage, intelligence gathering and Resistance operations. We are helping by providing agents who will train them and furnish supplies. So far, we have organized a small air support unit operating flying out of Tempsford just north of London, and another bunch flying out of Tangmere south of London."

"Squadron Leader Howarth and his men have been unofficially flying over our newly trained agents and supplies to the Resistance groups in a Lysander at night. The Lysander is a weird looking bird but is truly ideal for its covert mission. It is a single pilot aircraft that can carry a rear gunner or a passenger but not both. It can carry about a thousand pounds of cargo or a passenger/cargo combination. It is a very rugged aircraft that can land on rough terrain. It can land in 320 meters and take off in 250 meters. Its range is only 600 miles. It has two Browning 303 machine guns fitted into its wheel spats. Not much protection and they are fixed so the pilot must make himself vulnerable to even take a shot at the bloody bastards. Frequently, we have made small drops of supplies only to have our Lysander and the Resistance fighters on the ground be ambushed by the Gestapo or Abwehr. The Lysander can do little to fight off the Germans until the supplies are collected or help the escape of the freedom fighters. It's a very sticky situation that must be changed.

"They are also subject to German fighters. So far, we have been lucky on that point as the Germans fighters don't fly very much at night when we do. We have tried to use Wellington and Whitley bombers to increase the size of our supply payload as well as range, but that was disastrous. They are big, slow, and easy targets for both anti-aircraft and fighters. They have no maneuverability and cannot fly as low as the Lysander or low enough to avoid the flak. As Squadron Leader Howarth always says, "The lower, the safer!"

Coltrane raised his hand and said without being recognized, "Sir, the B-17 would have the same limitations. The Wellington is a good aircraft too, but both would be sitting ducks."

"You're absolutely correct, Captain Coltrane," said Squadron Leader Colin Howarth. "But the B-25 does not."

"B-25!" exclaimed Coltrane. "That bird is just now in test flight. No telling when and if it will be certified and accepted by the Army Air Corps, sir."

Dalton took the conversation back to himself, "The B-25 made it first test flight 42 days ago. The subsequent test flights showed no problems. The U.S. government has made an initial order and the British government has ordered one with an option on three others. North American Aviation has been directed to start immediate production of the bomber. The jig for aircraft 40-007BX was laid down yesterday. That will be your bird. It is one of the very first production models."

Everyone in the room was stunned.

"Shall we continue?" Dalton asked.

"Sir," asked Kelly Sharp, "the B-25 is a bomber but there is no bombardier in the room."

"Very good point Lieutenant Sharp and I shall explain in a moment," Dalton said as he took a sip from a glass of water. Then he looked over at General Andrews and continued. "You won't be dropping bombs. You will drop people and supplies. Occasionally, you will pick up passengers in the occupied territory and nip on back to London."

"Be patient and all of the pieces will fall into place," Dalton said. He took a breath then continued.

"This Operation is named 'Black Bart'. No, Captain Coltrane, not after you. It is named after a British Pirate John Bartholomew Roberts of Pembrokeshire, Wales. During the golden age of piracy, he was the most successful. He captured over 470 vessels before he was killed in battle in 1722. It is hoped that you will be our 'pirate' and steal success from the Germans. You are to make very low-level flights deep into occupied territory and drop off thousands of pounds of supplies, agents, communicate with the underground Resistance fighters, perhaps pick up a few for debriefing in London. If necessary, provide fire support so they can get the supplies and escape. Your B-25 will be modified especially for this purpose. Since it is cargo and personnel that will be delivered, there is no need for a bombardier. High-speed low-level flying is the order of the day, gentlemen."

"Anyone getting weak in the knees or want out?" asked General Andrews. There was no reply. The general smiled and set back down.

Dalton continued. "Black Bart missions are high priority as the Resistance units rely solely on our shipments to be able to conduct operations against the Germans. We must drop in our agents as well as extract them. There are very few places that you can land a B-25 in enemy territory, so I wouldn't expect that to be a big item.

"You will be based at Tempsford about 60 miles north of London. We have a large tent erected to put your bird out of the elements. Hangar space is full, and we don't want general knowledge of your operations known, even to our own personnel. My experience tells me that after a few missions the Germans will put a remarkably high price on your heads and for information on you and your whereabouts. One lone B-25 will undoubtedly attract a lot of attention anyway but let us not expose the mission any more than necessary.

"For the enlisted crew, we have a nice three-bedroom cottage for you in Tempsford. Yes, we are trying to reduce your exposure to the other crews. We don't want to put you on the spot having to lie to them as to what you do. Most are a part of the Lysander operation and will know. But many are support personnel and other RAF personnel that don't know and cannot be told. The Germans have operatives in England and would not hesitate to kill you or destroy your plane. The cottage is very cozy. You have a house lady that will come by every weekday morning to put out a breakfast, do your laundry and keep the place tidy. If you want her to cook for you too, you will need to take it up with her for a fee. Your hanger or should I say, tent, is within a brisk walk of your cottage, but we will have a lorry for you as well. Tempsford has several good places to eat and get a pint of ale. You can eat at the enlisted mess hall as usual. You work will be generally during the daylight as missions flown across the Channel are usually at night. You will maintain and repair the bird during the day.

"Our intelligence operation is being reorganized as we speak. The new designation is the Special Operations Executive (SOE). I am Sir Hugh Dalton, and I am the new Minister of Economic

Warfare under the SOE, headquartered at 83 Baker Street. You are a part of Section D which handles sabotage and its support. Section D is commanded by Lieutenant Colonel Lawrence Grand. Our Section D operations as well as yours will be office in the headquarters area at Dorset Square. You will have an operations room on the fourth floor. It is a four meter by twelve-meter room that has a small desk for Captain Coltrane along with four high security filing cabinets. On two walls you will find detailed aviation maps of Europe and the Scandinavian countries. It has two blackboards and a scheduling blackboard. In the middle is a one meter by four-meter conference table and eight chairs. This is where you will be working when not flying a mission. I would expect an average of three missions per week, depending on weather. Plan by day, fly by night. You can sleep on the train from London to Tempsford. You will be supported by an able bunch of chaps from the Military Intelligence Research Branch, MI-6. They will provide you the intelligence, order of battle, and mission coordination needed to fly your mission. We have made arrangements for you to rent hotel rooms in the Montague Mansions area, a short walk from the office. If you find something you like better in the area, feel free to move. You are paying for the accommodations out of your housing allowance."

"Any questions so far?" Major Dalton said.

"I am sure that your mind if full and spinning around with all of this. Not to worry, there's more! Starting at 0800 hours tomorrow, you will report to Squadron Leader Howarth who will start the task of going over the type of flying and operations that we … you … will be doing. Based on these tactics and mission details, you can start thinking of how your B-25 should be configured. Obviously, you won't need bomb racks for example. Day after tomorrow, you will proceed to the North American Plant near Inglewood where your bird is being built. You will meet up with Arthur Bede who is your factory representative. He will be the one you work with on changes and modifications.

"This bird has one purpose and that is the direct support and supply of the Resistance underground in Europe. Make the bird fit the mission. It is what gets you there and back alive. Now is the time to build it up your way. Listen to Colin Howarth. He has flown dozens of missions over there in the Lysander and knows what he is talking about."

"Mechanics," Dalton said in a commanding voice, "you are to be at the factory watching and learning everything you can about the bird. Every rivet, nut, and wire. If you see any modification that can help performance or maintenance, now is the time to say something. You will be working in a cold damp tent, so you need to make maintenance and battle repairs easy and efficient.

"Once the bird is completed and North American signs it over to the British government, you will be transitioned by the contractor into the bird. After you are qualified, Howarth will move all of you to Tacoma Field. I guess they have renamed it to McChord Field outside Tacoma, Washington. There Colin will give you an accelerated training course on SOE flying procedures and mission tactics. McChord weather is much like England and you can fly low level over the Pacific on navigation exercises. Short-field take-offs and landings, cargo drops and low-level flying in mountains. You will learn techniques of flying in bad European weather and many other procedures that we have learned the hard way. Usually that means at the loss of someone's life. Last chance to ask questions." He said in completion.

Coltrane stood up and asked, "Sir, our code name is Black Bart, but what is our priority code for parts, supplies and services?"

General Andrews stood up. "Thank you, Major Dalton for that excellent briefing, turning to Coltrane, "It's Silver Fox." Both terms are to be treated as top secret, need to know only. If there are no questions, I must depart for Washington. Good luck, gentlemen," he said as he left the room.

Chapter Nine

The two-car caravan arrived at the main gate to the North American Aviation Plant in Inglewood three minutes early for its 0800 hours meeting with Arthur Bede. The recent government orders for more aircraft and the fear that the U.S. could be drug into another war had the pace around the plant considerably more animated than it was a year ago. There were lots of new faces and all of them had a look of professional purpose. The security guard checked the ID of all eight of the occupants against the authorized visitor list. He motioned for his supervisor to come over. He showed him the annotation beside their names. He nodded and lowered his head so he could talk to Captain Coltrane. "Sir, I am to take you over to the security office to get you security passes, then to the conference room. Please follow me."

It was almost 0900 hours by the time the group got over to the assigned room where a balding man in his early forties was waiting with a middle-aged assistant.

"Good morning, gentlemen. Please take your seats so we can get started. I am Arthur Bede, your factory rep for this project. Today I would like to introduce you to the B-25 serial number 40-007BX, which is configured for Special Operations in England. First let me show you some film of recent flight test of our pride and joy," he said with the pride of a new father at a maternity ward.

The assistant in the back turned down the lights and started the projector. The black and white film showed the B-25 taxing out for take-off then leaping into the air like it was under great power. It showed several different airborne maneuvers including slow flight with landing gear and flaps extended. Coltrane was impressed. It then made a short field approach and landing. Then it took off again and performed several high-speed low altitudes turns and maneuvers in the hills east of Los Angeles. The film suddenly ended, and the lights came on.

Bede moved back to the front of the room. "I believe that this aircraft will do the job described in the letter from the White House."

Major Dalton looked over to Colin Howarth as if asking the question. Howarth smiled and nodded back. He then looked at Coltrane and asked, "Can you fly this speedster?"

"Sir," answered Coltrane, "I'd pay a month's pay to just kiss its tires. That is one hell of an aircraft. It can do the job that you described." Then he joined the group in a little laugh.

"Okay then," Dalton said to Bede, "Tell us all about the B-25."

The better of two hours was spent by Arthur Bede showing slides of the various systems of the plane and endless performance charts. When the engine, fuel, electrical and hydraulic systems were on the screen the three mechanics came out of their seats talking among themselves as well as asking Bede endless questions. Bede was excited about the high level of interest in his and North American's new creation. Bede had to call a halt to the questions for the lunch break.

After lunch, Bede had representatives from the plant who specialized in the engine and other critical areas of the aircraft present to go deeper into the details. The pilots and Howarth talked with design and performance engineers and the prototype test pilot. Five o'clock came quickly. It was agreed that the Black Bart maintenance team would come back tomorrow to work with the respective specialist on the aircraft systems and engines. The pilots would work back at March Field on tactics and objectives of the mission with Dalton and Howarth. They would return day after tomorrow to discuss suggested changes and modifications.

The drive back was one of elated chatter like that between kids in a candy store. They had seen a new and dynamic aircraft that they would get to fly. The ominous aspect of deadly combat wasn't even considered except as a non-emotional fact to be incorporated into the plane configuration and operation. The staff car somehow found its way to the March Field Officers Club bar, where the conversation about what they had been changed to life and housing in London. Naturally, Coltrane asked about the women.

The next morning everyone showed up early for the meeting. Major Dalton started the meeting by letting Colin Howarth go into great detail of the type of mission they would be flying. A great deal was spent on routes usually flown, low level tactics, weather problems, navigation procedures and problems, and of course the enemy anti-aircraft and fighter hazards. His vivid and detailed description and personal experience in the Lysander was chilling to everyone. This brought about discussion on the aircraft configuration and equipment.

Bart looked over at Dalton, "Sir, did you get confirmation that we can get the Wright-2600-13 instead of the dash nine engines?" he asked. Dalton nodded in the affirmative. "Great, that gives us a little more usable power."

Kelly Sharp looked at the blueprints of the plane laying on the table. "I'd like to get a Plexiglas sighting blister for celestial star shootings."

Dalton made a note, then asked what was next.

"We really need that entire package of deicing boots. We will be dealing with a lot of icing over there," Coltrane said. "I'm thinking that with the existing system that they are offering have two positions. The one proposed looks good, but I think that we should ask for a booster that can deliver an additional amount of hot exhaust to the boots in really bad ice. I know there is a heat limitation on the rubber, but if we could have the ability to really heat them up for two or three minutes during heavy icing, it could make a big difference."

Once again Dalton wrote notes.

"Mr. Bede, you show a cover around the bomb bay. We do not want that option. We must have full access to the bomb bay from front and back. Any problem with that, Sir?"

"None," Bede said as he took notes.

Kelly Sharp was next to the talk about the navigation and radio equipment being installed. "I suggest that they wire the bird for both the GEE and LORAN Navigation System. I know neither is available today, but within a year, they will and that will greatly expand our capabilities in bad weather," Sharp said in a questioning tone.

Robby West agreed, and the point noted by Dalton.

Coltrane asked Colin about armament. "Sir, if we are flying at low altitude over the Krauts, we really don't need a tail gunner or a bottom turret. All of that is useless weight to us at that altitude."

"Agreed," chimed in West and Sharp. "What about a top turret with two fifty cals in the back?' asked West. "If we get jumped by fighters, we will need that. Granted, it can't shoot downward, but the only thing lower than us would be our buttons. So rear coverage from a top turret is all we need besides the eight fifty cals in front."

Coltrane shrugged his head and shoulders and said, "Very true, but that turret cuts our speed by 30 knots. That could be the difference if we were trying to outrun the fighters. So, we cut out the turret."

Sharp lifted his hand without thinking and added, "What if we went with only the two side waist guns. If we get jumped, we can use them and pray we can out-run them. The weight savings is considerate."

"You have a good idea, Robby, Coltrane said, "That's the way we go."

Coltrane nodded in agreement and looked at Dalton who started writing.

"What about the bomb bay configurations," asked West. "We need to replace the bomb racks with something that is more consistent with our cargo."

Colin added, "Yes, he is right. We could put the individual release hooks that we are putting into the Lancaster bomber. We could then hang the equipment pods vertically. When they are released, the chute goes on top. Leave enough line on the ripcord to allow the pod to clear buy ten or so feet then pull the drag chute. That type of release could allow us to drop from a really low altitude."

"Sounds great to me," Bart said as he looked at the others.

"The only other thing that I can think of is instrument panel configuration and instruments. I can see that we will be flying a lot on the gauges," Coltrane said, looking at West. "What have you got drawn up, Robby? I saw you making diagrams earlier."

"Given the amount of anticipated weather or instrument flying, I suggest that we outfit the bird with dual instruments. In combat, one side could be shot up and if we only had one set, we could be sure out of luck in the clouds. Think about this configuration. We first put all engine and monitoring gauges in the middle so we both can monitor them. On each side we have an independent Radio Magnetic Indicator top front with the clock and gyro compass on either side. Below that we have a 4-inch altitude indicator, airspeed, and altimeter on either side. Below the altitude indicator, we have the turn and bank indicator and climb and descent indicator. Leave the auto pilot in the center with the engine instruments.

"That would give us both a navigation radio to monitor and cross-reference as well as full instrument panel."

"Wow," Coltrane said, "That would really be effective. Major Dalton, would you add that to your list?"

"I'll put it down, but we are running up a big bill. I am not sure headquarters will like it, but they are not flying the bird," Dalton said. "Is that all the changes?"

Everyone remained silent.

"Okay, then we will leave for Inglewood at 0700 hours. I think we have accomplished a lot today. I suggest a gin and tonic before I leave for London," Dalton said, as he raised his hand as if it had a glass in it. "Meeting adjourned!"

Chapter Ten

Bart Coltrane looked out of the window of the train as it passed through the train station in Tucson, Arizona and noted that there were very few Christmas decorations. *Why wouldn't they have decorations up?* he thought, *It's the 15th of December 1940. Christmas is less than two weeks away. Christmas... I wonder how they celebrate Christmas in London. Well, I'm sure as hell going to find out. I'll be there in a week.*

Coltrane leaned back in the comfortable first-class chair and thought about the past three months. They sure had gone by fast. There was the day-by-day oversight of the building and testing of the new B-25. Then there was the heart-stopping training that Colin Howarth had put them through in Washington, Canada, and those long-range over-water flights to Anchorage. Twice his special de-icing boot had come in handy. That was a real good bird in icing conditions. Then there was the mobilization phase at March Field. They had collected four spare engines, enough spare parts for another two engines, replacement parts for everything imaginable on the plane. Even two sets of spare tires. Short field operations were hard on tires and brakes. Bart silently laughed to himself about letting the smokers in the crew pack 200 cartons of American cigarettes in the shipped cargo.

The containers were sealed and delivered to the freight forwarding company that would ship the five containers by train to port. There they took the risk of being sunk in transit across the Atlantic to London. The process started on November 10th and 35 days later he had not been advised of any loss in transit. Maybe, just maybe, those loads got there on time and without being repositioned on the ocean floor by a German submarine. What bothered Bart was that things that must be together to work usually can't be shipped together and three containers went first on a different ship. Oh, well, he would find out when he got there. Tomorrow he and his crew would report in from the customary 30-day leave prior to overseas deployment.

Bart enjoyed his leave back to Sweetwater, Texas as much as he could given the never-ending thoughts about the missions over enemy territory that were ahead of him. It was great spending time with his parents. It was even better reviving his acquaintances with old girlfriends and other ladies of his checkered past. Now it was time to get some sleep. He would be in Los Angeles early in the morning, and then it was back in the saddle.

When Bart signed in from furlough, he ran across Curt Lemay who had recently made Captain as well. "Hey, Curt, how are you doing? I thought that they would have you in jail for spreading the truth about strategic bombardment."

"Not yet, Bart, but they're waiting for the opportunity, "Lemay said. "Colonel Olds finally told me the details about what you are doing overseas. That's going to be rough, damned rough. Be careful and use your head."

"I think that we're well prepared for this. They gave us a great bird to fly and the Brits we are working for are solid as a rock. That's about all we can ask for," Coltrane said, trying not to sound melancholy. "You think you'll remain here or deploy to a forward area before the war starts?"

"Hawaii – real soon! That's all I know," Lemay replied. "I've got to go see the old man. Take care."

"Don't make him mad. We have a meeting with him this afternoon. We deploy in the morning," Bart added.

It was 1600 hours when Colonel Olds came into the conference room. "Welcome back to the working people," Olds joked as he went to the head of the table. "You have an incredible aircraft and an opportunity to really make a difference in the struggle over there. The people in these occupied countries want to fight for their country and they need your help to do that. You are the vanguard for the United States. We will be entering the war in the not-too-distant future. I don't see any way of staying out. Have a safe trip and God speed." Olds shook everyone's hand as he left the room.

After the Colonel left, Bart told everyone to sit down. "Okay, has everyone completed their overseas paperwork, last will and inoculations?" Everyone nodded in the affirmative. "Tomorrow is the day." We check out of the orderly room at 0700 hours. Load up and ready to crank up at 0800 hours. We'll fly to Wright Patterson, refuel and standby for some VIPs who want to look at the bird. It has got the imagination of some important people who support strategic bombardment."

"If we are off by 0800, we should be on the ground by 1900 hours. We should be finished with the VIPs by 2100 in bed by 2300 or so. We'll crank and depart by 0800 local. It's 1,269 miles to Goose Bay. If the winds hold, we'll be on the ground by 1800 plus or minus. We'll refuel, rest and standby for a 0100-hour departure. That puts us into Keflavik about 1030 hours. We need to refuel and take off within an hour if the weather is okay. We must arrive in Prestwick prior to dark, so we don't scramble the RAF. We'll remain overnight and await Squadron Leader Howarth's arrival. He's going to fly with us in to Tempsford, so we don't get lost, land on the wrong airfield or scare the cows. Then it's show time! Any questions? Okay, see you at the bird in the morning. Dismissed."

"Hey, Bart," called out Kelly Sharp. "Want to grab a drink and supper at the club?"

"Maybe, let me make a quick call first," Bart said as he picked up a phone and dialed 9 for an off-base phone line. He dialed a number from memory. The phone rang twice before it was answered by a female voice. "Afternoon, may I speak to Captain Andrews?"

"I'm sorry, he is out on a trip until tomorrow," she said.

Bart changed his voice back to normal and said, "Want to give a guy a heart attack?"

"Bart!" she screamed into the phone. "Yes, I would. When and where?"

"Meet me at the Dew Drop in an hour. We can grab a couple of drinks first. I need courage before taking you on."

"You clown. I'll grab a couple of things and head your way. I hope that you took your vitamins today. Bye." She hung up quickly.

Bart hung up the phone and turned to Kelly, "Sorry, I have to meet a friend."

Kelly knew what that meant. The whore dog was on the prowl tonight.

The next morning, the crew was anxious to get going. They had signed out and went to the bird and started a detailed preflight check about 0645 hours. They had finished when Captain Coltrane arrived a little before 0800. He looked tired and sleepless. He threw his duffel bag into the open bomb bay to Jack Martin who tied it down with the other bags. He then handed his flight bag with its charts, paperwork, E6B flight computer and other items used by seasoned pilots. Martin stepped across the bomb bay and placed the flight bag in the pilot's seat.

Coltrane started a slow walk around the bird, carefully looking for anything out of the ordinary. Yank Royston came up to him quietly and stood by for any questions that the pilot might have about the plane. When he finished his preflight inspection, he looked at Royston and asked "Ya got any problems?"

"No sir, we're ready to go," Royston said proudly.

"Okay, let's go cheat death," Coltrane said as he climbed up the ladder into the aircraft.

Crank up and pre-take off checks were completed, and they were ready to start the adventure of a lifetime.

Coltrane called Royston over the interphone system, "Yank, make one last check of that ferry tank. I'll leave the bomb bay open while you check it inside and out. That's one thing we don't need problems with in-flight."

Royston looked at the connections, hoses leading over the auxiliary fuel connection point. Wires to the internal fuel pump were verified to be connected. There were no leaks visible. He climbed down the ladder and looked up inside the bomb bay and looked at the tank over one last time. No leaks or drips. He climbed back inside and put his headset back on.

"Crew Chief to Pilot. Ferry Tank secure and no leaks," he reported.

"Pilot to Crew, anybody got a problem or need to go to the bathroom before we depart?" Coltrane said jokingly. "Okay, let's get this show on the road."

He depressed the mike switch on the control yoke to activate the radio transmitter and in a calm professional voice, "Tower, Black Bart 007 a single B-25, ready to depart when cleared."

"Roger, Black Bart, you are cleared for takeoff. Depart heading 090 until passing 4,000 then cleared on course. Contact Los Angeles control after takeoff on 3105 megacycles. Altimeter setting 29.30, wind 040 degrees at one zero. Have a safe flight."

"Roger, Black Bart on the go," Coltrane said as he advanced the two throttles to maximum power, then put both hands on the control yoke. The co-pilot, Robby West, put his hand on the throttles in case of emergency and started reading the increasing airspeed.

"Airspeed coming up," he said in a loud voice as the airspeed needle started to move . He eased the right engine throttle back very slightly to ensure the manifold pressure did not exceed the maximum limit which could cause one or more cylinders to blow up. He then started reading out the airspeed, "60 knots, 70 knots, 80 knots, 90 knots, 100 knots, 110 knots." Just then, Coltrane eased back slightly on the control yoke and the nose wheel came off the ground. Seconds later the main landing gear lifted off and the bird was in flight. It continued to climb upward steadily. Coltrane couldn't help but say over the intercom, "The adventure has begun!"

"Gear up," commanded Coltrane as he turned to heading 190 degrees as directed by the tower. "Okay, pull up half the flaps."

"Gear up, flaps coming up" West advised.

"Los Angeles Control, Black Bart 007 is with you passing two thousand feet enroute to fifteen thousand and on a direct 090-degree heading," Coltrane reported.

"Okay, flaps up and give me 35 inches of manifold and 2500 rpm," he told West.

West immediately reduce the throttles to adjust the engine manifold pressure to 35 inches of mercury and the prop pitch of the propellers to a speed of 2500 rpm.

"Black Bart 007 you are cleared on course, no reported traffic. Have a good flight," the Control Center directed the departing B-25.

"Roger, LA, good day," replied Coltrane. Then he turned to a heading of 075 degrees as the aircraft continued to climb to its assigned cruising altitude of 15,000 feet.

As they pass above the mountains below, the air smoothed out and made the ride more enjoyable. As they passed through 10,000 feet, Coltrane ordered, "passing 10,000, go on oxygen." Everyone put his oxygen mask on as they went about their duties, or in the case of the crew chief and mechanics, laid down on anything soft that they could find and go to sleep. Kelly Sharp was busy marking their progress on his map. He got his E-6B Whiz Wheel flight computer out and dialed in some settings. After a few minutes got an answer.

"If anyone is awake at the wheel, make your heading 072 degrees. We have a nice quartering tail wind," Sharp said, teasing the two pilots.

"Roger, 072 it is," Coltrane said as he pushed the nose down and leveled off at 15,000 feet. He adjusted the throttles to 30 inches manifold pressure and 2000 rpm. As the aircraft adjusted its altitude and flight characteristics, Coltrane made slight adjustments to the trim tabs on the ailerons and two tail rudders. This smoothed the flight even further. He then turned his heading bug on his RMI indicator to 072 degrees. Once the plane stabilized, he turned on the autopilot. The autopilot kept the plane heading 072 degrees the wings level. Cruise flight conditions had been achieved. They were on their way to war.

After an hour and twenty-seven minutes, Sharp said over the intercom, "That should be Williams, Arizona out your left side."

Both pilots looked out to see the town as if it had any relevance to the flight other than a known point enroute.

Sharp added in a serious tone, "Come left to 070 degrees. That wind is shifting slightly to the north. We have a ground speed of 219 knots. Not bad at this power setting. I estimate Wichita in about three hours twenty-eight minutes. That will put us in Wright Pat 28 minutes early if the winds don't go against us."

"Roger that," Bart said then looked at West and said, "I am going to put it on autopilot." He then patted him on the head and said, "You have it." West smiled and put his hands on the controls to show acceptance of the controls. The plane was already on the autopilot, but Bart wanted to get up and stretch his legs and go to the rear for a piss call. As he got up and went behind Sharp who was leaning over his navigation table making calculations.

It was almost 1830 when Sharp patted Bart on the shoulder and said, "We're 20 miles out, better contact approach control."

Bart nodded and grabbed the control yoke and triggered the radio transmitter. "Wright Pat approach Control, Black Bart 007 is with you 20 miles southwest at 15,000."

"Roger Black Bart descent and maintain 5,000 expect runway 24 wind 255 degrees at 8 knots gusts to 10 knots. Altimeter 29.08, visibility 6 miles, clear with a haze layer at 1,500 feet. Report 5 miles southwest."

"Roger Black Bart is out of 15,000 for 5,000 will report 5 southwest. We have the numbers, weather and runway," Coltrane said. "Okay, Robby take us to 5."

Robby West hit the autopilot disconnect button and pushed the yoke slightly forward as he made a small reduction in power. The B-

25 started to descend to its assigned altitude. Minutes later West made a textbook landing.

"Great landing, Robby," Bart said as he requested taxi instructions to the transmit aircraft parking.

As they pulled up in front of the transit operations building, three staff cars pulled up. Bart observed what seemed to be a dozen senior officers and civilians get out of the car and start looking and pointing at the new B-25. He unstrapped and got up to go report to the VIPs while West shut down the engines.

The visitors were impressed with the new bomber. They asked where it would be assigned, and Bart could only tell them that he was flying tests. He couldn't say his real assignment with the British. They didn't stay as long, as he had anticipated. He and the tired crew were grateful. They made their post flight checks and servicing prior to heading for transit quarters.

The next morning the flight departed on time and the 1,269 nautical mile flight to Goose Bay was very uneventful and routine if not boring. That changed when they got on the ground in Goose Bay only to find that the Arctic storm in northern Greenland was moving southward and could affect the alternate airfield located in the far southern end of Greenland.

Coltrane was not initially concerned as they had no plans to land there except if their primary landing field in Iceland became below approach minimums. He decided to remain overnight and see what the weather was in the morning. If the storm didn't move south and affect their route of flight to Keflavik, Iceland, he would take off. If it did, he would wait a couple of days and let it blow through. Now it was time to find the Officer's Club and a couple of stiff drinks and supper before getting some sleep.

The next morning Bart, West and Sharp went into the Goose Bay Operations building. They went into the weather office to get the enroute weather along the planned route which took them over Narsarsuaq, at the very southern end of Greenland to their destination at Keflavik, Iceland. The Army Air Force meteorologist informed them that the storm had not moved much overnight, but the direction had shifted to a more southeasterly. They may not be able to get into the Greenland airfield, but Keflavik should be no problem. The old Sergeant looked at the data and a report from a Greenland weather outpost at Dundas had reported within the hour that the storm had started to move rapidly to the southeast. "You know, Captain, if they are correct, it could affect you along your route including Keflavik, sir," the Sergeant said to the weatherman.

"Sergeant, I doubt it. Those guys are more interested in their ice flow studies than flying weather. They have been wrong before on those Arctic storms," the weatherman said with some doubt in his voice. He then went back over to Coltrane and put the weather map in front of him. "Here is what we have as of now. The storm should not affect you except over Greenland if you get going soon. We did have a report from some ice flow scientist who inputs weather twice daily that the storm was moving to the southeast. I just don't see any problem getting to Keflavik. If you do have a problem, you don't have an alternate and you can't come back here. We are forecast to go below minimums here by late today. It's your call."

Coltrane turned to Sharp, "What do you think?"

"Well, we barely have enough fuel to go on to Scotland if these guys are wrong! It would be really tight."

Coltrane turned back to the weatherman and asked, "You did say we should have no problem to Keflavik if we go now?"

"That's my read of the tea leaves, Captain!"

"Okay, we will go right away and get ahead of the bad weather." Bart said with some reservation.

"Okay, let's crank!"

Three and a half hours later, Black Bart 007 was flying between cloud layers about 277 miles southwest of Narsarsuaq, Greenland in very rough and turbulent air. The weatherman's prediction wasn't even close. They had a 65- knot headwind that had slowed their progress and was eating up their fuel. It was rough, but Coltrane and the older crewmen had seen worse. But the conditions were getting worse. To make things worse, weather conditions at Goose Bay had deteriorated as forecast. They couldn't go back now.

"Hey, Bart, could you go up to 20,000 and get above that cloud deck? I sure could use a good navigational fix before we get really in the soup.

"Yeah, but the winds are a lot stronger up there, so don't take long." Coltrane increased the power to be able to climb up through the clouds above. It took about 11 minutes to get through the deck at 21,500 feet.

"Okay, Kelly, make it quick. We've lost a bunch of ground speed in this wind," lamented Bart.

Kelly Sharp quickly got his sextant into the plastic bubble above the cockpit and looked for navigational information from the stars and sun.

A few minutes later Kelly said "I got it, take her down. Give me a minute to get our position."

Coltrane pushed the nose over and went down quickly back to 15,000 feet. Suddenly he heard voice traffic over the 278-kilocycle frequency Narsarsuaq used. He grabbed the control yoke tightly and pressed the radio transmit button.

"Narsarsuaq this is Black Bart 007 with you at 15,000 feet to the southwest enroute Keflavik." He said, "What's your weather?"

"Roger, Black Bart. We have 200 feet overcast 2 miles visibility, wind 305 at 40 gusting to 55. Last report from Keflavik was 22,000 overcast, 14,000 overcast, 5,500 feet broken visibility 6 miles, and wind 280 degrees at 20 gusts to 25. Weather is deteriorating. What is your estimated time of arrival at Keflavik?"

Coltrane looked back at Sharp for the answer. Sharp said, "Five hours 37 minutes based upon current winds."

"Looks like five and a half hours. What is the projected forecast for then?" Coltrane responded.

"Black Bart they are forecasting VFR conditions, but that storm is unpredictable," said the voice over the radio.

"Okay, we're continuing on as filed. Give us a call if the conditions change," a concerned Coltrane replied.

Black Bart 007 was slightly more than two hours from Keflavik when he was finally able to reach Keflavik on the radio. The wings were starting to get a thin coat of ice on them.

"Keflavik, this is Black Bart 007. We are with you at 15,000 to the southwest. What is your current weather and your forecast for two hours from now?"

"Black Bart, our weather is deteriorating rapidly. We have less than 3 miles and blowing snow. Wind is 290 at 45 gusts to 55. Forecast is for instrument conditions and severe winter storm. The Arctic storm changed course and is expected to arrive here within two to three hours. Recommend that you proceed to alternate."

"Keflavik, our alternate is below minimums and not usable. Standby," a very troubled Coltrane said as he turned to Sharp.

"Kelly, can we make Scotland given the distance and the fuel used so far?"

"This is not good, Bart, let me check," Sharp replied. After a long four minutes, he responded. "Bart, the changing winds may save us, but we will be on fumes. Our fuel consumption going against the wind has screwed us. By turning to 115 degrees the wind will be on our tail and that might be just enough to get us to dry land. We will be in a lot of bad weather. I expect a lot of icing most of the way." He said with a deep tone of concern.

"Thanks, Kelly," Bart said as he pushed the radio transmit button. "Keflavik, Black Bart is turning to Scotland direct, climbing to 21,000 feet. Coltrane announced as he pushed the throttles forward and made a climbing right turn to 115 degrees." Robby, make sure that you get every drop transferred out of the ferry tank. We're going to need it."

Black Bart 007 had leveled off at 21,000 feet. The instruments indicated that the speed had picked up and the fuel flow had declined slightly. Coltrane had set the power settings for the maximum cruise efficiency. He was grateful to the fuel ferry tank in the bomb bay.

Without it they might get to try out that life raft in the back compartments.

"Hey, Bart, there seems to be something wrong with my airspeed indicator. It seems to be showing only 60 knots airspeed. Why?" asked Robby West.

"Shit!" exclaimed Coltrane, "We're taking on ice."

He looked out his window into the gray sky at the wing and engine. His heart sank when he saw a heavy build-up of ice that had collected on the leading edge of the wing, engine, and propeller. He immediately reached out and turned on the pilot tube heater, carburetor heat, and the other deicing equipment. He saw that it was collecting faster than the deicing boots could handle. He knew that he had to turn on the extra heat position that he had put on at the factory. This might be enough to buy them time to get to a warmer altitude where the deice equipment could handle the problem.

He pushed the nose over and hit the radio transmit button. "Keflavik control, Black Bart is out at 21,000 descending to 10,000. We have some heavy icing at 21,000 feet." There was no reply. They were out of range so there was nobody that could advise other aircraft of their position and altitude. *There is probably nobody stupid enough to be flying in this shit anyway*, he thought.

He could not see through the forward cockpit windshield due to the ice buildup. He put the windshield heat on then turned on the wipers.

He looked out again as he passed through 15,000 feet. It was getting better. He had to turn the deicing boots back to normal or risk burning up a boot or seal that attached the boot to the wing. Coltrane just hoped that normal heat would be enough.

"My airspeed is back to normal," West reported. Bart nodded and smiled slightly.

He leveled the aircraft at 10,000 feet and reset the power settings to the best cruise setting possible. He decided that 2,000 rpm at 30 inches of manifold pressure would be best at this altitude. He adjusted the heading bug to 115 degrees and turned on the autopilot.

He lowered his sweaty hands, wiping them on the legs of his flight suit. *Then were okay for now*, he thought.

"Kelly, we are stable. Work up a position and fuel report," he said with authority.

"Roger, sir," he said, understanding the seriousness of Bart's tone.

"Captain, we are 593 nautical miles from Prestwick. Our ground speed at this altitude is 242 knots. Time to Prestwick is 2 hours 27 minutes. If the winds remain steady and we can stay at this altitude, our fuel burn is 165 gallons per hour and we have 460 gallons of usable fuel, sir," reported Kelly Sharp. "In short, keep this altitude, no wind change, and we will make Prestwick with 25 gallons in the tank."

"Right", he said. "I'm not certain we can keep this altitude due to ice. I'll do my best. Be thinking about a suggested lower altitude based upon winds. Also, keep your eye on that line of islands on the west side of Scotland just in case we have to go down before Prestwick."

"Robby, you watch the gauges and fly for a while. I need a breather. Do we have any coffee left?" Coltrane asked.

"Roger that, Captain," Sergeant Royston said as he handed him a thermos and a white porcelain cup and filled it halfway to avoid spilling.

Coltrane stood hunched over behind Kelly looking at his map and calculations.

"We will be over dry land in an hour and 44 minutes," Kelly said without being asked. He had already learned how Coltrane thought.

"Thanks, that isn't too bad if …."

"Captain," yelled West, "We're building up ice again."

Bart quickly got back into his seat and strapped on his parachute and safety belt unconsciously as he looked out of the windows on each side to get a clear picture of the situation. It wasn't good.

"Okay, Kelly, can you live with 8,000?" he asked as he indicated to Robby to let the plane down to 8,000 feet. West nosed the bird down without making a power change. It took very little time to get to the new altitude.

"We will be chewing up some of that 25-gallon reserve, but we can still make it ... barely," Sharp said with concern in his voice.

Bart looked at the windshield and then at the wings to see the ice buildup. It was holding at this altitude mainly because the precipitation had decreased more than the slight increase of outside air temperature. He reached up and turned up the heat level in the boots to the maximum level. He noticed a quick response and turned it back off for fear of damage to the boots. *Maybe this altitude will work out*, he thought. He then looked over at the radio transmitter dials and cranked in the coastal defense approach frequency that he had been given. They were 6 or 8 hours ahead of schedule. He got his code book out as well. Satisfied that he had what he needed; he made the call. It was almost immediately returned. It wasn't very clear due to distance and weather conditions. Coltrane gave the proper identification code and authentications required. It was too bad that the new Identification Friend or Foe (IFF) device had not been installed. That would happen at Tempsford. He could see the needle on the radio direction finder move from pointing off to the right to almost straight ahead. *Kelly was on course ... as always*, he thought. Bart looked at the clock on the instrument panel and saw that they had less than an hour to fly before landing.

"Prestwick Control, this is Black Bart 007 with you at 8,000 feet," Coltrane said then waited for a reply.

"Black Bart 007 descend and maintain 4,000 feet. You should break out of the clouds at that altitude."

"Roger Prestwick, Black Bart is out of 8 for 4 thousand," he replied. Bart looked out west and pointed down. He lowered the nose to descend.

They broke out of the overcast and out of the rain slightly below 4,800 feet. Coltrane turned off the deicing equipment. He was amazed at the beautiful countryside surrounded the aircraft. It was the first Arran Island to the west of Prestwick.

"Pilot to crew, prepare for landing! The Yanks have arrived!"

"So have the Brits", Royston said in response. "Look at your starboard wing. That's a RAF Hurricane."

"We've got one on our port too," Andy Lightfoot said as he looked out the left side window where a machine gun normally would be mounted in combat.

Coltrane said, "Looks like an RAF Identification sortie to make sure we are not bearing a Swastika.

"American Bomber follow me to Prestwick," came the voice over the radio.

"Roger, take the lead. Black Bart 007 will follow. Be advised we are fuel critical," Coltrane advised.

"Roger on fuel state. Turn to a heading of 095. Prestwick is 8 nautical miles. Descend to 1,500 feet. Tune in tower 119.5. Good day, mate," said the RAF pilot as he dramatically increased his speed and broke off contact.

"Prestwick Tower, Black Bart 007 is with you descending to 1,500 feet 7 miles west. Request landing instructions."

"Black Bart, Prestwick Tower, enter a left downwind for runway 31, winds 330 at 20, altimeter setting 29.05. You are number one for landing, understand fuel critical, you are cleared to land" came the metallic voice over the radio.

Coltrane started through the pre-landing checks then said, "Let me have 10 degrees of flaps, advance the mixture controls, full prop pitch, as he slowed the bomber to 120 knots. Okay, give me the gear and flaps."

Robby West's hands flew across the instrument panel complying with the pilot's commands. "Gear is down and locked," he reported.

The plane made minor course connections on final approach to properly link up with the runway center line and the effects of the 20-knot wind on its right front. As it crossed the runway threshold, Black Bart gently touched down in Scotland.

"Black Bart 007 turn left on the taxiway and follow the 'Follow Me' Lorry to parking," ordered the control tower. "Welcome to Scotland."

"Roger, we are damned glad to be here," quipped Coltrane.

The aircraft came to a stop in front of a small transit aircraft terminal. Two men in civilian topcoats and hats left the building and headed towards Black Bart.

"Okay, let's shut her down and wrap it up. We will do dailies and services in the morning," Coltrane said as he pulled the mixture controls to the rear stops stopping the engines. He flipped the ignition and battery switch, and the aircraft became almost silent. With only the sound of the gyro compass slowly spinning down.

Bart immediately recognized Major Dalton and Squadron Leader Howarth.

Dalton extended his hand and said, "I take it your flight didn't go as planned."

"Not exactly, sir. We got caught up in some unpredicted weather storm. Had to bypass both Greenland and Iceland," Coltrane reported. "Bad winds and heavy ice really tested the old bird."

"So, I understand from Keflavik Control. They really didn't expect that you could make it in the bloody bad weather. May I offer you and your crew a stiff drink? You've certainly earned it," Dalton said in classic British humor.

* * *

An hour later in a small private dining room at a popular Scottish restaurant near the airport, the crew was starting the second round of drinks. The crew described to Dalton and Howarth the hair-raising trip across the Atlantic. The waiter came in with a third round ordered by Major Dalton along with menus. After ordering, Dalton nodded to Howarth who went to the door and closed it and stationed himself outside so nobody could enter or eavesdrop on the Major's briefing of the crew on their schedule for the next three days.

"Gentlemen, you will stand down for today and tomorrow for crew rest. Then on the 21st we will fly down to Croydon Airfield which is near downtown London. Howarth will fly copilot to help you get there without being shot down. A B-25 is an unknown to our blokes. There you will present yourself and aircraft to a few the General Staff and other Royal dignitaries. Then you will fly to Tempsford, just north of London. Your crew will take occupancy of their cottage. The B-25 will immediately go inside the temporary hangar for your operation. In this case, your temporary hangar is two large tents put together. Temporary probably means until after the war. Once everything is sorted, the three officers will depart by train for London. There you will check into the quarters at Montague Mansions. You will start detailed briefings on the 22 and 23 December at SOE Headquarters at 84 Baker Street. You have an office to work up missions there. All covert operations are planned there. On the morning of 24 December, you will take the 0510 train to Tempsford. The crew will be ready to fly at 0900."

"Squadron Leader Howarth will fly with you and give you an orientation on the local area, then take you across the channel and give you a familiarization on the coast and routes back to Tempsford and Tangmere. All SOE Resistance operations go out of those two airfields. Depending on fuel and weather you will fly north to RAF Sumburgh in the Shetland Islands. We normally go in and out of Norway and Holland from there. After that you will return to Tempsford. Keep your aircraft in the hangar unless you are going on a mission. We want to keep your base a secret as long as we can. You will then stand down until the 27th. Starting 27 December 1940, you will no longer be in the organizational category and will become a part of Section D. That's Lieutenant Colonel Lawrence Grand's command. He will be directing your missions. Good chap Grand, you'll like him. You will fly a short mission into France on the 28th after planning and preparations on the 27th. After that we will be working on the planning of many missions and probably some that may come up in urgency. Any questions?" Major Dalton asked. "No questions, then will someone collect Howarth? Good luck and good hunting."

Chapter Eleven

Kelly Sharp said over the interphone to anyone who was listening at 0405 hours, "When the Major said our first mission would be on the 28th, he failed to say it would be in the middle of the night."

Colin Howarth who was flying in the copilot seat retorted, "I say, you will find that it is much safer to fly at night. Today we are giving it a go in the early dawn so you can get a good feel for the countryside and the bloody Germans. I bloody well think that we can give them a little surprise on this one. They really don't know much about you yet. I am sure their Intel people know about you, but they don't know what you are doing over here with us. That will change in about an hour. Lieutenant Sharp, can you give us a time on this leg to Tangmere?"

"Sir, we will be over Tangmere in 8 minutes. Then we turn to a heading of 070 degrees for the channel crossing to the river delta area just south of Le Crotoy, sir," came the confident voice of the navigator.

"Bloody good. Now after you leave Tangmere, you will want to drop down to 500 feet for the crossing. It should be early dawn by the time we get over to France, so you should be able to see the Le Crotoy Delta," he said then continued. Lieutenant West, the usual copilot, was sitting on the jump seat just behind the navigator. "Lieutenant West, it's your job to keep a keen eye for check points and any fighters ahead of us. Sergeant Royston will watch for fighters coming from above and behind us. Once we're over the water or France you can expect fighters, flak and anti-aircraft fire. Don't let it bother you or let it distract you from your assigned task."

Coltrane could see the first improvement in his ability to see things on the coastline ahead due to the dawn's early light. He hoped that the Germans were sleeping in, just like he wanted to do when they woke him up this morning.

Sharp reported, "Coastline in two minutes." Coltrane looked at the approaching coastline of France and mentally concurred. *Sharp was dead on with his navigation*, he thought.

He resolved to find a better expression than 'Dead On!'

At 230 knots the plane crossed the shoreline quickly. Sharp said, "Course 135 degrees to Walrus."

He had no more said that when Coltrane saw several streams of tracers arching up ahead of them. "Shit, taking fire already."

Howarth smiled and said "This is nothing. It will get much worse. Put it out of your mind. You might want to drop down to 100 feet to reduce the volume of fire," as he looked over to Coltrane and smiled. "The lower you go the fewer of the buggers can get a shot at you."

Coltrane responded very quickly.

"Walrus in 60 seconds," Sharp reported. Howarth looked up and said, "I have it in sight, do you?"

Coltrane nodded as he gripped the control yoke more tightly. Fear was starting to have its effect on him.

Suddenly, six or eight streams of tracers from machine guns started up at him. He could feel an occasional hit on the aircraft. Coltrane glanced at Howarth, who looked like someone looking for flowers in the field.

"I say, you need to ignore the fire. You can't do much at this point. I have Walrus in sight. You'll be turning to 080 degrees then pop up to 1,000 feet and open your bomb bay as we planned. We kick out the first delivery pod on my command. Then we drop to 150 to 200 feet and turn to 062 degrees to overfly the clearing. Hopefully, the Jerries will be watching the first parachute and ignore us when we drop the real load in the clearing. Now don't get too crazy on me when we're up at 1,000 feet. They'll really be putting some fire power on us," he said in a calm voice.

Coltrane looked over at him and knew this man had seen much worse and lived to talk about it. "Bomb bay doors open," he ordered.

Sharp said that Walrus was ahead in 10 seconds. Howard said, "Pull up now," and he reached over and opened the bomb bay door himself.

"Okay, release." Then he pulled the release device that held the first supply pod from the bomb bay. Coltrane could feel the change in weight when the 300-pound dummy load went out. The sky was alive with tracers and puffs of black smoke just after a bright flash. Flak! Fear was starting to well up inside him again even more. He smiled at the thought that if the enemy is in range of your fifties you are in range too!

"Put it over and turn to 062 degrees standby for second release," he said. "I have the forest and the clearing."

As he descended to 150 feet the flak stopped and the machine gun fire almost stopped. He spotted the clearing and adjusted his course so he would be directly over the center of the clearing.

"Standby," Howarth said. "Ready, release!"

The 1,200-pound load of weapons, ammo and explosives dropped out the bottom.

Coltrane felt the bomber to lifted suddenly as the heavy supplies dropped out. The parachute immediately opened and slowed the pod down before it landed.

Sharp directed, "Turn to 120 degrees." Sharp felt the plane execute a hard-right turn to the assigned course. He looked to the right to watch the bomb bay doors quickly shut. "Turn to 185 degrees in 30 seconds, stand by … turn." Again, the plane turned to the right and descended to slightly above tree level.

Howarth pointed out the front of the aircraft after closing the doors and said, "Do you see that river up ahead?"

"I have it in sight," Coltrane said with a little more composure. The machine gun fire had decreased to just a few lines of tracers.

Occasionally, he would feel two or three rounds hit the plane. Still dangerous, but not as bad as it had been.

"Okay, follow it to the channel. Stay low, very low. We will go through a couple more bad areas." He could see the channel ahead about five miles. He also saw the tracers increase as well. He got the bomber down almost into the trees. The tracers nearly stopped. *The bastards couldn't get a shot at him at this altitude*, Coltrane thought.

"Now, there you go mate. Keep it low and stay alive," Howard said as if he were ordering a beer. "Sharp, how about a course back home?"

"Three miles offshore turn to 355 degrees," the navigator directed.

As Coltrane turned north and he climbed to 500 feet he felt relieved. The hard part was over. They were safe and on their way home. Then he saw a black dot in the sky ahead of them starting down towards them.

"Shit," Coltrane said as he reported, "Bandit 12 o'clock just above us. Coming down." He lowered the plane slightly to ensure that the enemy ME 109 couldn't go below him.

Howarth said nothing. He just looked at Bart and smiled slightly. He was evaluating the pilot and his actions in a one-on-one situation with the enemy.

Coltrane saw the ME 109 start to level off at the same or slightly higher altitude on a head-on course. The ME 109 still had a little more altitude advantage as it approached at a combined speed of over 600 knots. Bart flipped the cover up that covered the button that fired the eight .50 caliber machine guns mounted in the nose and sides of the B-25. He slightly raised the nose and hit the fire switch. The impact of the eight streams of .50 caliber bullets tore the ME 109 into pieces. Fire consumed the falling pieces of the fighter.

"Nice shot, Bart," Howarth said. "Those fifties are impressive." "Now be a good chap and take us home without any more excitement. You chaps are ready to go it on your own. Can I buy you a pint or a shot of whiskey when we get back to Tempsford?"

Master Sergeant Royston and his two mechanics walked around the B-25 looking at the bullet and black flak holes without comment. After they finished the walk-around inspection, Royston looked at his two assistants and asked the question that everyone knew was coming, "How long will it take you to get it ready to go again?"

Jack Martin looked at him and said, "If the engines check out you can have it back late tomorrow, maybe sooner, Sarge. They really didn't hit anything we can't fix quickly. There is a lot of patching and some minor damage, but that's it. You were damned lucky."

"Okay, I'll pass it on to Captain Coltrane. I hope they don't have any mission planned for tonight or tomorrow," Royston said with resignation.

"Speak of the Devil," Lightfoot said as Coltrane and Sharp came out of the operations building with Howarth.

Coltrane walked up to the group and looked up at the obvious damage. "Let me guess, I get it back tomorrow," he said with a smile.

Royston nodded with a short, almost silent laugh, "We were lucky, this time."

Howarth looked at the damage as they walked around the aircraft. "I'll be surprised if you could get back up by day after tomorrow. We'll stand down for a couple of days. Let's go get a shower and head for the office. We have an After-Action Report to complete. Then we have a talk with the boss to see what he has in mind for your next mission. Sergeant Royston, do you really think it will be ready for a mission tomorrow night?"

"Yes sir, it'll fly tomorrow night. Black Bart will be ready to go." He paused then asked Coltrane and Howarth, "Can we paint nose art on our bird like the other squadrons?"

"I see no reason not to," Howarth said as he looked at Coltrane.

Coltrane switched his look from Howarth to Royston, "What do you have in mind, Yank?"

"Just who we are sir, Black Bart!" We will put the original pirate flag on it too!

Coltrane smiled and nodded. "Okay with me."

* * *

The hour and a half train ride to London was occupied by sleep. The train had not left the Tempsford Station before all the flight crew was asleep.

It was a little after two in the chilly and damp afternoon. The first thing on the agenda was to debrief the mission to the key staff. In the past they would report the events of the flight to Lieutenant Colonel Grand, the head of Section D. This time, Sir Hugh Dalton, the new head of SOE came into the debriefing along with four others. Everyone quickly took their seats at the long conference table in the center of the new Black Bart operations office.

"Well, Captain Coltrane, Black Bart's first mission was even better than I had hoped for. My personal congratulations to you all. You delivered the delivery pods exactly on target, you shot down an Me-109, and you brought your crew and aircraft back alive and in flyable condition."

"Sir, I was nothing more than a bus driver on this mission. Squadron Leader Howarth directed every aspect of the mission and deserves the credit," Coltrane said.

Howarth leaned back in his chair and said, "Other than to spot the Landing Zone and when to drop the pods, I did nothing. I certainly didn't have a thing to do with shooting down the Me-109. I didn't even see it until you called the bloody bugger out." Lieutenant West will be quite able to fill in my place in future missions. I shall report that Black Bart is fully operational and bloody well ready for assignments," he said in a commanding tone.

"Very well, then, "Dalton said, "Then Black Bart will be operational effective immediately. Any questions for me?" he said as he got up to leave. "Well, then, carry on."

Lieutenant Colonel Grand stood up and turned to the four new people seated at the end of the table. "Let me introduce the operations and intelligence team that you will be working with. First, the big ugly gentleman at the end is Colonel Julian 'Hak' Smythe. He is the man that coordinates all field operations. He spent two months in Norway, two months in Denmark and four months in Belgium making contact with potential Resistance leaders. You are supporting his network and I might say he was right under Jerry's nose and lived to tell about it. He knows the ground operations side across the channel. Next to him is Group Captain Sanford Balfour, our Order of Battle specialist. He will give you his best guess on enemy location, strength, and aircraft positions. He works closely with the lady to his right, Major Annabel Beddows, who heads up our Intelligence Collection and Evaluation Section. Lastly, we have Lieutenant Commander Rupert Chapham who we stole from the Royal Navy. Rupert coordinates all air supply missions like yours. Essentially, he gets a request for supply or personnel drop from Colonel Smythe. He reviews the available intelligence and actual mission requirements and priorities, and then he schedules the mission. He assigns it to either one of the Lysander Groups at either Tempsford or Tangmere and now Black Bart. Once tasked, you and your crew will get detailed enemy information from Major Beddows and Captain Balfour," he said in conclusion.

Bart nodded with a smile as each was introduced. He was especially taken with Beddows. He thought this raven-haired beauty was stunning. He looked for wedding rings on both hands but didn't see any. This excited his salacious nature. His attention was broken by Lieutenant Girard.

"I understand that enemy battle damage has your aircraft non-op until late tomorrow." Rupert Chapham said. "Are you certain that it will be available for a mission tomorrow night?" he said with an irritating air of superiority and contempt.

Bart knew that he wasn't going to like this son-of-a-bitch. He had that Oil Can Harry villain look to him with his hair slicked back and a pencil thin mustache. "Not certain, but my crew chief believes it will be ready."

"Captain, we don't deal in 'beliefs.' We deal in certainties and absolutes," Chapham retorted.

"Alright, Commander Chapham, I will report when it is operational again. No matter what time it becomes operational!" Bart said in a tone designed to stand his ground and not cower to this asshole. Bart knew that this war may have many combat fronts and this man may be one of them.

"Very well, you do that. I'll be interested in exactly when you do report operational. We shall see how good your Crew Chief estimate really is," Chapham said contemptuously.

Lieutenant Colonel Grand saw the level of conflict start to escalate and intervened, "Well then, let's get down to mission details."

* * *

The debriefing took the better part of an hour. Being the first time to undergo this form of debriefing, the questions and answers were somewhat choppy at first. At the end, Chapham got up and left without comment or ceremony. The others left with polite farewells. Bart was still taken by Beddows, even though she was expressionless. *She was beautiful*, he thought.

It was almost 1700 hours in the afternoon when they finished and were very tired and sleepy. They left the building and walked over to their quarters at Montague Mansions. Bart went into his room. It was frightfully small. He went to the bathroom to relieve himself. He became irritated when the old pull chain toilet wouldn't work. Frustrated and tired, he went back into the room and lay down. He went to sleep immediately with his clothes still on.

It was almost 2100 hours when a hard knock at the door woke Coltrane up from a deep sleep.

His room was dark and still somewhat unfamiliar despite living there for almost a week. He flipped the switch on the wall to turn on the overhead light. It promptly flashed and went out. "Damned light bulb," he said in a low, angry voice. He opened the door and found both Sharp and West standing in the hall in civilian clothes.

West said in a flippant voice," We're hungry. We flipped a coin and you lost. You're buying!"

Shaking the cobwebs out of his head, he smiled and replied, "Yeah, me too. Let me change clothes. I'll meet you downstairs in 5 minutes."

Bart got off the old elevator to join the other two standing near the door. Okay, where do you want to go?" Please, no damned fish and chips. I have had my fill of that shit. I need a real steak or at least something different."

"Yeah," West said. "We asked one of the Lysander pilots who just came through here what was available in the area. He suggested either an Italian joint four blocks down or a German place called The Rathskeller over on Dorset. It's closer and it's getting damned cold outside. The wind is coming in off the North Sea."

"Rathskeller, it is. Besides being from Texas, I just can't take this type of cold weather. Lead the way, navigator," Bart said as he offered an open door.

The trio walked quickly over Dorset Street in the cold damp wind. They saw the empty outside tables and chairs just outside the restaurant. They went into a dimly lit room where there were about 20 locals drinking at the bar or eating at one of the four booths and four tables along the back and right-side wall.

West leaned over to Bart and asked, "Do we want an outside table?"

The heavyset man behind the bar saw them and waved them to an open booth at the very back of the bar.

"Greetings, gents! I take it you're here for the tourist sights," quipped the barmaid who was in her late 30's, but beautiful by any standard.

Bart replied at once, not taking his eyes off the buxom blonde's well-developed chest. "You bet! We're here on the American plan.

Tomorrow it's the Buckingham Palace tour if the damned Germans don't bomb it first."

"You're Yanks, great! How about something to warm you up?" She asked them while looking at Bart and said "… and I'm not on the menu."

"Killjoy! How about a double shot of your famous single malt scotch?" he retorted.

"Right-O, now how about you lads? She responded.

"Make that three," Sharp said. "Shots, that is. I have no idea what junior here wants. Better check his ID to see if he is old enough to be here," pointing to Robby with his thumb.

After the second round they looked at the menu. There were very impressed at the wide variety of foods and the almost total omission of the traditional fish and chips. It even had a breakfast menu on the backside.

The lady came back without another round and asked, "What's your pleasure, gents?" Then looked at Bart and said, "Forget it!"

Bart looked up at her blue eyes and smiled, "I don't get it. The world is under attack by the damned Germans and this German bar is going great in downtown London. What's the story, if you don't mind my asking?"

"Fair question," she said. "The owner is Heinrich Hoff, the big guy behind the bar. He came here in 1913 with his parents and sister. When the first war broke out, he volunteered to help Whitehall with translations and advised them on the German culture. He even helped recruit spies to go into France and Germany. Needless to say, he became a popular man to the government. After the war, he went into Germany to assist with the transition and implementation of the Versailles Treaty. He had a little money, and he took advantage of the war-torn situation. He made a lot of money over there. He came back after two years and bought this place. People really don't think of him as a German. Besides, he runs a great kitchen and hotel. You'll find the food to be outstanding."

"Did you say hotel?" Sharp interjected.

"Yes, he has eight apartments that he rents upstairs. They are large and have very nice furniture. He gets good money for them too," she said.

The crew looked silently at each other then quickly ordered supper. Sharp was the first to say what was on everyone's mind. "Are you guys thinking what I am? That dump we are in is really bad. This is not. This could be really great for us. Good place to live and food that doesn't make you want to throw up. With what we are getting for housing allowance and per diem, we could afford this, I think."

When the barmaid came back, Bart asked, "Are there any available flats upstairs?"

"Sure, we have four open. They rent for five pounds per night or 120 pounds a month," she responded. "That includes breakfast."

"Great, that's within our housing allowance. Could we see the space after we eat?"

"Sure, I'll tell Heine. He'll take you up for a show." Then she looked at Coltrane and waved a finger at him. "No, no, not me, forget it."

Bart smiled warmly. "Who are you?"

"I am Regina Whitehurst. Everybody calls me Reggie. And who are you blokes?"

Bart introduced the three of them. She was genuinely warm in her response. Then she turned to get the waiting food order.

A couple hours later, Heinrich Hoff finished showing the available flats to the three aviators and turned to them in anticipation of an answer.

Sharp was the first to say anything. "The bathroom is larger than my current bedroom. This is a palace compared to what we have now. I'm in!"

A smile came over Heine's face, then Bart and Robby West chimed in with their agreement to rent.

"Can we move in tomorrow?" asked Bart.

"Tonight, if you wish," Heine said. "Now, how about a drink on me?"

Chapter Twelve

On the night of December 29th, 1940, President Roosevelt sat at his desk in the oval office. A bank of radio microphones had been placed before him. He was preparing to give one of his fireside chats to the American people.

The President began: "This is not a fireside chat on war. It is a talk on national security; because the nub of the whole purpose of your President is to keep you now, and your children later, and your grandchildren much later, out of a last-ditch war for the preservation of American independence and all of the things that American independence means to you and to me and to ours."

The audience, seated in several rows of folding chairs arranged before the President's desk in the oval office, included Clark Gable and his wife, Carol Lombard. Anna Roosevelt along with the Secretary of State, Cordell Hull, were seated in the front row. John Roosevelt, the youngest son, stood behind and to the right of the seated guests. Several military types including General Arnold, several VIP civilian types and two newsmen occupied the remaining chairs.

The President continued: "Never before since Jamestown and Plymouth Rock has our American civilization been in such danger as now. For, on September 27, 1940, by an agreement signed in Berlin, three powerful nations, two in Europe and one in Asia, joined themselves together in the threat that if the United States interfered with or blocked the expansion program of these three nations - a program aimed at world control - they would unite in ultimate action against the United States. The Nazi masters of Germany have made it clear that they intend not only to dominate all life and thought in their own country, but also to enslave the whole of Europe, and then to use the resources of Europe to dominate the rest of the world."

Every eye in the audience was on the President.

"The people of Europe who are defending themselves do not ask us to do their fighting. They ask us for the implements of war, the planes, the tanks, the guns, the freighters, which will enable them to fight for their liberty and for our security. Emphatically, we must get these weapons to them in sufficient volume and quickly enough, so that we and our children will be saved the agony and suffering of war which others have had to endure."

The President raised his voice in firmness as he made his final points: "We must be the great arsenal of democracy. For us this is an emergency as serious as war itself. We must apply ourselves to our task with the same resolution, the same sense of urgency, the same spirit of patriotism and sacrifice as we would show were we at war. We have furnished the British great material support and we will furnish far more in the future. There will be no 'bottlenecks' in our determination to aid Great Britain. No dictator, no combination of dictators, will weaken that determination by threats of how they will construe that determination."

A short time later in a parlor in the White House, the select group of people who had been invited to sit in on the fireside chat, now sat with cocktails and hors d'oeuvres. Roosevelt was seen talking with several of the people, General Arnold being one of them along with the two reporters. Secretary Hull finished shaking hands with one of the VIP types, then moved to the President.

"An excellent speech, Mr. President," Hull said. "Ought to give our people in the Congress something to work with when Lend-Lease comes up for debate." President Roosevelt grinned. "Well ... let's hope so, Mr. Secretary," He turned to the reporters. "The American people ought to realize how vital it is to our own future security that England holds out against Hitler. Britain is bankrupt, but Churchill leaves no doubt they'll fight on … if they can be supplied. And … our American industry can do that!"

A reporter asked "But what about the Neutrality Act, Mr. President? Wouldn't direct aid to Britain, a belligerent in a war, be a violation?"

"The Lend-Lease proposal I'm sending to the Congress would allow us to lend England unlimited supplies and equipment, in some cases in exchange for leases on advanced bases of operation, all without violating the Neutrality Act or any other constitutional provision the Isolationists try to use against us," Roosevelt said.

"Well, Lend-Lease notwithstanding, it was a great speech, Mr. President. The Arsenal of Democracy … is the kind of phrase that finds its way into the history books!" John Roosevelt said.

"Thank you, John."

Gable and Lombard detached themselves from a small knot of people and approached the President.

"Great speech, Mr. President," Gable said.

"Thank you, Clark," President Roosevelt said. He turned to Carole Lombard. "You look positively ravishing tonight, Carole."

"Why, thank you Mr. President. You don't look so bad yourself,"

Roosevelt laughed. "Come now!"

Lombard held her champagne glass aloft before the guests. "A toast everybody." She turned to the President and smiled. "To the President. May America indeed become the Arsenal of Democracy, Mr. President, in spite of Charlie Lindbergh and the isolationists!"

The guests raised their glasses, and some exclaimed "Here! Here!"

A smiling President Roosevelt sipped the toast and then thanked his guests. "A President's day doesn't end at sundown, you know."

Roosevelt nodded to a secret service agent who stood nearby, indicating his readiness to leave the room.

The agent went to Roosevelt's wheelchair, grasped the handles to push the President from the room, all of this as Roosevelt spoke softly to Eleanor Roosevelt who had leaned over to kiss the President on his cheek.

"Harry will be along with the initial press reactions momentarily. I'll be in the library. Send him in there, will you?"

"Of course, Father." Anna gazed at her father admiringly. "It was really an electrifying speech, you know."

"Thank you, my dear."

President Roosevelt turned to General Arnold. "Oh Hap."

"Yes, Mr. President."

"I've got some work to finish off. Mind coming along for a few minutes?"

"Not at all, sir."

Roosevelt emerged from the oval office, being pushed by the Secret Service agent, General Arnold walked alongside the wheelchair. They proceeded through the reception area and on down a long corridor leading to the library, the President talking all the while.

"You know, Hap; we've got a long way to go in overcoming public apathy," Roosevelt said.

"Yes, Mr. President," General Arnold said.

President Roosevelt thought for a moment. "Well anyway … Marshall approved the Kilner-Lindbergh Five Year Plan. The Air Corps finally has *its* mission."

General Arnold grinned. "That's right, Mr. President."

"And … we've got Air Corps observers in England?" Roosevelt said.

"We have General Chaney and that B-25 experiment with the Special Operations Executive, Code name Black Bart. They flew their first mission yesterday. Made a drop to the Resistance and shot down a Me-109 as well."

"Good." The President paused, becoming reflective. "Hap, there's talk up here about a reorganization plan for the Air Corps. It's what we had in mind when we made you Acting Deputy Chief of Staff last March and kept you on as Chief of the Air Corps at the same time. I'm directing Secretary of War Stimson to place our Army Air Corps under a single commander."

"We've needed that kind of unity of command, Mr. President," General Arnold said.

"We're reviving the office of Assistant Secretary of War for Air. I've been thinking Robert A. Lovett would be an asset there. He's done a fine job as our special assistant on air matters."

General Arnold found it hard to believe what he was hearing. "Excellent choice, Sir!"

"The way we've got it planned, you'll become Chief of the Army Air Forces at that time, but you'll retain the title of Deputy Chief of Staff." He paused to gauge Arnold's reaction." That way, of course, you'll be able to serve as contact between the War Department General Staff and the Army Air Forces."

"I'm not so sure I agree with my involvement in the matter, but I think the plan itself is excellent! It certainly should help eliminate our perennial problems with the war department general staff."

"Exactly ... something we should have done years ago."

They arrived at the library door and General Arnold opened the door as the Secret Service agent wheeled the President into the library. The President gestured to a desk across from the library door and the Secret Service agent pushed the wheelchair to the desk where he was dismissed by the President.

"Thank you," President Roosevelt said. "I'd like not to be disturbed except when Hopkins comes up, of course."

"Yes, Sir", The agent said and left.

The President wheeled himself into position behind the desk where a stack of paperwork had been carefully laid out for his perusal and action. The President gestured to one of the several large chairs by the desk. 'Sit down, Hap." He pointed to a decanter on the corner of the desk. "Care for one?"

"Why ... yes of course, if you are, Sir." General Arnold said.

Roosevelt began pouring the drinks, talking all the while.

"Hap, Churchill's chiefs of staff are coming over here next week. They want to discuss grand strategy with our chiefs and their representatives."

The President passed the drink to Arnold who took the glass and settled back into his seat. Roosevelt contemplated his glass for a moment, and then he gazed at Arnold:

"Of course, if the press gets hold of this, they'll accuse us of making secret plans to go to war! Our goose would be cooked, you know!" President Roosevelt said.

"I understand, Sir." General Arnold said.

"The military consensus seems to be that we'll be forced into the war eventually. The mutual pact between Japan, Germany and Italy provides a pretty sound basis for their judgment," the President said.

"Seems rather obvious, Sir."

"In that event, our combined efforts would be directed against Germany first," Roosevelt said, "any action against Japan being fought more or less on an attrition basis until Germany is defeated."

Roosevelt leaned forward as he spoke, emphasizing the gravity of his words.

"Hap ... the War Department strategists are talking about conducting a massive air offensive against German industry ... if not Germany itself. It will be done from airdromes that we've established in England. Heavy bombers will drop hundreds of thousands of tons of bombs deep into enemy territory. They feel German morale can't withstand the pressures of aerial bombardment as the British have for so long now. Can we do it?"

"Of course, Mr. President, given the time," General Arnold said. "The strategic bombardment mission is what we've been working toward ever since Billy Mitchell and our tactical school developed the concepts."

"How much time?" President Roosevelt asked.

General Arnold paused. "Three years."

"Three years! You're talking about 1943!"

"Mr. President … it'll be late in forty-one before sufficient numbers of B-17s and B-24s are available to begin basic four-engine training programs here in the United States."

"But … three years, Hap?"

"Well … we're looking at another year to a year and a half to equip and train a sufficient number of combat groups to efficiently mount a strategic air offensive." General Arnold began to speak slowly to emphasize the importance of what he was saying. "Gunners … bombardiers … entire crews … they have to be trained in the equipment they'll fly in combat. Otherwise, our combat losses would be unacceptable."

He was silent for a moment, knowing the President was thinking about his words. "In the meantime, we've still to equip our heavy bombardment groups in Alaska, the Caribbean and Hawaii with B-17s, not to speak of the possibility of placing a heavy bombardment group in the Philippines. Most of those groups are still flying obsolete B-10s." The President gazed at General Arnold for a long moment. "Prime Minister Churchill wants a hundred B-17s the minute the Lend-Lease proposal passes the Congress … if indeed it does."

General Arnold stared at the President incredulously. "But Mr. President! That would be impossible!" General Arnold deposited his glass on the end table by his chair, leaned forward to emphasize his concern.

"The Air Corps has developed its entire strategic mission around the B-17. Production schedules will be strained to the limit in meeting our own requirements."

The President frowned. "The whole idea is to keep England in the battle, General. The longer they hold, the more time we buy."

"But, if England falls, Mr. President … what then?" General Arnold asked. "We're apt to find ourselves in a damned ticklish position over here if we are called on to fight or even to defend our own hemisphere. We've only got forty in the entire Air Corps inventory right now … that's throughout this hemisphere and the Pacific."

Roosevelt's anger subsided as he gazed at General Arnold and realized the integrity of his response. "Can't something be done to increase heavy bomber production even before year's end?"

"I've got the Douglas and the Vega people talking with Boeing. We're hoping to sub-contract B-17 production to them. They both have the capability."

"And ..."

"I'm optimistic, Sir. But it'll be early summer before any scheduling projections can be made realistically."

"Then I'd say we've got a serious problem on our hands, Hap," the President said.

Years of frustration weighed heavily in General Arnold's voice. "If you'll excuse me Sir, that's what we in the Air Corps have been trying to demonstrate to the War Department general staff for the past ten years now."

"Of course, of course," the President said. "Well, nothing has been approved between the Prime Minister and me at this point." He stopped talking to gather his thoughts. "Hopkins is off to England next week to begin arrangements for a meeting between Churchill and me. He'll be reporting on what the most pressing needs are over there ... and what kind of a timetable we're looking at." The President smiled. "I appreciate your candor, Hap."

"Thank you." General Arnold stood up. "Goodnight, Mr. President."

The President nodded, smiled briefly and then delved into the paperwork before him,

General Arnold went to the door, opened it, then turned back to the President. "Oh, and by the way, Mr. President. It was a whale of a speech."

Roosevelt nodded, and smiled again, then watched as General Arnold left the room. In the hallway adjacent to the library Harry Hopkins hurriedly approached the library door just as General Arnold had moved a few steps down the hallway.

"Well, General Arnold, are you prepared to deal with forty thousand airplanes a year?" Harry Hopkins asked and waved a sheaf of telegrams. "They say you're going to get them."

"I'm prepared … if we don't give them all away before the Air Corps gets what it needs," General Arnold said.

"He told you about Churchill and the B-17s?" Harry Hopkins asked

"Yes," General Arnold said. "I've got heavy bombardment groups sprouting up all over the hemisphere, Harry. They don't have a damned thing to fly!" The General continued. "We *must* keep *all* of our B-17s over here … at least until late next year."

"That may be a tough request to follow through on, General. Anyway … nothing's been agreed to yet." Hopkins clasped the general's shoulders. "I'll confer with you before I leave for England, all right?"

General Arnold only nodded, and then walked on down the hall. Hopkins gazed after him momentarily as he entered the library.

* * *

President Roosevelt was at his desk in the oval office signing the HR 1776 Bill. Secretary Hull, General George Marshall, Admiral Stark and three government VIPs gathered behind the desk, witnessing the signing of the bill, the HR 1776, known as the Lend-Lease Act. The HR 1776 empowered the U. S. to provide its Allies with weapons of war. Twenty-one mighty B-17 Flying Fortresses were already on the way to England. The President asked for an increase in overall aircraft production to forty thousand planes a year. The production of virtually all military items had been increased tenfold or more. All over America, industry responded by gearing up to meet production quotas that were considered impossible by some, but not by America's workers. For the young and the old alike, skilled and non-skilled, there was no question that the job would be done. Churchill asked for tools to finish the job against Hitler.

Chapter Thirteen

A gust of wind came into the Rathskeller the same time Bart and two crewmen entered. "Damn, it's cold! That humid cold air off the North Atlantic goes right through me," Sharp said. "Reggie, dear, could we have a round of whiskey, please."

"Sure, love," she replied as she stopped Bart. "You have a visitor waiting for you in the back booth."

"Thanks, male or female?" he replied.

"Male, you sexual pervert," Reggie answered with a sexy smile. "I saw you and that redhead over at the Barley Mow last night. Nice looking woman. Since she was out with you, I assume that she has no morals."

"How crass of you to insult the reputation of one of Britain's finest teachers! I will have you know that she was teaching me British history," Bart said in mock indignity before shyly smiling and saying under his breath, "She did keep me after school!"

As Bart got close to the booth, he saw the head of the SOE Hugh Dalton himself.

"Welcome back, Bart. Another great flight I understand. What's that make the total, twelve over Belgium, one flown to Spain and four over France, right?"

"That's correct, sir," Bart said as he sat down. He was handed his drink by Reggie as soon as he sat down.

Dalton looked up at Reggie and asked, "Don't let anyone disturb us, love."

She nodded and left. She knew who Dalton was. Now she wasn't sure about Bart Coltrane and his friends. The head of the Special

Operations Executive doesn't just talk to anyone, especially some American instructor pilots. *They must not be just instructor pilots*, she thought.

"I hope that you don't mind this bit of intrigue and informality. I understand that you and Rupert Chapman don't always see eye to eye these days," he said, then continued without letting Bart comment. "Rupert can get under one's skin, but he is a professional. I know that he means well, at least." Dalton stopped and looked Coltrane in the eyes. Bart knew to keep his mouth shut. Then Dalton continued, "I have a very nasty problem in Norway. I need a special delivery that will be more than difficult. You are my only real chance of getting some supplies and two SOE personnel into the area in time for a very critical operation. The Germans have a new processing plant in Norway that could eventually have a serious impact on the war and Ensign Christian Hange is trying to form a coordinated underground Resistance movement in Norway. The two SOE agents and supplies are going there for those two purposes."

"I can't afford delays, difference of professional opinions or obvious office conflicts. So, if you agree to take on the mission, I will make sure Rupert is on a trip for me. A valid trip but out of the office anyway. That prevents office or internal problems to affect the mission. You understand where I am going with this, Bart?"

"The only question is where and when are we going?"

"Not that simple, Bart," Dalton interjected. The weather over the entire UK area and the North Sea is abominable. Nothing is flying for the next three or possibly five days. I need the delivery to be made tomorrow afternoon."

Coltrane sat back and finished off his drink without saying anything.

Dalton casually looked around to insure there was nobody eavesdropping. "Bart, you would have to take off in almost zero-zero conditions and fly on instruments to a point off the Norway Coast where the weather isn't too bad. It seems that the base of the clouds is around 500 to 800 feet off the ocean some three to four miles offshore. That means your flight would have to stay at altitude above the clouds to keep out of icing conditions then descend to 500 feet exactly three miles off the coast. Then fly to the drop point through the valleys and avoid the cloud covered mountain peaks and return. The weather in Norway is also trashy but better than we have here. It's bad enough to keep the German fighters on the ground. The last part of the problem is where in the UK you could land given the adverse conditions? Sort of a bloody challenge, isn't it?"

Coltrane looked at Dalton as he thought through the problem. Then he spoke in a soft deliberate tone. "This must be damned important for you to even be here much less asking us to fly this type of mission. What do you say we go over to the office and plan this adventure? I doubt that anyone would be around to disturb us or ask unnecessary questions."

"Great idea! After we go over the details, I'll buy you blokes a well-deserved supper."

Bart got up and looked at his two friends at the bar. They watched him stick his finger into the air and give the crank-up sign. They quickly downed their drinks and got their coats on as Dalton and Coltrane walked to the door.

Fifteen minutes later they were in their warm SOE office. Bart thought it had the warmth and comfort of a West Virginia coal mine. They sat at the Black Bart conference table as Dalton went over the details of the mission. At the conclusion of his briefing, there was a sigh from the crew.

"That is a tall order, sir," Dalton said. "How much of a cloud base will you really need to do some sort of instrument landing back here?"

"If it was a flat area with no towers, obstructions, hills or buildings, I could put us a mile off the end of the runway at 300 feet possibly 200 if our altimeters are not too far off. We would need the help of someone to call around the selected airfields to see what they actually have for weather conditions and let us know."

"Smashing!" Dalton said, as he slammed his fist into the other hand. "We can do that easily."

"I can do my part if the boss is comfortable with it," Sharp said as he turned to Bart.

"Hell, I'm just a truck driver going where I'm told to go. It's almost as bad as being married," Bart said in a mock serious tone. Everyone broke into laughter.

Robby West was as the wall map looking at the probable course and return conditions. "Yeah, you are really on target with *smashing*."

Bart turned to Dalton. "Sir, we will have this planned and into your hands by 0500. We will be off Tempsford by 0900 but on our return course ... we'll need the airfield weather conditions updated every 30 minutes starting at 1200 hours. We'll call RAF Sumburgh operators to get the report. Perhaps we can even get in there. They'll probably clear before Scotland or the Midlands. At any rate, we'll depend on the weather report. Since we'll be the only aircraft in the sky, we shouldn't have to worry about any midair collision."

"You can depend on the very best report possible when you call in to Sumburgh," Dalton said with a tone of commitment.

"Well, then sir, if you will give us a rain check on that meal, we have work to do. Please have your drop pods to our hangar by 0700 and your passengers there by 0800. We will take things from there, sir," Coltrane said as he looked at Dalton.

"Bloody good! I shall leave you to your planning," Dalton said as he went to the door. "Gentlemen, thank you for your effort." Then he left.

"Okay, Prince Henry, how do we do this?" Coltrane asked.

"Actually, it's a piece of cake until we get to the landing part. That could be a little dicey. But, fearless commander, I have a plan!" Sharp said with fanfare.

Coltrane dropped his head and shook it a couple of times before looking back up at Sharp. "Why do I get the feeling this will be far beyond normal flying and established instrument landing procedures?"

"Take a look at this idea," he said as he went to the blackboard. He drew a horizontal line then four perpendicular lines. "Now," he stated his explanation, "this only applies to Tempsford. If we return slightly to the west of RAF Thurleigh turning towards their HF Non-directional Beacon (NDB) at one thousand feet, we'll cross over it on an established course of 107 degrees at 120 mph. That is critical! Immediately after crossing we establish a 175 feet per minute descent. That rate is critical as in the heading. You maintain precise 107 degree heading on the Tempsford NDB, but it is the Thurleigh NDB that is important. Winds should not be a factor in this trashy weather. Three minutes and forty-eight seconds we should be over the town of Tempsford. We might break out and see the runway a little over one mile ahead, but I doubt it. Four minutes and nine seconds after Thurleigh, we should be at 300 feet above the road west of the runway. We should be able to see the runway a quarter of a mile away. If you can't after four minutes and fifteen seconds, you put the power to her, and we fly out over the channel and bail out. We will be out of fuel and options by then. So how do you like the plan?"

Coltrane looked over at West who was hanging to every word said by Sharp. "Smashing, I guess." He said with a look of amazement on his face, "You can fly that close to tolerances?"

"Yes, but I'll need to focus totally on the instruments. Robby will need to be looking outside at all times to spot the runway and maybe the two checkpoints. When you see the runway, you'll take over and land. I won't be able to transition from the gauges to looking for the runway in time to land. Not at 120 mph for sure," Coltrane said as he leaned back in his seat and put his hands behind his head.

"I guess that we had better call Royston and tell him to get the bird ready to go. Okay, let's work up a flight plan for our three options. Then get some sleep before we launch into the white abyss," Coltrane said, as he got up to get closer to the wall map.

* * *

The visibility was absolute zero-zero when the Black Bart crew got off the train at Tempsford. Sergeant Royston was there with a jeep. Where and how he got it, Coltrane didn't want to know. He was just thankful that he had 'requisitioned' it. That British lorry was a rough riding machine.

Coltrane hadn't fully gotten into the jeep when Royston started talking. "Both passengers and cargo arrived before 0600. They don't say much, nor have they really identified themselves. I assume that they are spooks. They have three delivery pods which weigh a total of eight hundred sixty pounds. The Black Bart is ready to go except for the deicing boots. That hot air modification that you came up with is probably too much for the rubber and connectors. I wouldn't go up maximum anymore. They will hold for now, but I have put in a requisition for another complete set just in case. The radios and navigational instruments are good. I checked out the gyro compass and everything else I could think of. Apparently, we're going to fly on the gauges," he said as he took in a deep breath. Royston turned halfway in his seat as he directed his next comment towards Lieutenant Sharp. "I put in two more map lights over your new table. I also put in a couple other modifications to make the ride better for you in that cramped area."

"Thanks, Sarge. It's rather tight in there and dark as hell," Sharp responded.

As they drove up to the make-shift hangar, Coltrane could see two men standing next to the left main landing gear looking at the pirate flag and name "Black Bart" painted on the nose of the aircraft.

"Good morning, gentlemen. I am Bart Coltrane, your tour guide today," Bart said as he extended his hand. "May I see some identification?"

The smaller of the two stepped forward and gave him a leather-bound identification card identifying him as an SOE agent from the Special Intelligence Service of Section D. He then said, "I will vouch for this man. His identity needs to remain hush hush if you don't mind."

That peaked Coltrane's curiosity. "That's fine with me, Mr. X."

The man then said in perfect Southern Alabama English, "Thanks, it's just better that way. I work for Colonel Bill Donovan, if that helps you."

Coltrane immediately understood and nodded. "Okay, then. Did Sergeant Royston brief you on the flight and the way you'll depart?"

"Yes, sir, he was very thorough. We jump out of the bomb bay immediately after the pods." He said that we would go out at 500 feet. That's a little tight on altitude for our chutes," the agent said.

"It's better that way. Your chutes will deploy very quickly at 150 knots and you'll only swing in the air twice before landing. We've done it many times before without so much as a sprained ankle. The Germans are less likely to see you or your pods. Besides, the weather won't let us get much higher. The takeoff may be a little different than you may have experienced before. We'll use a max power short field take off procedure due to the bad visibility. We want to get off the ground as quickly as possible, given that we can only see maybe three hundred feet ahead of the aircraft," Coltrane concluded. "Okay, if you go with Sergeant Royston, we will get going in about 17 minutes," he said as he looked at his watch.

Coltrane climbed up into the forward entrance and looked at the three delivery pods hanging from the British type of release hooks hanging from the top of the bomb bay. He checked to see if the parachute static lines which deployed the chutes immediately after leaving the bottom of the B-25 were attached properly. He then looked past the pods at his two passengers and Sergeant Royston in the rear compartment. All was ready. He climbed up into the cockpit and strapped himself into his parachute and safety belt. He looked out of his window to see Martin standing by the left engine with a fire extinguisher. Then he looked out to see if Lightfoot was next to the right engine. Fire guards were set, and they were ready to crank.

It took almost ten minutes to start up and go through the checklist. Once satisfied with the aircraft's ability to fly safely, he hit the intercom. "Pilot to crew, confirm readiness." Then both pilots checked their altimeters to check accurate field evaluation, then cross-checked that against the reported barometric pressure. The difference was the adjustment or "K" factor.

One by one, everyone checked in and confirmed that all aspects of their job and equipment were ready to go. Coltrane gave the signal to the two ground crewmen to pull the wheel chocks so he could move forward. Jack Martin quickly got into the jeep and slowly drove forward leading the B-25 to the end of the runway. He then went down the runway and turned around and parked next to the runway facing the aircraft, so it gave Coltrane a visual reference as he took off. Coltrane set the parking brake and advanced the throttles to operating speed to check the magnetos and aircraft systems.

"Okay, Kelly, are you ready?" Coltrane asked.

"Just waiting on the bus driver," he said poking fun at Coltrane. "Fly runway heading and climb to 6,000 feet."

"Roger, fly 100 degrees, climb to and maintain six thousand," Coltrane responded in a serious tone.

Black Bart was at the very end of the forty-five-hundred-foot-long runway one zero at Tempsford. Coltrane advanced the throttles to maximum power. The aircraft shook as it strained against the brakes.

"Pilot to crew, prepare for takeoff," ordered Coltrane. "Okay, Robby, follow me up on throttles and controls," he said as he looked ahead at the barely visible runway and dim glow of the jeep headlights. *It was time!*

Coltrane released the brakes and the aircraft lunged forward and quickly gained speed. He had to make a slight heading correction to keep the plane in the center of the runway. Suddenly, the jeep flashed past, then he pulled back on the control yoke and the aircraft leaped off the ground and into the dark morning sky. Coltrane immediately adjusted his rate of climb and power settings to climb power. He kept his eyes on the altitude indicator and the compass to ensure they didn't go off course. He turned on the autopilot which kept his wings level and on the 100-degree heading. West had raised the landing gear and flaps when Coltrane gave him an indication with his hand. The plane became steady in its climb out to six thousand feet.

Coltrane noticed that it was starting to get lighter about the time they passed through forty-five hundred feet. Suddenly, they were above the clouds. It was mostly clear above with only a thin deck of clouds at 15,000 feet.

Bart was about to start leveling off at six thousand feet when Sharp was heard over the intercom. "Turn to 027 degrees and climb to one seven thousand feet."

"Roger, zero two seven degrees, climbing to seventeen thousand," Coltrane responded.

About forty minutes after leveling off, Sharp came up to the cockpit. "We're on course and on time. I got three fixes and three RDF (Radio Direction Finder) fixes to confirm. We're on our way and where we want to be ... I hope," Sharp said jokingly.

West looked at Sharp with a questionable look on his face.

"Relax, Robby, I know where we are," Sharp said. "It seems strange to be up here and not another aircraft in sight." After a few minutes, he went back down to the navigators table and prepared to run another set of position fix.

Two hours and eight minutes after takeoff, Sharp called out to Coltrane, "Standby to descend to five hundred feet on my mark at five hundred feet per minute." There was a pause, then Sharp said, "Descend now!"

Coltrane adjusted the trim tab to lower the nose for a power on descent to five hundred feet. When passing fifteen hundred feet, Coltrane reduced power and adjusted the altitude of the aircraft to continue the descent with the aircraft flying in a flat or level altitude. This would allow him to quickly advance power and stop the descent in case of emergency or premature sighting of the ocean surface or land mass. The aircraft had almost reached seven hundred feet when they broke out of the overcast. The visibility appeared to Coltrane to be about five miles or better. "This was good," he thought. He looked ahead and saw the Norwegian coast directly ahead. He could see the big island just to his left and the river directly ahead.

"Bingo!" he called out. "Absolutely dead on, Kelly."

"Can you see the river valley ahead?" Sharp asked.

"Got it. Right where it's supposed to be."

"Good, stay in the valley for 29.5 miles. You will over fly a small lake. Then turn to 010 degrees for forty-eight miles to drop zone," he instructed.

West was looking on his map and watching for key land points to confirm their position. This was made difficult by Coltrane maneuvering the aircraft through the twists and turns needed to say in the valley and below the top of the surrounding hills and mountains. Suddenly, West called out, "There's the lake!"

"Okay, take up a heading of zero one zero. You'll be coming out of the narrow valley and be in more open area with lots of hills popping up."

Coltrane kept the aircraft fifty to seventy-five feet above the very rough terrain as he followed the course to the drop zone.

Coltrane hit the intercom, "Yank, get them ready. We'll be there in five minutes or so."

"Roger," replied Sergeant Royston.

Sharp came over the intercom, "You're three minutes to drop zone … can you see the lake yet, Robby?" With any luck, they'd land just short of the lake and not in it."

"I've got the lake," exclaimed West. "It's five degrees to the starboard. Opening bomb bay doors. Standby!"

"Permission to drop," West asked Coltrane per the SOP.

"You are cleared to drop," Bart replied calmly. "Standby 15 seconds to drop."

"Ready," then a pause, "Drop!" Bart said.

West toggled the release switches one at a time. The plane shuddered as each of the pods and two agents departed the aircraft and the static line went tight and deployed the parachutes.

"Five good chutes," reported Royston.

"Great," said Coltrane as he turned toward the valley to his left.

"It's only 11.2 miles to the end of this valley then turn to 267 degrees for 70.55 miles. Then we're home free," Sharp said.

Home free, thought Coltrane. *We've had no enemy fire. We surely didn't catch them by surprise did we? Even if we did at the beginning, they would have communicated a general alarm. They'll be waiting at the coast for us!* He hit the intercom, "Better be ready for some heavy fire at the coastline. Kelly, keep us in the least defended area and a route that we can go across the beach at treetop."

"Roger," Sharp replied. "You will clear the hills about six miles prior to the beach on this course."

The next twenty minutes were silent as the B-25 weaved through the valley and hills until they hit the flat area near the beach. The visibility was still about four to six miles which gave the enemy a clear shot at them. Bart put the bird down to 15 to 20 feet above the ground. This was a little unnerving to West who could see trees and other obstacles come screaming towards the aircraft at over 235 knots, then disappear suddenly. It took slightly more than two minutes to cross the coastal plain to the North Sea. Again, not a shot was fired at them.

"I don't believe it!" Coltrane said. "We caught them by surprise! Maybe they thought we were just another German aircraft. Anyway, we cheated death once again … or should I say, so far!"

"Climb to ten thousand feet on a heading of 192 degrees. I'll contact Sumburgh for a weather report," Sharp said with a businesslike voice.

He came back up on the intercom about the same time the aircraft hit clear air again. The sun felt good on Bart's face.

"Stay on this course. Sumburgh is visibility zero, sky obscured. We can't go there. Prestwick and Tempsford are about the same," Sharp said pausing to arrange his notes. "They're reporting 400 feet overcast, winds less than 3 variable, visibility less than one mile. It looks like we get to use my new homemade approach."

"Oh joy," Robby said, sarcastically. "Now we're back to that smashing idea."

"Robby, take the damned controls and fly his plan," Coltrane said with irritation. "You think too damned much about the bad and not the true genius of his idea. Put your ADF upon the Thurleigh frequency. I have mine on Tempsford. That will be our crosscheck on our approach and our missed approach point if you cannot find the damned runway. We're too far out to receive the signal, but we will in about an hour and a half. Kelly, keep him on course, I am going to rest up for the approach."

* * *

"Come right to 205 degrees," Sharp said loudly over the intercom. Coltrane was suddenly awake from his semi-conscious rest. He sat up in his seat and turned the heading bug on the autopilot to 205 degrees. "Start your descent to one thousand feet at 500 feet per minute."

Coltrane reduced the throttles slightly to get the desired 500 feet rate. He looked over at his ADF tuned to Tempsford and Robby's ADF on Thurleigh. Both were registering their respective radio stations. "Okay, let's go through the pre-landing check while we aren't in a hurry. Prepare for landing."

As the Black Bart passed through two thousand feet, Sharp came on the intercom. "When I give you the word, execute a standard rate turn to the left. Establish yourself on a 107-degree inbound heading towards Thurleigh. You should be stabilized on course at 1,000 feet and 120 mph. Okay, look at your ADF. We're almost ready to turn. Get down to 1,000 feet, you're a little high and fast."

Coltrane made the needed adjustments. He saw the needle reach the turn point and quickly checked to make sure he was at 1,000 feet and 120 mph. All was where it should be.

"Turn," came the command from the navigator. Coltrane made the turn slowly and precisely. West had his sweaty hands on his thighs in nervous anticipation. Coltrane leveled up the plane on 107 degrees while still at 1,000 feet and 120 mph. "Very good, we're two miles from Thurleigh. Remember the runway will be slightly off to the left when we get to decision height. Get ready to start your descent at

175 feet per minute," Sharp said.

The ADF needle in front of Robby fluctuated slightly then turned 180 degrees to the bottom of the instrument. He heard Sharp say, "Station passage, start descent and start your stopwatch." West quickly hit the timer function on the clock mounted on the instrument panel.

"Give me gear and flaps!" Coltrane ordered. West quickly complied then directed his attention to the ground and in front of the descending aircraft. His eyes strained for any sign of the ground or runway. He became increasingly nervous as the altimeter slowly wound down to the 400 foot decision height.

"Are you sure there are no towers or church steeples around here?" West asked. Nobody replied.

Sharp said softly, "We should be over Tempsford, now. Anything in sight?"

"Hell, no," Robby said. "We are at 500 feet, looks like we are going to hit the silk over the channel."

"Time!" Sharp said loudly. "You should see something."

Robby West strained his eyes out front then something caught his eye. It was the road, and then he saw the runway. "Runway! I have the aircraft!"

Coltrane pulled his hand away from the throttles as Robby grabbed them and reduced the power as he corrected the path of the aircraft slightly to the left to the center of runway 10. Then he chopped the power and the B-25 settled to the ground. The landing was a little rougher than what Robby liked, but very acceptable. The bomber slowed to a stop then turned on to the taxiway. A jeep suddenly appeared in front of the bird. 'Follow me' was a large-lettered sign on the rear.

Sharp came up behind the two pilots as they taxied to their hangar on the southwest end of the field. "Nice landing. Looks like my idea worked," he said with a big shit-eating grin.

Coltrane set the parking brakes and shut down the engines. As the propellers started to slow down, the ground crew replaced the chocks and started to look for the anticipated bullet and flack holes. They were surprised to see none.

Sharp opened the hatch and lowered the built-in ladder. He looked down and saw Hugh Dalton's face looking up at him. He had Lieutenant Colonel Grand with him.

"Have a nice flight?" he said in jest.

"Not bad, but the in-flight meals were terrible," Sharp said in a mocking tone.

They got down and gathered at the front of the aircraft. Dalton shook everyone's hand with a big smile. "Bloody outstanding!" he said. "There will be no debriefing on this mission today. You can write it up tomorrow afternoon. I want to meet with you at half past three in my office. We got a short wireless from our man that you landed them exactly on target and there were no injuries or damage to the equipment. Now go get a shower and head to London. I'll buy you that promised meal at 2000 hours at my club. Be sure to wear coat and tie. The Reform Club is real sticky about that. Now get out of here!" he said like a proud father.

It was almost midnight when the crew of the Black Bart got back to the Rathskeller. Sharp closed the door behind the trio and started for the elevator at the back of the bar, when West said, "I was so tired that I couldn't enjoy such a wonderful meal at one of the world's most exclusive clubs."

Bart was taken by the extensive use of Mahogany and Cherry wood walls and ornate trim. The walls were covered with exquisite paintings and historical documents dating back to the early 1100s. This sure wasn't Sweetwater!

Sharp couldn't even find the energy to respond. He just kept walking to the elevator. Bart was no better, but he did notice a gorgeous Reggie leaning on the bar accenting her substantial cleavage.

"I may be dead tired, but I had to say how good you look tonight," Bart said as he continued to walk to the elevator.

"I tarted up just for you, mate," she said. "I was going to give myself to you tonight, but you're too bloody exhausted to do me any good."

Bart smiled and turned back towards her and responded, "Got any strong coffee?"

"I am afraid that you're far beyond coffee, love," she said as she got up and walked away laughing. 'You've had your chance."

"Thank you, I will cherish your offer forever," Bart said. "But I am walking dead." He then entered the elevator and closed the door.

Chapter Fourteen

Coltrane had just arrived at his office upstairs after their official meeting with Sir Hugh Dalton congratulating them on their successful mission in Norway when Major Annabel Beddows and Captain Balfour entered the office.

Bart was quick to stand up and walk over to them, "Good afternoon, and to what do we attribute having you join us today?" he said as he shook their hands.

"We came down to personally get your After-Action Report on your 'unscheduled mission' yesterday," she said in a terse and professional tone. "You didn't bother to coordinate with us prior to your departure. That is not the way we do things here in Section D."

Bart was starting to get really irritated at this point. He moved closer and towered over the five-foot six Balfour and quietly said, "I do what I am told by the Head of the SOE. If you don't like it, take it up with him." Balfour quickly became intimidated and backed away saying, "Yes, of course. Now could we get the details on key points of intelligence?"

"Sure," Sharp said as he came over trying to defuse the situation, especially since Beddows had not given an inch. "Here is a copy of our actual flight path with times. We did not see a single German the entire trip," he said as he handed the map to Beddows who was still staring at Coltrane.

"Thank you," she said as she and Balfour looked at the map. Balfour pointed to the point on the map where Black Bart left Norway over the North Sea. "Our information indicates that they had two anti-aircraft companies along this area."

"They could have, Sanford," Coltrane injected. "We may have caught them by surprise, or they couldn't see us due to weather and the low altitude that we were flying, or they had not been briefed on the B-25 and thought that we were one of theirs. No telling!"

Beddows said in a cold and disinterested demeanor, "Well it worked. There is nothing in your report that I need." Then she left without further comment.

Balfour and the others just looked at her as she left.

"What the hell is wrong with her?" Bart asked.

"Don't be offended, she is just that way. Her nickname around here is the 'Ice Maiden'." Her husband, the Duke of Estis, was killed in the initial Polish attack in '39. He was doing a threat assessment when he bought the farm," Balfour said in typical British form.

"Duke? Was she married to royalty?" Robby asked.

"Yes, quite! She is the Duchess of Estis, but she doesn't flaunt it like most of the blue bloods around here," responded Balfour. Her parents were killed in an auto accident when she was 19. They left her with a great deal of money, property and several large and successful manufacturing concerns."

"She was left quite well off by the duke as well," Balfour said as he took a shallow breath, and then continued. "He had more money than god. You would never know that she was either a blue blood or very, very rich. She never uses her title or shows her wealth. She drives a ten-year old Bentley. On the other hand, the duke always drove a new Rolls. She is just a very nice woman down deep. On the outside around here, she is the Ice Maiden. I guess that I had better get back to work." He reached for the door lever when the door exploded open with Annabel Beddows storming in behind it. She marched in a direct line to Bart Coltrane and stopped just inches from his face.

"You said that if I don't like it, I could take it up with Hugh Dalton. Well, that is exactly what I am going to do. This affront to myself and Rupert shall not go unanswered. I shall demand that you be formally rebuked for not following procedures and policies," she said in an angry and forceful voice. "Do you have anything to say?"

"You bet, lady, or should I say Duchess. You go to Dalton, and you will end up on the same shit list that Rupert is on," Bart said in a calm but commanding tone.

"What kind of bloody talk is that? Rupert Chapham is a brilliant professional soldier of the highest caliber. I seriously doubt he is on anybody's bloody list! He is everything that you should be as a military officer."

Coltrane almost broke into a laugh, which was noticed by Beddows and made her even madder. He then said "Rupert is a pompous REMF that has never seen hostile fire or lead men in combat. He is quick to send men in harm's way without considering what his orders could jeopardize. He is what combat officers fear more than the enemy."

This outraged Beddows. Others in the room were inching away before her next vocal assault. She had reached a level of anger that she could not say anything then collected herself to ask, "Your arrogance is incredible! What is a REMF?"

He chuckled as did the others. "Well, you did ask. It means Rear Echelon Mother Fucker. It's a term used in the American military to express total professional disrespect for an incompetent officer. Now that you have heard nasty words from my mouth, let me help you out of our office and into the hallway that will lead you to Dalton's office." Bart gently grabbed her elbow and ushered her to the door. She was speechless.

Bart turned to the others and said, "Okay, I'm taking bets on who calls me first Dalton or Rupert. Any takers at 20 pounds?"

Balfour was the first to produce a twenty-pound bill. "I'll take Rupert," he said as he gave Bart the money. Then Robby put up his money on Dalton. Sharp said, "That's a no brainer. Dalton will just laugh at her. Very silently, but he will die laughing. Rupert is another thing. He may cause you more grief."

Balfour started towards the door shaking his head. "REMF! What a term."

"Now, if you get another midnight call to fly off, do give me a call. No matter what hour. My job is to keep you alive, if possible. Got to go, chaps, Cheerio!"

Chapter Fifteen

It was almost five in Berlin when Admiral Wilhelm Canaris, head of the German Abwehr got a call from Reichsfuhrer Heinrich Himmler, who was the head of the SS, asking him to come to his office. Upon arrival, he found Dr. Joseph Goebbels, the minister of public enlightenment and propaganda already there seated in a leather chair before the fireplace.

"Good afternoon, Admiral," Himmler said warmly, "Please take a seat. Could I offer you some Schnapps?"

"Thank you, Reichsfuhrer, that would be wonderful," Canaris said as he carefully watched the two close Hitler confidants. He was always on guard anytime these two were friendly. It was totally out of character for them to be friendly to anyone and he was compelled to watch as they poured the Schnapps. He would drink it ... if they did first!

Himmler walked over to the window then abruptly turned and took a seat at his desk facing Canaris before speaking. "During the past few months, we have been quite successful in keeping the Danish Resistance movement from becoming organized and cooperating with the SOE in London. Several of the SOE attempts to drop spies and supplies to various Resistance groups have been stopped. This effort has discouraged both inter-group communications and coordination of attacks. They are also disappointed with London. Well, until recently they were disappointed. It seems the SOE has been quite successful recently delivering both large amounts of supplies and qualified British agents. This has not only encouraged them, but they are starting to conduct more aggressive and damaging acts of sabotage. At first, we could not understand how this could be. We have been quite effective against the SOE Lysander aircraft. They are slow and very limited in capability. Our troops would joke about hearing them approach from the North Sea with enough time to smoke a cigarette before they were over land and shot them down. Now there is a new aspect that has changed the equation. They are using a different aircraft.

"The Gestapo headquarters in Odense, Denmark has advised me of a new situation there that could be of interest to both of you," Himmler said as he walked up to the fireplace sipping his schnapps. "It seems that one of the Resistance members was captured last week. When he was interrogated, he said that they were being supplied and supported by the SOE on a regular basis. We know it couldn't be by Lysander, so our man in Odense pressured the man to disclose that it was an American B-25 that was sneaking in and supplying them," Himmler said as he carefully studied the facial expressions of his two guests. "That should interest you, Admiral, as there are four to six SOE agents operating in Denmark now. Dr. Goebbels, I am not sure who is flying the B-25, but it is a clear violation of America's stated policy of neutrality. If it is flown by Americans instead of British pilots, that could be of significant use by your propaganda ministry. This public revelation would certainly be embarrassing to Roosevelt.

"I would suggest that Admiral Canaris contact his sources in Great Britain and the USA to determine where this plane is based and who is flying it. Meanwhile, the Gestapo will continue to investigate the matter. Perhaps we can set up a trap that will allow us to shoot it down and exploit the matter in the world press. I know that such an article would make our Fuhrer very happy. "Do either of you have any questions or want to say anything?" Himmler asked in a soft, but very intimidating tone.

Canaris was the first to respond. "I think not, Reichsfuhrer. I understand the problem and shall take immediate action to find out who is flying these missions and where it is based. I shall keep the good Information Minister informed of my findings as well as your office, Reichsfuhrer."

"Yes, that is most promising, and I will start to work on the structure of the news release while I await the Admiral's report," Goebbels said as he stood up and raised his hand and gave his perfunctory "Heil Hitler!"

Chapter Sixteen

Bart was looking at a series of bullet holes in the left side of the Black Bart. Much to his dismay, they damaged the pirate and crossbones flag on the side. Had they been a foot higher, they would have gone right through him. Unfortunately, the rounds had severely damaged the cartridge carrier that took the fifty caliber bullets from the ammunition can to one of the nose mounted machine guns. "That can be fixed," he thought as he continued to look at the damage from the last mission over Denmark. He turned to Sergeant Royston and asked, "Okay, how long will we be down?"

"Well, sir, they did a lot of damage this time. Nothing really bad, but it's going to take us at least two days. Just a lot of little things that take time to fix right," he said with resignation.

"Very well, I guess we could use some time to catch up on the paperwork and try to plan ahead on the next mission," Bart said.

Sergeant Lightfoot came up to Coltrane, "Sir, you are to report to Lieutenant Colonel Grand's office immediately." Bart looked down with a sigh. "Yank, you had better cut some time off that time estimate. The boss apparently has a mission for us."

Coltrane reported to LTC Grand at 1400 hours precisely.

"Good afternoon, sir. I understand that you are looking for a fourth for poker."

Grand smiled and told Bart to sit down. "Our boys across the hall at MI-6 have apprehended a foreign gentleman who has been asking a lot of questions about your operation. It seems Berlin is not happy with your performance and the moral lift that you have given some of the Resistance units. He and his associates here in the UK have been instructed to check you boys out. We know that we couldn't keep you under wraps for long, but here we are," he said in a very happy mood. I have some good news for you and your crew. It seems as if your President and the War Department are impressed with all of the missions that you have been flying. You and your crew are advanced one rank to Major. Congratulations! Grand became a little more serious. "We have been handed a hot one from Sir Hugh Dalton. It's a dicey one again. Back to Denmark I'm afraid. Well, as soon as you can repair your plane from the last trip there."

"I need to bring Lieutenant Zak Middleton and Colonel Julian 'Hak' Smythe into this," he said as he picked up the phone and called Middleton. "Be just a minute, he's just down the hall with Hak." Moments later a stocky man in his late 30's came into the office along with Hak Smythe.

"Ahhhhh, here they are now," Grand said as he got up to make the introductions. "Zak is a big fan of yours, Bart. He and Hak seems to think your chaps have given a great deal of encouragement to the Resistance fighters in Denmark. From the look of the intelligence reports, there is a significant increase in sabotage and attacks on German convoys."

"A pleasure to meet you and congratulations. I understand that you were promoted to Major. What he didn't tell you is that I would kill someone just to fly a mission in your B-25," Zak Middleton said with a lustful tone.

"You don't have to go that far. If you want to take a chance, you're welcome to fly with Black Bart any time," Coltrane said as he soaked in the praise.

"Actually," Lieutenant Colonel Grand injected, "Zak has been flying Lysanders for us into France and Belgium. Denmark is pretty much out of range except with drop tanks. Then the payload is minimal. He has flown over 200 missions. Some were real sticky wickets." He paused then continued. "On to the mission."

"There are four key Danish Resistance leaders and two of our own SOE agents over there that we need to bring back here to sort out the problems between them and to establish a coordinated program against the bloody Bosch. The bloody Germans have virtually closed off all air and sea routes for us to use. They can't go south into Germany or even go north to Norway. The Gestapo knows who these men are and are searching high and low for them. Especially, since they have increased their fight against the Germans with the supplies that you have been supplying them. We have a possible solution. Zak here can tell you his idea."

"Actually, it's quite simple. You fly in and pick them up," Zak initially said with a straight face, then broke out into laughter when he saw the shocked expression on Bart's face. "Let me explain. There is an island called Laeso, just off the northeast coast of Denmark. It is a fishing center where fishermen can bring their catch for further shipment down to Copenhagen. The Germans only have a platoon of 25 soldiers guarding the island. They all are at the seaport town of Vestero Havn. They have a daily patrol that drives around the island just before noon and three guard posts in the dock area and town center. This is all they do. To support them and provide for a rare visit from higher headquarters, they constructed an airfield in the center of the island. It is not guarded and can stand the weight of your B-25. Additionally, it's going to become one of the main operating and supply bases for the Resistance if we can get them unified and coordinated at the meeting here in London. The mission is to get them back here and then return them a few days later before they are missed by the Germans. If we can get them organized and establish a supply distribution center there, it can be of enormous help. The fishing boats can deliver the supplies all along the coast."

Zak looked at Coltrane to see his reaction then continued. "The plan would generally be that you fly in over the water over the tip of Denmark at dawn and land at the airstrip. Drop off more supplies and pick up the six passengers and return to Tempsford. You would have to land and taxi all the way back to the end of the runway, so you will have the wind on your nose. That is a short runway for a B-25. So, the wind will be important. There are some low hills between the landing strip and town which will mask some of your noise. What are your thoughts?"

"Well," Bart said. "It's doable, okay. We will be tight on fuel since we can't use a ferry tank. If all goes well, we can be on the ground at first light and off with the passengers in five minutes. If the Germans don't hear us come in, it will be a piece of cake. Even if they do, it will take them twenty or so minutes to get out to the airfield. By then, we'll be long gone. The key will be to come in from the northeast over water and return the same way. I don't think there will be enough time for the Germans to get a report of our over flight in the north to scramble fighters from Aalborg or Skrydstrup to intercept us. Even if they did, they would still have to find us and catch up for the kill. Time doesn't work for them."

Lieutenant Colonel Grand asked, "What about going south instead of west and drop off some ammunition and explosives to that group you supplied yesterday. They really do need the rest of the supplies?"

"Sir, the southern part of Denmark is getting to be extremely hard to fly through. They have significantly increased their heavy automatic weapons and ack-ack. The holes in the Black Bart are testimony to their defenses. Beside the danger to your people that we are bringing back is too great. You sure don't want to get them killed or wounded on a supply mission." Bart said as he tapped the wall map.

"Right-O," Grand said as he looked at the map point shown by Coltrane's finger. "Well then, when can you fly the mission?"

Sir, we got shot up pretty bad yesterday in southern Denmark. I'd hate to try the mission of this importance before we complete repairs. Can we do it at dawn day after tomorrow?" Coltrane asked.

"Yes, quite! Work out the details with Chapman and his people," ordered Grand. "I'll be gone for three days for a hush hush headquarters task."

"Make the best of it with Chapman. He'll be in charge in my absence. Say there, Bart, take Zak with you as an observer. Then I can get him off my back about flying with you."

"No problem, sir, Black Bart will be glad to give him a thrill," Coltrane said with a smile as he slapped Zak on the shoulder.

* * *

As Zak and Bart walked down the hall, Zak asked Bart a series of questions about the B-25 and their tactics. Then he got a little more serious and asked, "How many missions have you flown across the channel?"

Bart thought for a moment and responded, "Not really sure, but in the ten months we've been here we've averaged between ten and fifteen missions a month. A little less than that back in January and February due to bad weather and the ramping up of the Resistance groups."

"That's bloody incredible! How many times have you been hit with ground fire?"

"Actually, less than you might think. At the first, when we were not known and could fly past them at low level, it was not very often. Recently, everyone knew about us and is really trying to knock us down. It is sort of a challenge to them, I think," Bart said calmly.

"Yesterday was the worst. When we crossed the beach inbound, the alarm went out to watch for us. They were better prepared the longer we were over land. They even scrambled fighters out of Aalborg trying to find us. Someday we'll have to deal with the fighters as well. The Germans are not stupid."

"What about giving Chapman and his crew the mission requirements then go after a pint?" Zak suggested.

"Sounds good to me," Bart said as they entered the operations and intelligence section office.

Bart immediately saw the beautiful Ice Maiden standing next to Rupert Chapman.

"Good afternoon, Commander Chapman and Major Beddows," Bart said in a friendly and formal way. We have a mission for day after tomorrow to work out with you."

Rupert responded in his usually irritated and pontifical manner, "Yes, yes, I got the word of your high-priority hush hush mission. I'm busy right now, but Major Beddows can take down the details from you and we can meet at 1000 hours tomorrow morning with the flight plan."

"Great, I'd much rather deal with her than you," Bart said in a warm tone.

For once there was a hint of a smile on Annabel Beddows face. "Come on, cowboy, let's get the mission details," she said in a pleasant voice. This was the first time in all these months that she was remotely friendly.

Bart and Zak laid out the mission requirements given to them by Grand. "Given the importance of the passengers we will get in and get out, hopefully we can avoid any hostile fire."

Bart looked up and saw that she was looking at him and not the map. He saw something in her face that had not been there all these months … warmth and tenderness. Then she suddenly became all business again and looked at the route outlined by Coltrane.

She thought for a moment then said "What if you flew to RAF Sumburgh just after midnight and refueled. This time of year, it is getting light about 0530 or so. Sunrise is somewhere around 0600, so you would take off from Sumburgh about 0400 hours. That would put you about 30 miles south of Norway as you enter the Skagerrak Strait and away from any possible detection from either Norway or Denmark. Fly northeasterly until you clear any listening post or radar at the tip of Denmark, then still over water fly directly to the east end of Laeso. You would be there and undetected. Assuming you get there and pick up the passengers undetected, how would you return to Tempsford?"

"I would go a course of 250 degrees to the west. If I went south of Frederikshavn and north of Hjorring, I would be put over flat farmland and away from any German forces. We'll fly out about forty or fifty miles and then turn south to Tempsford. That's pretty straight forward. If we're detected as we pass over land, we'll be far out to sea before they can scramble the fighters to find us. Being at tree top altitude and 200 plus knots gives us a big advantage. We're hard to find that way. That's especially important given who we are bringing back," Bart concluded.

"I can arrange the welcoming committee tonight," Hak said with a deep-throated voice.

"Excellent, I'll work up your flight plan and threat assessment based upon this plan," she said in a professional manner. "Sanford is over at Whitehall getting the latest information and should be back here in an hour or so."

Zak Middleton was watching the uneasy interaction between Beddows and Coltrane. He thought he would help to break the ice between them. "I say, Major Beddows, you have some time before he gets back. Why don't you join us for a quick bite to eat over at the Rathskeller?"

Annabel immediately stiffened up and was about to say 'no' when she changed her mind. *Why not?* she thought. It couldn't do harm and she had missed lunch. "Very well, it would have to be quick, however."

The three of them walked over to the Rathskeller at a brisk walk. Zak and Annabel were walking ahead of Bart who was walking behind them trying to figure out why Zak would ask the Ice Maiden to join them.

Nobody took much notice as Bart and Zak entered but the entrance of Beddows didn't go unnoticed by Robby West, Kelly Sharp and Reggie Whitehurst, who was washing beer glasses at the time. She almost dropped the slippery glass when she saw Beddows and who she was with.

They took a table near the front of the Rathskeller. Reggie was quick to get over to the table to get their order and to see how this oil and water mixture was working out. *Why would she come here with Coltrane?* she thought.

After ordering, Zak turned to Bart and asked, "Bart, how about telling us a little about you. Other than what's in your file, we know nothing about you."

"Not much to tell. I am from Sweetwater, Texas, which is in the western part of Texas, some 220 miles west of Dallas. My father was a cotton farmer. We had very little money, so I got a job working after school for a crop-dusting company. As I got older, I learned to fly and did crop dusting jobs after school and later through my college days at Abilene Christian College. I didn't want to be a cotton farmer, so I joined the Army Air Corps in 1934. That's about it." he said in a low tone.

Zak noticed that Annabel had not missed a single word of Bart's history. "I say, do you have a girl back in Sweetwater?" he asked, knowing that was a question on Annabel's mind.

"No girl back home," he said. "I never was in one place long enough to develop a relationship with anyone," Bart said with a sigh.

Reggie showed up with their order just as he finished. "What about you, Zak?" Annabel asked as if she really cared.

"Grew up here in London," he said. "My father was a solicitor for a while before entering Parliament. The bloody devil is almost seventy and won't give it up especially since there's a war on. After the usual prep schools, I went to Sandhurst and got commissioned a lieutenant. From there I went into the Intelligence Services. I never did put on a uniform, as I was officially discharged to perform the usual cloak and dagger lot. I got restless and got an appointment to flight school. After graduation, I flew transports for a while, and then came the Hurricane fighters. I was just getting the hang of that beast when Mr. Hitler started his trouble. I got called in to volunteer for Lysanders and its bloody missions across the channel. After Hitler went into Poland, they pulled me back into uniform at my original Lieutenant rank. They're trying to get my civilian time credited and used for promotion to Lieutenant Colonel with the rest of my Sandhurst mates."

Beddows had finished her meal and looked at her watch. "My, my time flies. This is really wonderful, but I must get back and get your mission planned out," she said with a slight smile as she stood up to go. "See you at 1000 hours tomorrow morning."

Both men stood up and walked her to the door. Then he returned to the table.

"I guess she got an ear full," Zak said as he picked up his scotch glass.

"Probably more than she wanted," Bart said as he looked at the front door that she went through.

A big smile went over Zak's face, "I don't think so, mate. Now, tell me about the B-25," he said changing the subject.

Chapter Seventeen

It was just after lunch in Berlin when a knock was heard by Reichsfuhrer Himmler on his office door.

"Come!" he said in his usual commanding voice.

"Sir," his aide-de-camp said, "Admiral Canaris is here to see you. Colonel Feldcamp is still waiting to see you."

"Feldcamp can wait. I will see him after Admiral Canaris," he said.

Admiral Canaris came into the office and gave his perfunctory "Heil Hitler."

"So good to see you, Wilhelm. Please have a seat," the Reichsfuhrer said in an attempt to be friendly, a personality trait that was hard for him to display to others. "I take it that you have news for me on that American B-25 that is disrupting our operations from France to Norway."

"Yes, Reichsfuhrer, I do. The British have just the one B-25. It is a loan to the RAF, as are the American crew. They are there to train the RAF on the B-25. But we are not certain who is actually flying the missions. We believe that the training is a mere cover story. We believe that the Americans are actually flying the support missions. They fly very differently than British pilots. We almost had supporting information and documents, but our agent in London was arrested," Canaris said, pausing slightly. "They are not consistent on where and when these supply missions are flown. They have been of annoyance and problem to us in Denmark. The Resistance attacks have more than tripled in the past four months. It is Standartenfuhrer Feldcamp's position that it is a direct result of these impressive supply missions by the B-25. We have learned that it has a mission call sign of Black Bart. That is a historic British pirate. We have had reports that it has operated out of Tempsford and Tangmere. It has been seen refueling in the Shetland Islands as well. Our forces in France and Belgium have damaged the plane on numerous occasions but have not been successful in knocking it down. We did learn that it was responsible for the shooting down of one of our Me-109s last December. It is a very formidable aircraft."

This was of great interest to the Reichsfuhrer. He was fascinated by the concept of a medium bomber that could successfully win an air engagement with a Me-109. "What has been done to shoot this plane down?"

"Sir, it flies very low to the ground at over 400 kilometers per hour and usually at night or in the early dawn hours. Gunners have mere seconds to spot and shoot at the B-25 before it is gone or out of sight. We scramble fighters once the plane is spotted, but it is gone before they can find and destroy it," Canaris said.

"Very interesting," Himmler said. "Do you think that Standardenfuhrer Feldcamp has done a satisfactory job in Denmark in destroying this menace to the Third Reich?"

"Sir, there is always room for improvement for all of us. I would say that he has done an adequate job so far, I am sure that he will find a tactic that will work to destroy this B-25."

"Yes, yes, of course," Himmler said. "I wasn't sure until now of that. Your report gives me hope that he won't need to be replaced just yet. He is outside waiting. Bring him in and let's see what new tactics he has planned to defeat this one aircraft that is becoming an embarrassment to the Third Reich."

Moments later a very scared Standartenfuhrer (SS Colonel) commanding the German Gestapo in Denmark was standing at attention before Reichsfuhrer Himmler's desk. "Standartenfuhrer Feldcamp, my time and patience are very short. What do you plan to do differently to destroy this B-25?" Himmler asked in an intimidating tone.

"Reichsfuhrer, I believe that our past efforts were based upon the conventional method of scrambling fighters to seek out the B-25 according to where the report originated. By the time we got our fighters up, the B-25 was gone, and we had no way of knowing where to look. We are starting a new procedure when the alarm is given. The fighters will fly out to the North Sea and from a line across the probably flight paths back to England. Once one of our fighter aircraft spots the B-25, he will notify the others and it will engage to prevent it from escaping. This will give our forces a chance to find and destroy this Black Bart once and for all."

"Excellent, Standartenfuhrer. See to its implementation immediately," the Reichsfuhrer ordered. "You are dismissed."

"Admiral, shall we walk down and advise the Fuhrer of our news about the American-flown B-25 and our plan to destroy it. I am sure that he will want Goebbels to get a worldwide news release on this violation of American neutrality," the Reichsfuhrer said as he got up from his desk. As they walked toward Hitler's office, Himmler said to Canaris softy, "This is well timed as the Americans are about to get into this war, and they don't even know it. They are looking at us to start hostilities, but it won't be us. Our allies, the Japanese will throw the first blow…and soon."

* * *

Missy LeHand tapped on the door a couple of times as she informed the President that Colonel Donovan was on a secure line and wanting to talk to him and Admiral Leahy if he had the time?

"I'll take the call," said the President as he activated the speaker phone.

"Mr. President, Admiral, I had a call from an old client in Hong Kong a few minutes ago and I thought his comments would help you with your evaluation of Japanese intentions. He said that an aircraft carrier, two cruisers and five destroyers suddenly left Hong Kong during the night. They were reportedly to be in Hong Kong port until next week. This is unusual and may fit into your jigsaw puzzle on Japanese intentions. This ties into the fragments of intel you are getting from your code breakers. I believe they are gathering someplace for an attack on us. The question is where? It could be Pearl or Wake Island or Midway but not the west coast. Yamamoto knows better than to hit the mainland. When he was Naval Attaché here a few years ago, he and I talked about the Germans attacking the east coast and he was certain that the Germans or any other force would be doomed. There are too many civilians with guns for such an attack to succeed. America is an armed country with 130 million citizen soldiers."

"Thanks for the news, Bill. That fits in with our information," responded the President. "Keep up the good work." Then he replaced the receiver on the cradle.

Chapter Eighteen

Slightly after 0900 hours, Zak entered the Rathskeller and saw the crew of Black Bart eating a continental breakfast. He went over to the serving counter and poured himself a cup of coffee and sat down with them.

Robby West looked over at Zak and jokingly said, "Ahhhhhhhhhh, our thrill seeker. You just weren't satisfied with certain death in Lysanders. You had to become a member of the Suicide Squad."

"Right-O mate! Why wait for the grim reaper when you can do the job right away?" he retorted. Let's head over and get a head start on the operations and flight plan."

Coltrane was quick to get up and head for the door. The action was noted by Zak and Kelly Sharp. They looked at each other and smiled, Sharp said quietly, "That's a first. I wonder what has his interest. It surely couldn't be Annabel!"

When they got to the Black Bart office, they were surprised to see Commander Rupert Chapham there with Balfour and Beddows.

"Morning, gentlemen, quickly take your seats," Chapham said in a monotone. "I have your revised mission plan and flight plan."

Everyone immediately noticed that he had the flight path marked differently than planned. It had the departure segment going due south to an unscheduled drop point then across southern Denmark to the North Sea, then to Tempsford.

"As you can see, I am including an additional supply drop to the mission plan. It won't affect your fuel by any significant amount, and it will save an additional trip later," Chapham said as if the change was insignificant.

Coltrane stood up and went to the map with the route marked with red yarn and stick pins. He looked at the map then the printed flight plan. He looked at both Beddows and Balfour who looked away instead of looking him in the eye.

"You obviously realize that this route takes us over some of the worst flak and anti-aircraft emplacements in all of Denmark. This one area here," he pointed on the map, "is where we got our ass shot up on the last mission. You obviously know this. You also are aware that this significantly jeopardizes our primary mission of safely delivering sensitive and important people to our higher headquarters," Coltrane said in anger.

"Are you refusing to fly the mission, Major?" Before Coltrane could answer Chapham continued "Actually, Major, if you follow my flight plan you should be able to avoid the nastier areas."

"You idiot, that assumes the fucking Germans follow your plan and the four fighter squadrons don't get lucky and find us," Coltrane said with obvious anger. "I am putting you on official record that this plan of yours endangers the primary mission and has a significant potential of failing all together," Coltrane said as he turned to Beddows and Balfour. "Do you two fully understand what I have just stated? I suggest that you write up your own memorandums for the record to cover your ass later," he said in a calmer tone. Then he turned back to Chapham. I am personally holding you responsible for anything that happens after we depart the island. My officers and I will be filing our own memorandums objecting to your decision. If Grand was here, he would override you, but he is not here to do so."

Chapham appeared unshaken by Coltrane's comments. "It would appear that you are afraid to fly a difficult mission. You have the right to decline the mission if you are too afraid to fly it," he said.

Beddows was shocked at what Chapham had said. She looked at Balfour and said "I do want to write a memo. Care to join me, Sanford?"

This did get a slight and unexpected reaction out of Chapham.

Coltrane walked up to Chapham with his face less than six inches from his. "I accept the mission! Because to decline will set the whole SOE development plan in Denmark back perhaps a year. I must fly the mission for the best interest of the war effort. I will be back, and you and I will address the matter with Grand and Dalton," he said as he picked up the flight plan folder and handed it to Sharp. "Zak, you cannot go. It is far too dangerous to put you into unnecessary danger."

"Hell, Major, I wouldn't miss this one on a bet. Count me in," Zak said.

Nobody said anything as Coltrane left the room followed by the others. Beddows saw him leave the room and go down the hall. She knew that he was going to fly the mission when she saw Sharp with the mission folder. She had a very sick feeling. The same feeling when General Langham and a chaplain arrived unexpectedly at her home with the news of her husband's death in Poland. She turned away to hide the tears that were forming in her eyes.

* * *

"Bart, Bart, it's time to go," said Sharp as he shook Coltrane to awaken him. They flew to Sumburgh just after dark. This gave everyone time to get some sleep before the mission and avoid any potential ground fog developing after dark.

"Scrub the mission. I want to sleep," he said jokingly.

"Yeah, right," Sharp said. "That would absolutely make Chapham very happy. I think he wants to get rid of us any way possible. This mission is just his first attempt."

"Yep, he's every combat pilot's worst nightmare," he said as he got up from the makeshift mattress made of three parachutes. He looked around and the others were getting up as well. "Robby, make a quick walk around inspection with Sergeant Royston to make sure we still have two wings and two engines. I'll start the preflight checklist. Okay, folks, it's show time!"

About an hour out of Sumburgh, the cloud deck above them had gone allowing the moon to cast a shimmering glow on the North Sea below. This gave the pilots an additional reference point to help keep them from crashing into the cold water below. There was a hint of sunlight showing on the horizon.

"Two minutes to the Skagerrak Strait turn. You'll turn to 030 degrees on my mark. Standby … turn," ordered the navigator. Nineteen minutes on this course."

The sunlight in the east continued to increase. The winds at the surface were coming out of the southwest. *That was good*, thought Coltrane. They could make their approach from the east and not have to fly near the German garrison. The departure would be different. They would be close enough for anyone awake there to at least see them as they took off and turned south.

"Turn to 185 degrees on my mark … turn," came the familiar voice of Kelly Sharp. After Coltrane made the turn, he turned to Robby. "Call the reception committee and tell them we're 5 minutes out. Be on the northeast end of the runway."

Zak Middleton was between and to the rear of the pilots. "There," he said. "Slightly to the right. It's almost a perfect alignment for your approach."

Coltrane nodded as he saw the short runway. As he turned on final approach to land, he said to Robby, "Gear and full flaps." The plane slowed to 120 mph and slowly decreased its speed until it made contact with the very east end of the runway. Bart quickly slowed the plane and made a 180 degree turn so he could quickly return to the east end of the runway. He got to the end and turned around again facing down the runway ready to take off quickly if attacked. Robby had already opened the bomb bay doors as a dozen men came running up to the plane.

"I hope those are our friendly chaps," Zak said as he looked out the cockpit side window. Then he turned around just in time to see three of the four delivery pods drop to the ground. The men on the ground quickly carted them away to a grocery truck that had driven up. At the rear of the aircraft six men climbed up the rear ladder into the compartment.

Coltrane was looking at the last pod being carried away when he heard Sergeant Royston report, "We're ready in the rear with six more souls on board."

"Close bomb bay doors," Bart ordered as he advanced the throttles to the maximum setting allowable in these conditions. Okay, Robby, you have the aircraft, take us to Horsens," Coltrane ordered.

The chance of a tactical take-off was a thrill to Robby West. "Roger on the go," he said as he released the brakes. The big bird started down the short runway. Coltrane read off the ever-increasing airspeed to West. Then West gently pulled the control yoke back and the plane leaped off the ground.

Sharp called out, "Turn left to 168 degrees for 18 minutes then 205 degrees for 11 minutes. Your drop course will be 255 degrees. Robby started his turn once he was fifty feet off the ground. "Roger, one eight zero degrees."

* * *

Three miles to the West, German Obergrenadier (Private First Class) Claus Herbert was taking a moment from walking his guard post on the Vestero Havn dock to relieve himself when he heard the B-25. He quickly turned to see the aircraft turning south. He immediately ran to the guard shack telephone some 1,100 feet away. He was out of breath when he got to the phone. He lifted the phone and contacted the Sergeant of the Guard. "This is post number three! Black Bart, Black Bart," he screamed into the phone! The voice on the other end told him to slow down and tell him again what he saw over five minutes ago. When the Sergeant understood that post number three had an actual sighting of Black Bart, he too became excited. He hung up the phone and called his platoon leader at the local headquarters. He did not answer. The Sergeant thought for a moment then called the local restaurant where the German Lieutenant took his morning breakfast. It took what seemed forever to the Sergeant for that damned officer to get off his ass and answer the phone. Precious time was being wasted.

"Ya, ya, this is Lieutenant Hoenfels, Heil Hitler," replied the unexcited officer. "Sir, this is the Sergeant of the Guard – post number three saw Black Bart back towards the east about ten minutes ago," the Sergeant said as he looked at his watch.

With a little more interest, the officer asked which direction he was flying. "It was to the south, sir," said the Sergeant.

"Very good, Sergeant, I shall call headquarters." The German officer then dialed a number in Aalborg. It took 8 rings before the phone was answered. "Gestapo headquarters Aalborg, Schultz speaking."

"This is Lieutenant Hoenfels, Heil Hitler. I am the commander of the guard detachment at Laeso Island. Black Bart was seen 12 minutes ago over the island heading south or southwest."

"Excellent, Herr Lieutenant! I shall handle it from here. Goodbye," said the Gestapo agent.

By the time the Gestapo agent had called his superior and then the alert fighter squadron at Aalborg it was enough time for Robby to make his turn towards Horsens. He was still far offshore and flying about fifty feet off of the ocean. This was a real thrill for him.

Most of his flying the past few months had been the easy long over water segments of the flight which were boring. He did do a couple of drops over Belgium and France, but they were not in bad anti-aircraft areas. He was a happy camper today. This was a hot mission, and he was on the controls.

"Okay, Robby, turn to a heading of 205 now," came the voice of Kelly Sharp who was recalculating the final course to the drop zone that would keep them away from the effective range of the higher concentration of anti-aircraft fire. The preferred course was still going to be bad enough. Zak had squeezed around so he could look over his shoulder at the map.

Zak looked at the map and pointed to an area just to the east of Horsens. "Stay away from this point. That is a bad flak area. I don't care what Chapham said. That is a real bad area. Fly to the south a little and it will be better … not good, but better."

"Hey, Bart," called Zak over the intercom. "If we cut short this next leg by about five miles and turn inland near Samso Island, we can miss some of that heavy flak on the west side of Horsens. We would approach the drop zone from the north instead of the east. That will minimize the AAA near Rask Molle. What do you think?"

"Good idea. I wasn't looking forward to flying over the top of those emplacements near the drop zone. Kelly, go with his plan," Coltrane directed. "Okay, Robby, you'll turn to the new course just before you get a beam of that island. What is his new course, Kelly?"

"It will be 198 degrees. You will have flak on your right, so don't cut the corner," Sharp advised.

"Strange that we haven't seen any fighters up looking for us," Bart said as he scanned the sky.

The phone rang on Colonel Feldcamp's desk in his Odense headquarters. "Standartenfuehrer Feldcamp, Heil Hitler."

"Sir, this is the duty controller at Aalborg. Two squadrons are airborne and are headed for their position across the western side of Denmark. We have another squadron ready to launch in 30 minutes to replace aircraft that are running low on fuel. Times are staggered for fuel concerns. Each aircraft will have a twenty-five-mile area to cover. We should be able to spot and destroy the B-25 on its homeward leg, sir."

"Very well, keep me informed," he replied.

Sharp came on the intercom and said, "Standby for right turn to 198 degrees. Ready … turn!" Robby West made a smooth turn and descended to twenty or so feet above the ground.

The two pilots saw the tracers coming up towards them as soon as they crossed over the shoreline. It was heavy and getting worse. Coltrane felt a few hits.

"Crew Chief to pilot, we have taken hits in the rear. One of the passengers got hit. Not serious. Wow, we just got hit again," Royston said.

Black puffs started appearing in front and to either side of the B-25. Flak was from the anti-aircraft battery just outside the small town of Rask Molle. Suddenly, the aircraft shuddered as the close by flak detonation sent pieces of hot metal into the right side of the fuselage. Coltrane looked at the instruments searching for signs of damage to systems that operated the airplane. Then another hit and another. Several bursts of machine gun rounds hit the aircraft.

"Kelly, contact the reception committee and see if they are ready for the drop," Coltrane ordered. "We're five minutes out!"

"Roger, contact made. Ready for drop! Prepare to turn to 225 degrees in about one minute," Sharp said.

Coltrane was almost deafened by a loud explosion just outside the right side of the cockpit. He felt a warm liquid on his face along with little Plexiglas cuts. The aircraft jumped up then down. It was about to hit the ground when Coltrane grabbed the controls from West. "Dammit, Robby, you are getting too close to the ground!" There was no reply or the feeling of Robby on the controls. He looked at West and saw that he had massive facial wounds with blood spurting out of his face, neck, and chest, then it stopped. He was dead! "We lost a passenger back here. He took one in the chest," Royston responded.

"Zak get up here and pull Robby out of his seat. He's bought the farm."

"Turn to 225 degrees – now," Sharp said. "You're four miles to drop."

Coltrane opened the bomb bay doors as Zak and Sharp pulled Robby West's mangled body out of the copilot seat. Zak got into it and strapped himself in.

"Zak, look over there at one o'clock. Is that the drop zone?" Coltrane asked as he gained a few feet of altitude for the drop.

"No, it's right on the nose. You're shooting for that open area in the middle of those trees," he replied as another stream of tracers reached up for them.

"Get ready, drop!" Coltrane said as he hit the solenoid release system. The last delivery pod departed normally.

"Good chute!" cried Royston.

"Turn to 233 degrees, 62.5 miles to coastline," responded Sharp.

The Black Bart was receiving almost continuous ground fire. Hits were felt, but no systems failure as of yet. Flak bursts started appearing in front of them as they approached the coastline.

Coltrane kept the aircraft as low as possible to reduce the exposure to hostile fire. The coastline flashed behind them. The ground fire ended. They had made it ... so far.

Zak tapped on the starboard fuel gauge. "Hey Bart, I think we have a problem. There are holes in the starboard fuel tank. We're losing fuel," he said.

"Great, just what we didn't need. Coltrane retorted. Use the fuel cross feed system and transfer as much to the port tanks as possible then use up the remaining starboard fuel before it leaks out."

A flicker in the distance caught his attention. It was much higher and getting closer. "It was a fighter! Just like before, only there had to be more than this guy," Coltrane thought. He had to do his best to get away from the coastline and this Me-109. He advanced the throttles and prop pitch to gain as much speed as possible. Like before, he would get as low as possible so the fighter couldn't get below him and his unprotected belly. "Close off the cross-feed system. I don't want to risk an air bubble while we're maneuvering," he said to Zak.

"We have to take his first pass," Coltrane said to the crew. Yank, you get on one of those waist guns and get a passenger on the other." "You have to keep the 109 from getting a clean shot. I'll swing the tail when you need it so you can have a good shot. Once he has passed, I'll see what I can do with the eight fifties up here. I'll be doing some wild maneuvering, so be careful."

As predictable as sunrise, the Me-109 flew over the B-25 and made a steep turn to get on the tail of the B-25. As he got closer, Coltrane moved the plane back and forth to make a hard shot for the German.

Royston yelled, "Give me some right pedal!" Bart did so which gave a clear shot at the Me-109, who was now starting to fire. Royston's aim was good, but he had not hit the 109. Tracers were flying by the cockpit window and making splashes in the sea in front of them. "He is almost on us," Royston said. "He'll overfly on the left."

Coltrane chopped his power and dropped the landing gear to quickly reduce speed, and then he raised the gear just as the Me-109 flashed by above. Bart added power and the speed started to increase quickly. The 109 started to make a climbing right turn just as Coltrane had hoped that he would. He immediately made a tight right climbing turn and pointed his eight fifty caliber machine guns just ahead of his flight path. He pushed the fire button and eight streams of tracers bolted out ahead of the 109. It literally ran into a wall of Coltrane's fifty caliber bullets. Just like the first German he shot down, this one broke apart as the rounds tore through the aluminum skin and fuel tank. The fuel tank explosion finished off the kill.

"Now, let's get some distance between us and the other fighters that have to be enroute," he said as he straightened out the Black Bart for Tempsford.

They had barely crossed the English shoreline when the right engine quit from fuel starvation. The holes made by the flak had emptied both main and auxiliary fuel tanks in the right wing.

"Feather number two," Bart said to Zak, who pulled the throttle and mixture levers to the full rear position. He then turned off the ignition switch on the console. Black Bart flew very well on one engine," Coltrane thought.

"Okay, everyone get strapped down, this could be a rough landing with one engine and this amount of weight."

Zak made the radio calls to Tempsford advising them of their condition and the need for an ambulance for a wounded passenger and two dead comrades.

Bart made a long, slow turn to the left to not induce a spin by turning into a dead engine. He straightened up on a long final approach for runway 10 just like he did when we returned from the Norway mission. He kept his speed up for safety given his bad engine. As he crossed the runway threshold, he slightly reduced power and let the Black Bart settle on to the runway. They were home!

* * *

It was almost noon by the time they got Robby's body off and into the ambulance. Coltrane took a shower in the Operations building and went back down to the hanger to get a detailed list of the damages to the aircraft. The list was three pages long. It would be at least a week before Black Bart flew again. That was fine with Bart. He was tired and very depressed at the recent events. They had been over here eleven months. They had flown over 120 missions behind enemy lines and were credited with two Me-109 kills. "Not bad, Bart thought," especially since the United States wasn't even at war … yet. Judging from the news reports and the classified intel that he got from Sanford Balfour, America's entrance into the war was not far off.

Coltrane walked over to Sergeant Royston. "Go get a drink or twenty. This will wait until tomorrow," he said holding up the damage list.

Royston nodded, then pointed his thumb over his shoulder and said "They'll get started right now. I'll join them in the morning. After a big success like this, the brass will only be pushing harder, and we must deliver."

By the way, Major, while we were on the ground, one of the Resistance guys asked if we could get them some American cigarettes on the return trip. I gave him two cartons of Camels and he was overjoyed. I asked him if he could sell us a couple kegs of their really good beer if we paid for it and brought more smokes to them. He agreed! Is it OK with you if we bring back the beer?"

Coltrane thought for a minute and said to Yank, "Sure, but let's do it right. I'll get Hak to send word to them that we want four kegs. Two for your place and two for ours. We also can do that with the Resistance we supply in southern Germany. Now that's good beer!"

Coltrane smiled and reached out to shake the Sergeant's hand. "See you tomorrow, Yank."

The train ride back to London was usually a time for sleep, but this afternoon there was only silent reflection and grief. When they got back to the Rathskeller, Reggie ran up to the three men and hugged each of them. They had no idea what prompted the affection. "What's the big deal, Reggie?" Zak asked.

She held up the afternoon newspaper. The headlines read "YANKS FLYING FOR RAF." The news article generally described the B-25 and the behind the lines supply mission. While vague, the German news release was fairly accurate. This proves that America had violated the Neutrality Act and had taken Britain's side in the war.

"I knew that you chaps were something more than instructor pilots," Reggie said, as she and Heine came out from behind the bar with a tray of caviar and champagne.

Bart and Sharp tried to put on a happy face, but their heart just wasn't in it. Zak told them of Robby's death which promptly put a damper on the celebration.

The trio was a little livelier after supper. Zak was describing the maneuver that allowed them to shoot down the Me-109. Heine was totally elated at the story. He was proud to have the crew of Black Bart staying at his Gast Haus. Heine knew that he and Reggie could not tell anyone without the risk of the crew being killed by German agents. That was fine with him. He could keep a secret.

It was a little after 2100 hours when Rupert Chapham came into the Rathskeller. He made a direct course to the bar where Bart was having another scotch and it was by no means his first.

"Well, you survived," he said to Bart who had his back turned to him. The sound of Chapham's voice stirred an angry emotion deep inside him. He didn't reply or react. He just remained there with his elbows on the bar.

"Well, Major, if you had followed my flight plan in detail, your mission would have been totally successful. You probably would not have lost anyone as well. You didn't follow my instructions and flight plan; therefore, you must bear the full responsibility for the losses and failure."

Coltrane was enraged, but still had not moved or said anything. Others in the room had started to take notice of the situation. Zak and Sharp stood a little closer but were not about to interfere.

"I say, turn and face me, you bugger," Chapham said as he pushed on Bart's right shoulder. Bart still didn't move.

"What's wrong, can't you face me and admit that you failed to follow my plan which got your mate killed? It's your fault and yours alone that Lieutenant West is dead. Admit it!" he said as he once again jabbing at his right shoulder. This time Coltrane spun around like a coiled spring to his left and unleashed a powerful punch to Chapham's left jaw and cheekbone. Those close by could hear the bones shattering. Blood from his nose and three inch cut on his upper cheek sprayed everywhere. Chapham fell to the floor unconscious and bleeding badly. The left side of his face was gruesome and deformed.

Coltrane turned back to the bar and picked up his drink and after taking a big gulp, he looked over at an astonished Reggie and said, "Perhaps you could call him an ambulance."

Chapter Nineteen

Heinrich Himmler was walking down the hall of Gestapo headquarters at Prinz-Albrecht-Strasse when he saw SS-Colonel Knoff. Knoff, had a reputation for strict allegiance to his admired superior Himmler and for his cruelty. Himmler stopped him in the hall. "Standartenfuehrer, I have a special assignment for you. You are to go immediately to Odense and arrest Standartenfuehrer Feldcamp for disobeying my order to terminate the Black Bart operations. He failed! You are to place him in Schutzhaft (protective custody). In my name, you are to appoint his second in command as commander. He is to take whatever actions necessary to kill or terminate the Black Bart missions. If he fails, he will be joining Feldcamp. Do you understand?" Himmler asked in a harsh command voice.

"Yes, Herr Reichsfuehrer. What do you want me to do with Standartenfuehrer Feldcamp?"

Himmler gave him a cold, hard look without saying anything. Knoff saw the look and replied, "I understand."

* * *

"Missy get Colonel Donovan on the phone please," asked the President with a tired and weak voice.

Moments later, "Sir, he is on the flashing line," Missy reported from her office as she juggled the phone in one hand and a bundle of loose papers in the other.

"Good morning, Bill." said the President. "This is not a social call to be sure. We have lost contact with all those ships that you mentioned to me along with a lot more. Things have become very serious, and I need your help here as we once discussed. Hitler and his Axis attacked Russia of all things a few days ago. That may be his undoing in the long run. We may not be at war today, but it is only a matter of time. When can you report for duty here old salt?"

"I need some time to hand off my clients to my partners and take care of some personal matters," replied a serious Colonel William J. Donovan to the President of the United States. "How about the week of the 11th of July?"

"That will be fine, Colonel," replied the President, then hung up without ceremony.

Roosevelt could see the catastrophe that was coming, and he was doing everything he could to prepare for the inevitable. The strain of the eminent war was taking a toll on his health. Bill Donovan knew the situation had become serious when Roosevelt was short and to the point and not his jovial self. The winds of war were getting stronger.

Chapter Twenty

There was a knock at Coltrane's door. Heine spoke loudly through the door so Bart could hear him. "Bart, you're wanted at the office. You need to go see Lieutenant Colonel Grand immediately."

"Okay," Coltrane said as he rubbed the sleep from his eyes and tried to fully wake up. He finally got up and headed to the shower.

Thirty minutes later, he arrived at Grand's office. He knocked on the door. "Good morning, sir," Bart said with genuine voice.

"Thanks. I might be a bloody private by sundown. We have no time to talk. Sir Hugh is waiting, and he is livid over the mission and subsequent events," Grand said as he led Bart out the door. The two quickly entered the office of the head of Special Operations Executive (SOE) and took seats as directed while he finished a phone call with the Prime Minister.

Sir Hugh's office was magnificent Coltrane observed. It was paneled in a rich mahogany wood and was steeped in his many citations, degrees, and framed photos with world leaders. His thoughts shifted to his own office upstairs which had the warmth of an abandoned warehouse complete with a dead rat on the floor. He then focused on Sir Hugh as he ended his call.

"I have read the reports, memorandums and various stories about yesterday. What the hell happened to your command, Lawrence?" Dalton asked with stress and irritation.

"Sir, it seems that Chapham exceeded his authority as acting commander to change Major Coltrane's mission flight plan to accommodate an additional supply drop in southern Denmark," Grand said professionally.

"Knowing the critical importance and sensitivity of the primary mission, I can't understand why he would bugger the mission with a routine supply drop. His decision caused two deaths, one wounded, not including him, and a badly shot up B-25. Why didn't Beddows and Balfour inject themselves into the matter? They are just as responsible as far as I am concerned."

Coltrane interrupted Dalton. "Sir, they tried. They did attempt to explain the problems with his revised mission plan. They did all that was possible under the circumstances. Chapham was acting commander and he wasn't going to change his decision or listen to his subordinates even if it was a temporary command. I suspect that there was a certain amount of personal animosity as well."

"So, you feel comfortable with Balfour and Beddows?" he asked.

"Absolutely, sir. They make a great team. I am speaking for the others when I say that we have full faith and confidence in them. The problem was Chapham," Bart said with confidence.

Dalton leaned back in his chair and looked directly at Coltrane. "Why did you accept the mission given the unwarranted dangers?"

"Sir, it's really simple. First, the primary mission was critical and beyond the good of any one man or crew. Secondly, I am Regular Army; therefore, I always obey those appointed over me. I sure wasn't going to give the son-of-a-bitch the personal satisfaction of me declining in fear or disobeying a lawful order."

Dalton was silent for a moment and then he spoke in an official tone, "Then I can tell the Prime Minister that the problem is isolated to one person, and he is going to be in the hospital for months prior to his discharge from active duty for medical reasons." Grand and Coltrane both agreed.

"Very well, the matter is closed," Dalton said authoritatively. "Now to the matter of a new co-pilot for you."

"Sir, can we keep Zak Middleton? He was great on the last mission and fits in with the Black Bart crew," Coltrane asked.

"Bloody good idea. Done! Now about the two bodies. The American Embassy will take charge of Lieutenant West's arrangements. It seems that we must bury the Dane here. It would be difficult to send him back to Denmark."

"Sir," said Coltrane. "Black Bart will take him back when we take the others back when they are ready. That would go along with the Danish underground."

"First, what makes you think that you are taking them back instead of a submarine?" "Secondly, can you get a coffin in the aircraft?" Dalton asked with a degree of authority.

"Logic says it's a Black Bart mission. A sub would take a long time and they'll be anxious to get the new operation into action. We took them out under fire, and we must show our resolve to fight with them despite the danger. Besides, sir, we want to," Coltrane said respectfully. "And yes, the coffin will fit into the bomb bay."

"Very well, it's your mission," Dalton commanded.

"Do you have anything to add, Lieutenant Colonel Grand?"

"No sir, we're ready to move forward."

"Good hunting, gentlemen!"

Grand and Coltrane went back to Grand's office chatting about the problems dealing with the new German tactics employed to get Black Bart. As they got to the fourth floor, they ran into Annabel Beddows in the hall. Grand excused himself and left Bart and Annabel talking.

"How did it go with Sir Hugh?" she asked.

"Very well, I guess. I'm not scheduled for a firing squad. We'll be taking the Dane's body back to Denmark when they're ready to go," Bart said softly.

"Good, I'll look forward to making up that flight plan," she said as she started to walk away.

"Wait," Coltrane said, "how about joining me for supper at the Rathskeller tonight? We can eat early and then go our separate ways. Strictly platonic!"

She smiled as she lowered her head and started off down the hall. "I don't think so, thanks anyway."

It was almost 1900 hours. Coltrane was sitting in his usual booth at the back of the Rathskeller drinking scotch and reading The Times about the Japanese diplomats negotiating in Washington, DC. when a woman walked up. At first, he thought it was Reggie, until he looked up and saw Annabel Beddows.

"The supper offer still good?" she asked.

"Absolutely," he said as he got up. "Please have a seat. Can I offer you a drink?"

"Sure," she said. "Scotch neat."

"Reggie," Coltrane said, "could we have two of your best single malts, neat, please?"

"I understand that you stood up to Sir Hugh on behalf of Sanford and me. Thanks. I thought certain that we would be political casualties. I really do like what I'm doing, and I wouldn't want to be transferred to a regular unit." They had just finished the first round and reviewed the menu when Bart waved towards Reggie. She and Heine were listening to the radio. Reggie looked over and said, "Come quickly. The Japs are bombing Pearl Harbor!"

"Well, we're in it now!" Bart said.

"It's about bloody time. You've been at it almost a year," she said with a warm smile.

Coltrane looked at her smile and then into her eyes. He saw what he had hoped for in them.

"I must go," she said abruptly. "I have two Lysander missions to prepare for." She got up and departed unceremoniously.

At first Bart just stood there watching as she went out the door. Then he went after her in long strides. He worked through the unusually crowded sidewalk to catch up with her a half a block away. He gently grabbed her arm and turned her around. He pulled her to him and kissed her passionately. She did not react. She truly was the Ice Maiden. Then suddenly, she threw her arms around his neck and returned his kiss.

* * *

The props were still turning when Zak turned off the two engine ignition switches after his pilot in command and crew competency check ride. Zak turned to Bart who was standing on the steps behind the two pilots and asked, "Will that pass muster?"

"Zak, you and your crew were qualified long before the check ride. This is a formality, and you know it," Bart said as he started down the ladder to the airfield tarmac. "You're cleared to start flying missions starting tomorrow. It will be nice to have help. I'd say that it would give us a break, but if I know Dalton and Grand. They'll just increase the mission load."

"No doubt," Zak replied. "What do you have planned for the next 72 hours? It must be nice to have some time off."

"Annabel is taking me up to her family house up near Bolton. I think she's a little concerned about my reaction to her obvious wealth," Bart said with concern.

"How do you feel about being in love with a woman who is worth over one hundred million Pounds Sterling?"

"Hey, you know where I come from. I'm happy just being with her. The money really doesn't excite me. It's her money, not mine," Bart said with a tone of certainty.

"Well, like it or not you'll be around nice things and with a long list of British royalty and blue bloods. She can't change that either," Zak said as he started walking to the Operations building to get a shower. "Can you adjust to that environment from time to time?"

"Yes, I can spit out my chewing tobacco, clean the cow shit off my boots, and take a shower every Saturday," Bart quipped. "I can do anything required to be with her."

"Right-O!"

Chapter Twenty-One

Bart was enjoying the ride through the English countryside. He loved the rolling hills and diversified trees, cultivated fields and pastures. It was a far cry from west Texas that was as flat as it was desolate. "Cotton fields for as far as the eye could see," he thought.

They passed through a large stone gate and on to a blacktop road that went across a beautiful pasture with cows and half dozen beautiful horses. He looked ahead for the house, but it wasn't in view. Perhaps it wasn't as big as he thought.

"How big is the estate?" he asked.

"It's slightly less than 4,500 hectares," she replied.

"That's over 11,000 acres, very impressive," he said.

Just then they went over a hill and the house came into view. "It is a monster," he thought. It was a three-story mansion that looked very much like the Schönbrunn Palace in Vienna, only much smaller. Its size was still humbling to Coltrane. "Do you have parties here very often?" Coltrane remarked is a joking way.

"Before the war, we would have three parties a year and formal suppers six or eight times a year," she said softly. "This year the annual Children's Christmas Party was held in London due to the war. It's a social occasion that raises funds for Christmas presents given to children in hospitals and orphanages. The other annual charity ball that I host is the St. Dwynwen's Day celebration. It's a Welsh holiday for the Patron Saint of Lovers. The Duke was part Welsh. It raises funds for disabled veterans from the Great War. It comes up on the 25th of January. I'll have it in London this year as well. The war, you know. I hope that you'll be my escort and host," she said with a smile, looking at him briefly.

"I'd be honored, but I am not sure that I could be polished and sophisticated enough for the occasion," he said with a tone of reservation. I'll do what I can. You'll have to educate me on proper etiquette and customs."

"Just be yourself. If you're honest and sincere, you'll do fine. Do you have your formal dress uniform here or is it in the States?"

"It's in the States," he said. "It's packed away at March Field. It doesn't fit very well. I bought the cheapest uniform that I could get. We don't wear them often and I didn't want to pay a bunch of money for something that wasn't worn more than once or twice a year."

She thought for a moment then said "You have a birthday in March. My present to you will be a new dress uniform. Okay with you?"

"That's a little much for a birthday, but I'll need it if I'm going to help you with the St. Dwynwen's fundraiser," he said in appreciation.

"Then it's settled. When we get back to London you can go over to The Huntsman and Charles will fix you up. He has done uniforms for many, many officers including Black Jack Pershing."

"Where is this tailor shop?" he asked.

"Why, Saville Row, of course. You certainly don't want something off the rack that will make you look like a potato," she said almost laughing.

Bart laughed at her analogy. He knew about Saville Row. A necktie there would cost him more than a month's pay, much less an officer's dress uniform.

They came to a stop in front of the massive home. She looked at it then said "I'm thinking of selling it and buying a larger place in London. Elizabeth's uncle Henry made me a very nice offer last week."

"Really, last week you say? The devil! He knows that American combat units will be renting houses like this for their headquarters.

They will pay very, very well for a place like this. I'd hold on to it until after the war before selling. You will make a nice rental fee until the duration," he said.

"I bet you're right. He's quite the businessman. I was wondering what possessed him to buy a place like this during a war. I should have thought about the U.S. military. Damn, that was so obvious, and I didn't see it. I guess that I am not as good an intelligence agent as I thought I was," Annabel said in a mock terse tone. "Now, lover, collect the bags in the boot while I open up. I gave all the employees the weekend off, so we won't be bothered. Now let's go see if you are as good on the ground as you are in the air."

Chapter Twenty-Two

Coltrane had just arrived in London from the mission to take the Danish Resistance leaders and fallen comrade back to Laeso along with four kegs of great tasting beer. He had arranged for Yank to drive the kegs of Tuborg and Julebryg to the Rathskeller. He knew this would make Heine very happy and they could get a pleasant change from the English beer. He went into the Section D building on Baker Street and ran into Sanford Balfour just inside the entrance.

"I take it that you had a good mission," he said smiling. "The boss wants to see you. Better not keep him waiting."

"Right," Bart said as he gave Balfour a friendly slap on the arm. He went to Lieutenant Colonel Grand's office where Dalton and Beddows were already in the office and seated.

Seeing Coltrane, Grand motioned him on into the office and to a chair. "I take it the mission went off as planned," he asked.

"As you would say, it was frightfully boring." Bart said lightly. "It went just like Major Beddows planned it, sir."

"We were discussing the fact that you've been here for a year without any holiday at all and Christmas is coming. Ho, Ho, Ho and all that rubbish. I have a mission for the Black Bart crew and three of our staff officers here. It seems that our second B-25 is ready for pick up in California. It is just like yours except it has the suggested improvements that you have forwarded to North American Aviation. The next two that are ordered will be ready in March. That will give Black Bart four aircraft for its mission," said Grand, pausing to cut the tip off his cigar.

Dalton then spoke. "You and your crew will fly back to California day after tomorrow on a B-24 that they are using to shuttle VIPs and diplomats back and forth between London and Washington. You will find your own transportation from Washington to Los Angeles. Use your "Silver Fox" priority. That should work rather well for you."

"When you get to Washington, please assist Major Beddows and the three other SOE staff get over to the new OSS Headquarters. They have a series of intelligence coordination meetings to attend. Once the Major is finished at the OSS, she will catch a commercial flight to Los Angeles. She will deliver the final purchase documents for your last two B-25s. Perhaps they will make a right-hand drive version," he said joking. "I would appreciate it if you would give her a lift back to Washington Bolling Field in the new B-25. She has wanted to fly in your Black Bart, but her combat loss would be far too great to SOE. She'll take the B-24 Shuttle back from there." Dalton said, then remembering another item. "Oh yes, while you're at the War Department you're to stop by General Arnold's office. He wants to see you again. Now don't let him take you back. You have another year with us by agreement."

"Not to worry, sir," Bart replied. "They couldn't get me out of SOE with a crowbar."

Dalton, being a sly and cunning intelligence officer, had become aware of the budding relationship with Major Beddows. This pleased him. She deserved another good man in her life.

Lieutenant Grand interjected, "Her flight is on 20 December. She can't miss that flight. Seats are hard to come by and she has certain social obligations at Christmas time as the Duchess of Estis.

"Not a problem, sir," Coltrane replied.

"Well then, we have our plan then, thank you," Dalton said as he got up.

Everyone started to leave the room. Dalton grabbed Bart's arm and leaned closely and said "May I suggest that you have a refuel stop in Sweetwater. I think that your parents would like to meet your crew."

Coltrane looked Dalton in the eyes and knew immediately who he really wanted him to introduce to his parents. He smiled and said, "That's a great idea, sir."

* * *

The B-24 came to a stop in front of the Bolling Field Transit Aircraft operations building. The weary passengers deplaned and went into operations to check in and get individual instructions or travel orders. After the long and bumpy ride across the Atlantic, the group wanted to get a room and take a shower and sleep. Before departing the field, Coltrane arranged for he and his crew to fly out the next afternoon to the west coast.

The next morning Coltrane and the four British officers met in the VOQ office to arrange transportation to the War Department.

Beddows looked at the message attached to her arrival package. It directed her group to go to an office building near The White House, where they would meet the President's Coordinator of Information, a Colonel Donovan. He would take care of all arrangements from that point. She looked at Coltrane with a confused expression.

"Don't worry or say anything. You are going to meet this country's top spy. He's a real leader and knows his business. Work with him, as he has the President's ear. You can be sure that you'll see a lot of his personnel in the near future," Coltrane said softly. "I have a meeting with General Arnold, then I have to catch my flight. I won't see you until you get to Los Angeles. I'll meet your plane." Bart looked around to see if there was anyone around them, then he kissed Annabel.

Promptly at 0900 hours Coltrane entered the outer office of General Arnold. The Sergeant escorted him to a small conference room where there were six staff officers. Also, there was a full Colonel named Bradshaw, who introduced himself and the other staff officers around the table. Coltrane did his best to remember their names and staff function.

"Major Coltrane," the Colonel said, "We've been reading your Operational Reports and these letters and reports from the SOE. Very impressive to say the very least. Your program has exceeded the highest expectations. We understand that you're here to pick up a second B-25 and two more in March.

"We're in the war and Colonel Donovan expects to participate with the SOE in developing more Resistance activities. We are currently designing the force and operational procedures for what we're calling 'Operation Carpetbagger.' We should be deploying to RAF Harrington in July or, sooner, if we can get the B-24s modified and our intelligence agents trained. Today, we would appreciate you talking to our planning staff so they can draw on your experience. The bunch around the table have been excitedly awaiting your arrival. But first I need to take you to see General Arnold. Please follow me."

Bart entered the General's office and marched to a position directly in front of his desk, saluted and reported, "Sir, Major Coltrane reporting as ordered."

Arnold returned his salute as he came out from his desk. "It is a pleasure to see you again. You've become a distinguished combat aviator. Your outstanding operations for the SOE have made us proud. You have done a wonderful job over there this past year. We have a team anxiously waiting to debrief you in the conference room. We sure could use you here right now training our guys headed over there soon. But you're under an agreement with the Brits for another year unless you want to be relieved of the assignment."

"No sir, I'm doing a lot of good for the war effort there. I'll be ready to join up with one of our B-17 Groups when I'm finished."

"Very well, then. I am delighted that you feel that strongly about what you are doing … and we'll have a B-17 waiting for you," Arnold said as he turned to his desk and picked up a sheet of paper. "It is with pleasure that I present you with your orders promoting you to the rank of Lieutenant Colonel. If there was anyone who has earned this merit promotion, it is you. Now, please help my staff gear up for the war."

"Yes, sir," Bart said as he saluted and returned to the conference room. Coltrane barely got away from the endless questions in time to catch his flight west to meet up with Annabel.

The military C-47 stopped, and the passengers deplaned at the March Field transit terminal. Annabel was the first off, the plane. Bart's heart started beating more rapidly. As soon as she entered the building, he pulled her into the empty room adjoining the main reception area and kissed her passionately. "I have missed you," he said.

Annabel looked at him and said in a formal and proper tone, "And who are you? Yes, you idiot, I've missed you too." Then she noticed the silver leaves of a Lieutenant Colonel on his jacket. "My, my, they are giving away rank in the Army Air Force, aren't they?" she said jokingly.

"So true. Now let's get you checked in at the visiting female officer's quarters. Then we need to go over to North American. They're expecting you today instead of tomorrow. I can't explain the screw up ... the war you know. If we get the aircraft signed for today, I can show you Southern California tomorrow. We'll head back to Washington the day after tomorrow," Bart said without taking a breath.

* * *

The wheels of the B-25 barely squealed as they landed in Sweetwater, Texas. They parked the B-25 in front of the civilian fixed base operator. Several civilians came out of the old hangar to take a closer look at the new B-25. It was a novelty to them as military aircraft seldom landed in Sweetwater. Bart asked the fuel truck driver to fuel the aircraft while they went to get a bite to eat. The young kid nodded as his wide-open eyes took in the B-25. He sheepishly asked Bart if he could climb up the forward crew ladder and look in the cockpit.

Bart replied warmly and said, "Sure, just don't tell the War Department."

His parents had walked out to meet them. "I'd like to introduce my parents, Frank and Doris Coltrane. This is Major Annabel Beddows of the RAF who we work with very closely over there." He then introduced the crew of the Black Bart.

"Nice to meet you all," they responded. "Now, I understand you're limited on time, so let's head over to Lowaki's for some Texas hospitality and a damned good steak dinner," Frank said. The hurried steak lunch conversation was dominated by Bart's mother and Annabel. That was fine with everyone else, as they just wanted to concentrate on the delicious 16 oz. steak and trimmings. They hadn't had a steak that delicious before and they savored every bite.

After they stuffed dessert down, they returned to the airfield. As they walked out to the plane, Bart's mother hugged him goodbye and whispered into his ear. "She's the one, isn't she?" Bart smiled and nodded. Then he shook his father's hand before climbing up the ladder into the cockpit.

Chapter Twenty-Three

January 25, 1942 was a typical winter evening in London. It was cold, damp, and overcast with the persistent wind which had a way of going through any clothing and chilling a person to the bone. The ballroom of the Connaught Hotel in Mayfair was warm and alive with a host of political and business dignitaries from all parts of Great Britain. All of whom had come to this annual event to leave large amounts of money to support the less fortunate and disables soldiers and sailors that fought in World War I or the Great War as it was more popularly referred to.

Annabel Beddows of Bolton, Duchess of Estes, headed the official receiving line with her official escort, Lieutenant Colonel Bart Coltrane, US Army Air Force. At first Bart felt out of place, but quickly adjusted to the situation and became a warm and genial figure standing next to the chairwoman of this traditional charity gala in his new dress uniform. He was impressed at how well it fitted him but then again it came from Savile Row, it should. His attention snapped back to a tall, handsome military man being introduced to him.

"Colonel Coltrane, may I introduce a very good friend of mine, Prince Henry, the Duke of Gloucester."

Bart was quick to look this famous English figure in his eyes and extended his hand to his. "An honor to meet you, sir," Bart said with obvious respect and admiration.

"So, you're the bugger that figured out my land deal with Annabel. Very shrewd, young man," he gently leaned over and quietly spoke in Bart's ear. "I am grateful to you for bringing happiness to Annabel. She has been a hermit and very depressed until you came into her life. All the best to both of you." Then the Prince continued down the receiving line.

The official receiving line was about to close when two men in plain business suits came into the room and looked around the room then took posts at the door and midway along the wall. He was concerned as he couldn't figure out why two obvious bodyguards would be at a charity function. Then he saw why. His boss, Sir Hugh Dalton, had entered with the US Ambassador, the Foreign Minister, and a short man he could not seem to identify. Suddenly he was shocked to see the Prime Minister himself. It was Churchill!

Churchill and Annabel exchanged hugs and the traditional kiss on both cheeks like they were long-term close friends, and they were. Then Annabel turned to introduce Bart.

"No introductions necessary, my dear. I hear about this young man almost daily. Black Bart, it is an honor to meet you and to thank you on behalf of the British Empire. You have been of great service to our island nation and do great honor to your country," the Prime Minister said in his unmistakable voice which had been overheard by those close by. This brought spontaneous applause from the guests. Churchill being the consummate politician saw a political opportunity and grabbed Coltrane's hand and raised it high. "Ladies and gentlemen, I give you Black Bart, the man who the Germans fear more than their own leader." The applause became louder and then died away when Sir Winston continued down the receiving line.

Right behind the Prime Minister was Sir Anthony Eden, the wartime Foreign Secretary. "My congratulations, Colonel. My sources in Berlin tell me that you have become the most hated bunch of pirates to the Third Reich. Herr Hitler has lost a lot of sleep thanks to you and your men. Keep up the good work and we can bring an end to this bloody mess."

"Thank you, I shall take your news to the Black Bart Pirates," Coltrane said proudly.

The American Ambassador was next to pass through the line and expressed the President's appreciation to Black Bart for their efforts prior to and post declaration of war.

Sir Hugh Dalton came through considerably quieter than the others. "There is nothing that I can say to top the Prime Minister. Looks like you have won in the air and on the ground," nodding to Annabel. "I take it that you did stop in Sweetwater."

"Yes, sir, it was a great place to refuel and get lunch."

Annabel made like the regal social butterfly and went from guest to guest, greeting them and making social conversation. She kept looking over at Bart to see if he was doing okay with the guests. She saw him talking to the various guests, as well, and without any difficulty. Any question that she may have had about him not fitting into the social strata was soon dispelled. He was working the crowd like a professional.

Chapter Twenty-Four

Coltrane was leaving the Intelligence Office of Headquarters, Eighth Air Force, at High Wycombe, England when he almost knocked over Colonel Curt Lemay.

"Excuse me!" He said, then recognized Lemay. "My God, Curt, what are you doing over here? I heard you were getting ready to go to North Africa."

"Good grief … Bart! It's great to see you again. North Africa? No, I cheated. I deployed the 305th here before they could redirect us. I really pissed off some Senators and Montgomery when I did. They had visions of using the 305th as cannon fodder. I screwed their plans by leaving two days early for England. Hell, our entire ground element, and supply trains were either here or geared for here. What the hell are you doing? I thought you would have rotated back home. You sure did a great job from what I heard. My God, you're famous for your Black Bart missions. You can have any assignment you wanted."

"No, I'm still here. My two-year commitment to the British isn't up until next month. Then I'm going to take you up on the offer to put me in a B-17."

Lemay looked at him in thought, "How many combat missions have you flown over here?"

"Well, the first year I flew 136 combat and this year only 82. We now have two B-25s with two more in March. I have good crews that are carrying the load now. There is a lot of squadron paperwork and planning that keeps me down more and more. That's one reason I want to become one of your B-17 pilots. I just want to fly and leave the paperwork to you."

"You have to be kidding about 218 missions. That's an incredible number of missions over enemy territory. The odds of you surviving that many combat missions are incalculable!"

"No, that is a real number. Those are all actual combat missions flown over Norway, Denmark, France, Belgium, Spain, and a few over Germany. We fly almost any day the weather lets us. Those Resistance fighters and SOE spies must be supported. The mission and their lives depend on our delivering the goods," Bart said in summary.

Lemay shook his head. "I knew that you were flying a lot of high priority missions, but never that many. I see you're a Lieutenant Colonel now. That much experience and that high of rank limit me where I can put you. But I'll find a place for you. Would you consider a staff position?"

"Staff? Actually, I belong in the air. I've never been good at admin type jobs. I'm thankful the Brits aren't big on paperwork. I'd take the job if I had your promise to get me a flying job within 6 months. Also, I'd better tell you, off the record, that Churchill asked Roosevelt to make me a full Colonel when I have our Change of Command next month. That may complicate things for you."

"Maybe not. I have an idea that I'm working on and there's something big coming. The B-29. It's designed to take the flight directly to the Japanese homeland. I may be going that direction next year. I can see where you can really be of help to me especially if I get the B-29 command."

"Bart," Lemay said as he put his hand on his shoulder. "Use whatever pull you may have to get assigned to my staff. From there, I'll get you into the air. This crash meeting may be very fortuitous for both of us. You're exactly what I need and need badly."

"That's music to my ears," Bart said with relief.

"Just one question," Lemay asked. "With your record and experience, you could rotate home and sit out the rest of the war sitting on your ass at the War Department. So why do you want to stay on and fly here?"

Coltrane looked around and leaned closer to Lemay and said, "I've met a wonderful British lady and we plan to get married when we can. She's on active duty with the RAF working intelligence for the SOE. It's complicated and it'll take time to work out the details."

"Wait," Lemay said. "I remember seeing your picture in the *Times* at a charity event with a gorgeous woman. A wealthy blue blood as I recall. Is that the lady in your life?"

"Yes, but please don't tell anyone. It's tough enough and that bit of publicity would be very damaging to our plans."

"You have my word on the job and my silence," Lemay said. "Now don't go and get yourself shot up before you get over here with me."

"Thanks, Curt, this means a lot to me. See you in a couple of weeks. I'll contact the Prime Minister's office and General Arnold and make my request for a transfer to your staff. My second in command, Zak Middleton, is ready to take over. Black Bart operations are going very well, so my departure won't hurt anything. Can I bring my American crew with me? They wouldn't know what to do without Black Bart."

"Please bring them. They're welcome to join the 305th."

Chapter Twenty-Five

The sound of hobnailed boots across a marble floor, followed by a loud click of boot heels, was heard just before Colonel Knoff cried out, "Standartenfuehrer Knoff reports to the Reichsfuehrer, Heil Hitler!"

Reichsfuhrer raised his hand in the appropriate Nazi salute and looked carefully at the Gestapo Colonel before him. "Can I assume, Standartenfuehrer, that your mission was successful?"

"Yes, Reichsfuehrer, the matter has been dealt with. However, an interesting development has come up that you may want to know about. It seems that a young Lieutenant named Schultz was interrogating a recently captured Resistance member. Lieutenant Schultz was most efficient in his efforts to obtain information about a supply drop by Black Bart. He says that they will get a large number of explosives, radios, and ammunition. Approximately 1,500 kilos of supplies," Knoff said pausing.

Himmler became totally focused on the Colonel. "Go ahead, Standartenfuehrer."

"With your permission, sir," Knoff said as he unfolded a map.

"According to the individual, the drop will take place in far north Denmark. They have used this area many times before as it is remote with few residents in the area, and our closest troops are over ten miles away. It is in a large clearing and has excellent access by road. It offers the Resistance force many ways to escape. They feel very comfortable in using this area and will do so just before dawn the day after tomorrow," Knoff continued.

Himmler was still listening carefully and nodded for Knoff to continue. "Lieutenant Schultz and I drove out to the location. It is perfect for an ambush to get the main core of the area Resistance members and once and for all destroy Black Bart," Knoff explained.

"Yes, yes, go on. What's your plan?" Himmler said impatiently.

"Sir, I took the liberty of having a machine gun platoon and two rifle squads go out there and very carefully dig foxholes and machine gun nests here," pointing to a tree line on the north side of the clearing and on the east side of this road. "They will undoubtedly use the road for vehicles to haul off the 1,500 kilos of explosives. It is probable that they will also come through this area of trees on the west side and hide while awaiting Black Bart. The plan is simple. We wait until Black Bart drops the load. While the Resistance goes out into the field to recover the supplies, we radio the Luftwaffe at Aalborg who will be waiting on strip alert for our call. As soon as we call them with the time and directions that Black Bart is headed, they will launch and take up the picket line between England and Black Bart. They will cover the area with a minimum of two flights of eight fighters flying in a staggered fuel plan. We will launch every fighter and saturate the area so he can't get away. He cannot get away this time. Meanwhile, once the Resistance has got to the supplies in the middle of the open field, Lieutenant Schultz will give the order to open fire and eliminate those bastards. They will be in a crossfire from which there is no escape."

"Outstanding plan, Standartenfuehrer. I must meet this exceptional Lieutenant Schultz," Himmler said. "You are to return and see to the details. Take no chances. This is a very good opportunity to slay two flies with one swatter. If you are successful, you and Lieutenant Schultz are to come back here and give me a detailed report. I may want to bring Schultz to Berlin."

"Yes, Herr Reichsfuehrer. Heil Hitler!" Colonel Knoff said as he clicked his heels, gave his party salute, and departed.

Chapter Twenty-Six

The weather in Tempsford was starting to turn cold and damp. It was typical weather for late November and early December. Coltrane looked away from the Black Bart scheduling board and towards Zak Middleton. "Let's shift the new boys in 'Fancy Dreams' to the milk run near Bordeaux. I'll take the run to Denmark. I know the area and you can bet the Luftwaffe will be trying to get whoever flies the mission in their picket line trap. I'm not comfortable with the new guys taking on that hard of a mission just yet."

"Agreed! You know with the weather getting trashy, this could be your last mission with Black Bart," Middleton said as he handed Coltrane the latest weather forecast.

"It sure could be. Change of command is scheduled for 1300 hours on Saturday," Coltrane said with a tone of sorrow in his voice.

"It's high time we Brits get you Yanks out of here and add a little class to the operation," Zak said jokingly as he slapped Coltrane on the shoulder.

"You're damned right! You need to purge the Crown of all the Colonials. Now let me take you out and corrupt you with alcohol and supper when I get back," Bart said in a joyful tone.

It was a little after 0600 hours when the Black Bart broke out of the overcast and the clear air some twenty miles west of the northern tip of Denmark. Captain Willard Sims was at the co-pilot controls straining to see the coastline ahead. Sims had been one of four chosen out of over 200 volunteers to transfer from flying Lancaster and Wellington bombers to Black Bart. Captain Willard was to become an aircraft commander when Bart departed on Saturday. Today his job was to learn as much as he could about northern Denmark and the hazards involved in flying in the area especially given the new tactics employed by the German Luftwaffe.

Sharp was trying to show his replacement how he had been doing things as navigator. It was quite difficult for his replacement to see everything because of the cramped quarters. Sharp was impressed with the new British GEE Navigation System but preferred to rely on his own navigation and use the GEE to confirm. "I have a go code from the reception committee," Sharp said as he adjusted his earphones. "Turn to 192 degrees. You are 7 miles to the drop zone."

"Roger," Coltrane responded. "I have the controls," he told the Sims. "Start looking for a single white over two red lights. That will be our friends waiting."

Sims suddenly said, "I have the lights, 2 miles."

"Roger, open bomb bay doors. Stand by to drop on my command, "Coltrane said calmly. Coltrane saw the large open area and mentally timed the drop. "Ready, drop!" he commanded. Sims hit the four release switches one second apart.

"Cargo away," Sims reported. Then Royston reported four good chutes.

Coltrane made a hard-right turn to head back to England when he heard screams and gunfire over his headset.

"It's a trap! They have us pinned down on two sides in a crossfire. We've been compromised. There's no hope for us. Let London know," said the nameless voice with a definite Cockney accent.

Coltrane made another turn to the north. "Where are they shooting from?" asked Coltrane.

"They have machine gun nests on the north tree line and in the trees next to the road on the east side. There are troops on either side of the machine guns.

"Okay," Coltrane said. "Stay down and let me know how my first gun run works out."

"Do not come back. The fighters will be looking for you. You must escape now while you can. We're finished! Don't take the bloody chance," came the resolved voice of what must have been a British SOE agent.

Bart climbed up to three hundred feet to get a better look at the area and situation in detail. Then he descended to less than 100 feet and turned east toward the north tree line. As he crossed the main road going to Skagen, he opened fire with all eight fifty caliber machine guns. He sent a continuous burst of rounds and tracers into the line of Germans literally devastating the entire force on the North side of the clearing.

Sims exclaimed in an excited voice, "Wow! Those fifties chewed them up like grannie's bloody mincemeat pie. The only thing left of them is hair, teeth and eyeballs!"

Suddenly, he was over water. He went out a half mile then turned south for a couple of miles while observing the area on the east side of the clearing, then he made a descending turn back to the right and straightened out his course that would take him over the remaining German force that was partially firing on the still trapped Resistance fighters and trying to pull away from the incoming fire of Black Bart. This time Bart used his rudder control to very slightly move the intense machine gun fire back and forth in a slightly wider path. That caught both those still fighting and those Germans trying to leave. Once again, the first run on this line of Germans was devastating. The German force was destroyed. Only a half dozen could be seen staggering away from the firing position.

"Okay, get your supplies and go," Coltrane said.

"Thanks, Black Bart, you saved our bloody ass. We have a traitor in our group. We'll make contact with London as soon as we can find the bloody bastard and kill him. You must go now! The fighters must be getting close."

"Roger, we're out of here," Coltrane ended.

Coltrane was thinking to himself, *one good thing about the Germans, they always follow a plan and orders, not opportunity.* He looked at his watch as he turned east back over the water. If they were going to come after Black Bart at the ambush site, they would already be here. That means they are following orders by flying the airborne picket line. They are up there in force looking for them and burning up fuel. That gave Bart an idea. He turned southeast and got as low over the water as he felt safe. The heading took him to the far northeast end of Laeso Island. It took about twenty minutes to fly the distance to the island.

"Okay, guys," he said over the intercom. This is what we're going to do. We're going to land at the German strip on Laeso Island. We'll go to the end of the runway and wait 35 to 40 minutes until the Germans start running low on fuel. Then we'll take off and hope they're in the middle of relieving fighters in their staggered refuel plan. If they are, maybe we'll get lucky and sneak through. They have to be spread thin if they are."

Bart kept the aircraft at the lowest altitude possible. He landed at the vacant strip and turned the bird around and taxied back to the far east end of the strip. He set the brakes and throttled back as far as he could without killing the engines. The crew looked out every window for the first sign of German troops from the local garrison or fighters. After 25 minutes, Bart was getting uneasy about staying any longer and was concerned about his fuel remaining. So, he said, "Time to go. Watch out for fighters. Any fighters no matter how far away they are!"

The throttles were advanced, and the bomber took off. Bart had not gotten the plane more than 20 or 30 feet off the ground when he raised the landing gear and flaps. He leveled off at 30 to 40 feet then turned hard to the south to avoid being seen or heard by the German garrison. He flew about four miles before turning northwest to avoid the fighter base at Aalborg. Eleven minutes later, he was over open water in the Skagerrak Strait.

He turned and saw a cloud deck and climbed into it to avoid detection. He flew in the clouds for about 30 minutes before breaking out into the clear air above the overcast. The warm sun felt good. "Sharp, give me a course for home," he said in a cheerful voice.

"Turn left to 205 degrees. You are 563 miles to your first scotch," Sharp said in a light and happy tone.

* * *

Precisely at 1300 hours on 13 December 1942, the drum major of the Coldstream Guards Drum and Bugle Corps struck up a series of typical British military tunes. The sun was trying to show through to warm the cold audience who were present to watch what would otherwise be a less formal occasion of changing the command of a flying squadron from one officer to another. This was not such an occasion. Today, an American led volunteer aviation unit would turn over its mission and aircraft to the host British forces. This unusual event was visited by numerous American and British officials including the Defense Minister himself, along with American General Hap Arnold and Colonel Curtis Lemay.

The normal ceremony had been augmented to add appropriate pomp and ceremony befitting its honorable guests. After a short speech by the defense minister and General Arnold, who promoted Bart Coltrane to full Colonel, the Coldstream Guard Drum and Bugle Corps passed back and forth in front of the remaining five members of the original six members of the American Black Bart unit and the twenty-eight new members who were in a formation directly behind them.

A British major in his dress uniform stood before the formation and read the general order that directed that Colonel Coltrane hand over the British pirate flag that had become the unit flag to Lieutenant Colonel Zak Middleton. The change of command was complete, and the formation dismissed. The cold and shivering official guest went into the Tempsford operations building for a reception of fine wine, caviar, and champagne.

The Defense Minister came up to Coltrane and said, "I must run. The war you know. I do understand that you're staying with us to fight on." He looked at Major Annabel Beddows, who was standing by his side and remarked, "I can see why and wish you the best." Then he departed with most of the dignitaries.

Lemay walked up and said "That was very impressive. I hope that you don't expect the same ceremony when you get to that squadron at Chelveston. You will be lucky if the First Sergeant greets you. I need you to train them for combat. They've flown eight terrible combat missions. The commander was relieved yesterday. The hand-picked one the War Department is sending over will not be here for three months. Until then, it's yours. Then I have a special operations problem for you to solve for me. Yes, you'll be flying too!"

"Thanks, Curt," Bart said. "That sounds wonderful to me. I'll check in on Monday morning, if that's okay."

"Fine with me," Lemay said turning his attention to Annabel. "What are your thoughts on all this?"

"I am fine with it. There's a war on and we all have to do our bloody part. I wish things were different, but they're not. I accept that Bart is flying in harm's way. This is his duty, and he loves it almost as much as me," she said squeezing his arm. "It had better be 'almost as much as me,'" she said chuckling.

"Do you have any wedding plans yet?" Lemay. asked.

"We've not set a date yet," she replied, "but maybe in the spring depending on the war and what he's doing. I don't want to be a two-time war widow."

"I can't promise anything," Lemay. said, "but I plan to have him on my staff after he cleans up that mess at Chelveston. He still wants to fly, and I'll do what I can, but he has combat experience and common sense that I badly need at the headquarters. The staff job I have for him still keeps him flying some, but not the day-to-day missions."

"That's great," she said. "Now we can set a date!"

Chapter Twenty-Seven

It was a cold foggy morning with low visibility and a damp cold wind that went to the bone. The gate guard at RAF Chelveston handed the three military ID cards back to Master Sergeant Royston, who was driving the jeep taking himself, Colonel Coltrane, and Lieutenant Colonel Sharp to their new assignment. Royston drove through the gate and went towards the squadron headquarters over a very rough and muddy road. The entire base looked sloppy and rundown to Coltrane. It wasn't nearly as well maintained as Tempsford, and Tangmere. As they entered the ubiquitous Quonset hut that was the squadron headquarters, Coltrane noted how dark and drab the interior looked.

The First Sergeant was the first to see the new Commander enter and called the room to attention. A Major in a flight suit quickly came forward and reported, "Sir, Major Jack House, Squadron Ground Exec reporting, sir."

Coltrane returned his salute and extended his hand. "Good to meet you. At ease, gentlemen," he said with relaxed authority.

Coltrane turned towards Sharp and Royston. "This is Lieutenant Colonel Sharp and Sargent Major Royston. They will be joining us as well." Coltrane walked over to the old Squadron First Sergeant and shook his hand, "Top, I know that you have orders to High Wycombe, but I would ask that you delay your departure a week so the transition between you and Sargent Major Royston can go smoothly. Let's not disturb things any more than necessary," he said with a kind tone.

"Can do, sir!"

Then he turned to Major House, "Since there are no flights today, everyone should be available. So, would you set up a meeting with all aircrews and NCOs for 1300 hours?"

"Yes sir," he said as he looked at the two Squadron Clerks who were quietly watching the events before them. They grabbed their hats and coats and departed at a run.

"Now can you show us to the mess hall. I am starved," Bart said with a smile.

"This way, sir, we can slip in the back door to the Commander's table. The Mess Sergeant will bring us trays," House replied.

"Thanks, but I want to go through the line, so I know what the crews are seeing and eating," Coltrane said. Then he followed House across the road to another Quonset hut which was the mess hall. As he entered, the room was called to attention. Corporal Shapiro spilt hot coffee on his leg as he got up. "Damned officers, how many of these damned visitors are going to come see this hard luck bunch? We're no better than an amusement at a bloody circus!" he said to another Corporal to his left. He looked up and saw a full Colonel and a Lieutenant Colonel. He turned to the other Corporal and asked, "Do you recognize either of them? The full bull has some decorations, so he isn't our inbound Commander. Why can't they give us a commander with some combat experience?"

The Corporal said quietly under his breath, "Shapiro, shut up, you jackass. That's Black Bart himself."

"You're shitting me," Shapiro said.

There was a hushed murmur of chatter going throughout the mess hall as word spread about the visitor.

Shapiro looked up at Coltrane then down to his meal tray. "Black Bart, now that's what this unit needs. Somebody with experience and balls. Too bad that he's only visiting. Who is the half Colonel with him?" Shapiro said as he ate the beef stew. The guy next to him just shrugged not knowing.

Coltrane went to the chow line and grabbed a tray. This caught the Mess Sergeant by surprise. "Sir, if you will sit down, I'll get your tray for you."

"Thanks, but I'll handle this one myself." Coltrane then looked at the Mess Sergeant and pointed to the serving table which had numerous patches of spilt stew and other meal items." Sergeant, the men might appreciate your efforts more if the serving line didn't look like the latrine floor after a Saturday night beer bash! The salad wasn't properly drained after washing. It's standing in an inch of water. That shouldn't happen, should it?" Coltrane said.

"No sir, it will be corrected," the embarrassed Sergeant said.

Coltrane then took his tray to the Commander's table. He looked around at the men and was amazed at how young they were. Some couldn't be old enough to shave but would be killing Germans at 25,000 feet or being killed.

After lunch he went to the Mess Sergeant. "Sergeant, the quality of the meals is to get better and quick. Find a good scrounger and let's get him wheeling and dealing for steaks and anything else you may need to make some great meals for these guys. You have one week to bring up the quality and atmosphere or you can go cook for the infantry," Coltrane said then left before the Mess Sergeant could respond. Then stopped, looked up then back to the Mess Sergeant who was still in shock. "Get some white paint and more lights, this is a place to eat, not a cave!"

Coltrane entered the headquarters, "First Sergeant, I assume that you have a good scrounger in the squadron. Get with him and have him help the Mess Sergeant get some real food for the men. He needs some white paint and more lights as well. He looked up then at the old First Sergeant and the incoming Sargent Major Yank Royston. "Get enough paint and lights to brighten this place as well." Then he left for the briefing room … another Quonset hut!

Precisely at 1300 hours Colonel Coltrane entered the Operations Briefing Room. "At ease, take your seats. I'm Colonel Samuel Barton Coltrane, your new commander. Joining me is Lieutenant Colonel Kelly Sharp and Sargent Major Yank Royston. Our mission is to make you combat ready and an effective combat element of the 305th Bombardment Group. So far, your first eight missions have been less than adequate, in fact, dismal. My job is to change that. The practice of evasive action or jinxing from the IP to the target will stop immediately. You will fly your assigned position in the combat box and focus on bombing the target. Did anyone not understand what I just said?"

"Obviously, you haven't flown combat or have gone against flak or anti-aircraft fire," came an unidentified voice from the back of the room.

Major House got up and stepped in front of Coltrane. Excuse me, sir," then turning to the group. Whoever said that is an idiot and has no idea who this is. For those of you who have your heads in a rectal defilade, Colonel Coltrane is better known as Black Bart."

There was silence in the room.

Major House continued. "Both Colonel Coltrane and Lieutenant Colonel Sharp have been flying for the RAF for over two years. They have both flown over 200 combat missions over enemy territory. They have flown against flak and anti-aircraft ground fire over Norway, Denmark, France, Belgium, and Germany. They flew these missions at altitudes less than 500 feet, not at a safer 25,000 feet. They are also credited with two Me-109 kills, and they did it from a B-25 bomber. Now, anyone here have any questions about their combat qualifications?"

One young Captain stood up and asked, "Sir, welcome to hell, sir! I do have a question about what you have said." Coltrane nodded and the captain continued, "Sir, how do we avoid flak on the bomb run if we maintain straight and level flight?"

"Captain," Coltrane said, "that's a damned good question! First, the short answer is that you don't. We, or should I say the British, have learned that the gunners can't tell if you're going up, down, right or left from the ground. They aim for the flight and fire as many rounds as they can at your altitude hopping for a lucky hit. Moving or jinxing only throws your bombardiers off target. That means we must come back again and again until we reduce the target to rubble. The distance from the IP to targets have been shortened as much as possible. That will reduce your time of flak vulnerability. During those few minutes you must focus on steadying up on course, tighten your formulation so your bomb pattern will be effective, and concentrate on placing your bomb load exactly where it belongs. Look, these guys on the ground are not aiming at a specific aircraft. That is like shooting at a hummingbird with a deer rifle. They are shooting at the group and hoping for a kill. It's a function of luck and numerical probability. Before and after the bomb run, it is vital that you confine your evasive maneuvers so as not to open up critical openings in the combat box."

"The box works and gives you and the planes around you the best chance of getting home when the fighters attack. It's that simple! Are there any questions on the bomb run or combat box?" he said as he looked at the men. "Okay, tomorrow we'll fly a mission and see if there's any improvement. It should be a milk run, but it will give us both flak and fighters to deal with. Once I feel that we're ready, we'll be tasked with much more important missions. I'll be flying tail end Charlie tomorrow to see how well you fly and bomb the target. Colonel Sharp will be flying as the navigator for the lead ship. There will be a three-day pass to London for the crew that has the best on target bomb pattern. Aircraft commanders who violate the two new rules about jinxing on bomb run or breaking the Combat Box will have their orders appointing them as Aircraft Commanders revoked, demoted to co-pilot and transferred out of the unit. No exceptions," Bart said with a bold and commanding voice. "Dismissed!"

Chapter Twenty-Eight

Coltrane looked over at the outside air temperature gauge in front of the co-pilot. It was slightly less than 40 degrees below zero at 28,000 feet. It didn't get any warmer in July and now it was February 1943. It gave him a shiver to think about it. Then a real shiver came over him when the top turret gunner called out "Fighters at 9 o'clock, level." Bart looked to his left but didn't initially see them. *There they are*, he thought to himself. He looked around at the squadron formation. It was in a tight combat box. The past eight missions had shown them that the combat box really worked. They had lost only four men to hostile fire and no aircraft. The bombing accuracy had steadily improved to become the best in the 305th group. Not a bad improvement for the ten weeks that he had the squadron. This would be a real test today. They were going after the marshaling yards and dry docks at Antwerp. The fighters would be merciless and the flak heavy enough to walk on.

"IP in three minutes," Sharp said over the intercom. "Course will be 073 degrees."

"Roger, watch for fighters at our 9 o'clock headed for the low squadron," Bart said calmly. "The sneaky bastards may hit them first and catch us from behind."

Flak dots came up in front of them. The fighters were confirming the proper altitude for the gunners on the ground. *No amateurs*, Coltrane thought. *Well, neither are we.*

"IP, turn to 073 on my command," called out Sharp. "Now, turn. Target 6 miles."

Internal chatter was increasing due to the high number of German fighters attacking the two squadrons. Coltrane was pleased that he heard fear in their voices, but not panic.

"Fighters breaking off," came the cry as the Luftwaffe was getting out of the way for the flak barrage that was about to start.

Coltrane could see the first burst of flak ahead of the two groups of bombers. It got heavier and heavier as they approached the targets.

"Bombardier to pilot, I am ready. Target in sight," said the bombardier.

"Roger, it's all yours," Bart said as he engaged the autopilot.

The autopilot was now slaved to the Norden bomb sight that gave the airplane its steering commands to take it to the target.

"One minute to release," came the report.

There were constant explosions around the aircraft tossing it up and down like a cork in a lake.

"They got the 'Purple Plane,'" came the right waist gunner. "Direct hit!"

Coltrane shook his head. The first loss since he got there. Suddenly, he felt a hard hit to the control yoke. An alarm went off indicating a fire. The bomber yawed to the left. He looked out his window and saw the left outboard engine on fire. They had been hit!

"Chop power and feather number one and pull the fire extinguisher on the son-of-a-bitch," Coltrane said in a strained, commanding voice.

The bombardier called out, "Give me some right pedal for ten seconds."

Coltrane pushed the right pedal which controlled the rudder. "How is that?"

"Great, just hold it a few seconds more. "Bombs away! That should delay the trains for a few days."

Coltrane was trying to keep control of the B-17 as it started a steady yaw to the left due to unequal power on the left side. He increased the left inboard engine to as much as it could take without blowing a Jug. He reduced the right outboard engine slightly to further reduce the yaw. The plane became more stable but at a slower speed. He knew that he would have to fall back. "Bandito, this is Black Bart. Take the lead, we are hit and on three engines."

"Roger, Bart, Bandito has the lead," came the voice over the radio. "Execute right turn, now."

The right turn gave Coltrane the chance to turn into his good engines and cross under the protection of the high squadron and so he would end up on the right side of the squadron once it had made the slow right turn into the combat box formation. He just had to fight off the fighters as he limped back over the North Sea towards England. The Germans would certainly go after any crippled aircraft like Black Bart.

The top turret gunner called out, "Here they come. They smell blood in the water. Come on, you bastards, come and get us. We still have a big sting waiting for you!"

Sharp called out over the intercom, "Here comes the Calvary to the rescue!"

Bart looked out and saw British fighters engaging the Germans. They would keep them off long enough to escape. *We've cheated death once again*, he thought. He then turned his attention to the condition of the bomber as it limped home. He looked at what was left of the engine and far tip of the wing, or where the last three feet of wing tip should have been. The engine was slightly hanging downward; Coltrane assumed from the heat of the fire. That would slow them down some but otherwise of no importance ... he hoped.

The flight home was uneventful, and they were able to keep up with the squadron. Bandito had reduced formation speed to accommodate the three damaged aircraft struggling back.

As the Black Bart came to a stop at its parking position and the three working engines shut down, a staff car drove up. Bart knew that must be Lemay or someone higher. So, he got out quickly and went over to the car.

Lemay rolled down his window and said, "Get in, Bart."

Coltrane got in the car only to find Lemay and the new First Bombardment Division Commander. Lemay introduced Coltrane and immediately went into the reason for his visit. "Bart, we're getting ready to take the battle to the enemy war machine itself. On the 27th of January we had a great attack against Wilhelmshaven. It was only the first and you did great on that mission. If you can stay alive, I want your squadron to spearhead the attack on Nordenham. After today's mission, you certainly deserve it. Reports from the Air Recon boys indicate that the rail yards no longer exist. It will take a month to repair and rebuild. We could have done better on the sub pens, however. That's not your problem, yet!"

"Yet?" Coltrane said.

"Well, your replacement is on his way over. He should be ready to take over soon after the Nordenham mission. I still have a position for you on my staff, or have you forgotten? I'm sure Annabel will remember."

Bart hung his head down for a second or two then looked at Lemay. "I guess that I got caught up in the squadron and forgot that this job was just temporary. I am just 'summer help' here," he said. "I'll be ready to join you whenever you say, sir."

"Actually, the Division Commander here wants you to be his Operations Officer. It means a star for you, and you would be working out of London until the Division is officially formed in a couple of months. Then you'll move to an outlying airfield like Grafton. I can't offer you a star or that level of a staff position. It's a great career move, Bart," Lemay said.

Bart shook his head, then looked at the three star General and said, "Sir, the offer is tempting and probably what I want, but my head is swimming with the last mission and getting ready for the St. Nazaire. Could I have a couple of days to collect my thoughts and give you my decision, sir?"

"Sure, Colonel, here's my direct phone number, call me by the end of the week. I do realize how overpowering all of this is after this mission. I'll be waiting for your call," the General said.

"Thank you, sir," Bart said as he got out of the car. He stood there for a minute and watched the staff car drive off. Sharp came up behind him and asked, "Was that Lemay?" Coltrane just nodded as he turned and got into the jeep with Sharp. Coltrane put his foot on the dashboard and said, "I need a fucking drink."

Chapter Twenty-Nine

It had been two days since Lemay and that three star discussed the operations job and Bart was torn between two emotions. The staff job with some flying for Lemay, or the operations job and a brigadier's star at Air Division headquarters in London. Bart pondered, *that would allow him to be with Annabel all the time and be a safe job so they could get married.* The problem was Lemay needed him very badly for some special operations project. He owed Curt. He could not overlook what he had done for him and what may be ahead. *Lemay was just too good of a man and a leader to be let down*, he thought. *I guess that I must put the greater good of many and Curt Lemay ahead of myself*, he decided. *Oh well*, he thought, *I have until tomorrow to make a final decision.*

His concentration was broken by Kelly Sharp. "Boss, your Supreme Commander just called, and she needs for you to meet her at the Rathskeller at 1500 hours today. She said that it was extremely important that you be there and on time."

"From the sound of things, you're already married," he said, teasing Bart. "Things here are in good shape and I can handle the store if anything comes up. Why don't you catch the 1305 train, so you won't be late and get your ass in big time trouble?"

"Thanks, Kelly. She wouldn't have called unless it was damned important," Coltrane replied. "Besides, I need the time to think over that job offer. The train ride will give me the opportunity to think through the matter without being disturbed or distracted."

* * *

By the time it took Coltrane to get to the Rathskeller, he had made up his mind. He would stay with Lemay. He could still get married but would only see Annabel on a regular basis between whatever projects or missions Lemay have for him. This was best especially given the turn in the war against the Germans. They now had the aviation resources to conduct a proper bombing campaign against the German war industry."

As Bart walked into the Rathskeller, Reggie came out from behind the bar and gave him a big hug and said, "That terrible woman who took you away from me is in your usual booth with a couple of civilian gentlemen."

He walked back to the last booth and saw Annabel. She got up and gave him a long and passionate kiss. "Welcome, dear to the conspiracy." Then she pointed to Curt Lemay and Hap Arnold who were sitting with their backs to him in civilian clothes.

"My sweet cowboy, I want you to give what these gentlemen have to say serious consideration. I don't know what the details are, but the overall idea puts me at the altar on 2 June of this year. I hope you can make it," she said with sarcastic humor. "Love, I must go do my duty for God and King. So, you guys work out the details. Cheerio," she said as she kissed him goodbye.

Bart sat down across from the two men not having a clue what was going on with Annabel or the two senior officers.

Lemay was the first to speak. "Bart, this meeting never happened … agreed?"

"Yes, sir, I understand," Bart responded.

"First of all, both of us want you to take the operations job at First Division. We were the ones that got the general to ask you. He has absolutely no idea about what we're going to discuss. Sorry, too, for getting Annabel involved, but it was the best way to get you here without attracting the attention of others. All she knows is that we are trying to get you a staff position here in London. Beyond that, she knows nothing. She's a strong woman that knows what she wants and that is you ... you alive. To that end, she'll do whatever it takes. She told me in no uncertain terms that if I didn't get you out of high-risk missions, she would pick up the phone and call her friend, Mr. Churchill, and get it done through him. Well, she doesn't have to make the call. You're headed to London as Deputy Chief of Staff: Operations of the First Bombardment Division. You do have to make the call to the general accepting the position."

"Now let's talk about the rationale behind all of this. You need to sit back and listen to what General Arnold has to say about the larger picture. It is the future of strategic air power here, in the Pacific, and the future," Lemay said, as he sat back and nodded to Arnold.

General Arnold casually looked around to insure nobody was listening. Then he started. "Bart, strategic bombing is winning this war. We are now equipped with enough B-17's and B-24's to take the war deep into the Fatherland. You have seen firsthand since you got here in late 1939 the vast improvement in aircraft and joint air/ground operations. You flew a mission two days ago that proves that we can systematically destroy the enemy's capability to produce weapons of war and his will to fight a losing war. It's going to take another 18 to 24 months to destroy his industry and support the ground invasion. The outcome is clear, and our results from strategic bombing have made the powers in Washington true believers in aviation. You have been a key part of that success in your Black Bart missions and now in B-17 bombings.

"While we're here bombing the enemy night and day, our Army and Marine ground pounders are marching up the islands of the western Pacific. The Japanese are not only creative and resourceful; they are fanatical in their war efforts. They, too, must be bombed into submission. Unfortunately, the B-17 cannot do the job. We do have a plane in the works that can do the job, the B-29. It will have the range and capability to destroy their industry and war machine. It will be late this year or early next year before it can be put into operation. Curt here will be taking on that mission in the fall. That fact is only known by a handful of very senior officials. There is another project that is even larger than that. It is a means to bring the war with Japan to a decisive conclusion. I can't say anything more than that at this time, sorry! If you look at the enormity of the size of the Army Air Force on a global scale, it is enormous and getting larger as well as becoming responsible for the long-term defense of our country. I am talking beyond the current war."

"Curt and I both feel strongly that after the war we will have other smaller conflicts to deal with as well as a larger threat. Russia and China are both becoming very strong economically, and, most of all, militarily. We must look beyond the current conflict towards keeping the global peace and the protection of our country from the threat posed by these powers. There are very favorable discussions and planning towards the establishment of a separate branch of service for the Army Air Force. Curt will tell you about new aircraft that are on the drawing boards that will amaze you. Strategic bombing is just in its infancy, as you will see in the next few years. Air power is an essential part of our nation's defense. Curt and I want you to be a part of that future. Your posting to the First Division is just a step, a very short step at that. You will do exactly what was set forth by the new Commander. We want you to get the unit fully organized operationally between now and when it officially is activated in July. It will also be your job to assist the 801st Bomb Group (Carpetbaggers) get operational at RAF Harrington by September. They are the US equivalent of your old SOE missions. In early August, you'll receive orders assigning you to a special inter-service coordination office supporting Project Matterhorn. That is the code name for the deployment of the new B-29s to India. From there, Curt will bomb the hell out of Japan. You'll officially be working for me, but in reality, you'll be secretly working for Curt. He needs someone that knows the plan and can help him prepare for the air war in the Pacific. It is a job for someone like you who has the reputation and rank to get things done. That's why we want you to take the operations job. That will give you the promotion to Brigadier

General. You'll need the horsepower to deal with the various people, companies, government agencies and foreign governments. Especially with Leslie Groves involved. Is all of this starting to make sense to you?" Arnold asked in conclusion.

"Actually, yes, sir. I can clearly see the program now and in the future," Coltrane said in a serious tone. "Who is Groves?"

The General continued ignoring the question, "Very well then. You will fly the next bombing mission into Germany then be reassigned. We can't afford to lose you in combat. You are the key to the endless coordination of so many critical projects. Are you on board with us?" General Arnold asked.

"It's hard to say no and it's a dream come true. You can count on me, sir," Coltrane said still dazed from the general's explanation. 'Looks like I'll need a little flexibility to get married. She's a socialite and a part of the British aristocracy. I have nightmares about the magnitude of the wedding itself." Both men laughed. Then Bart looked over at Curt and said, "Since you got me into this mess, would you be my best man?"

"I'd be honored," Lemay said, "But I'm scheduled to be in Washington and Wichita, Kansas in June. Perhaps General Arnold will do it for you. It sure can't hurt the social standing to have an American four-star General as your best man."

"Sure, I will. I'd be delighted to be a part of your wedding," Arnold responded.

"That's assuming he's still alive," Lemay said sarcastically. "He's been pushing too hard. He's already had one heart attack."

"I'm fine, Curt," the General retorted. "Now, I need something to eat besides the damned British fish and chips."

"Sir, I highly recommend this place. I lived here before assignment to Chelveston. The food is great!" Bart said, as he waved to Reggie for menus.

Chapter Thirty

"Bombs Away!" was the cry from the Black Bart bombardier squatting over the Norden bomb sight in the nose of the B-17. Bart breathed a sigh of relief as he switched off the auto pilot slaved to the bomb sight. He took control of the aircraft and looked for the lead squadron to make its outbound course taking them back to England. The lead started his turn to the right as expected. He then went on the intercom and asked the tail gunner to give him a report on how well the squadron had done hitting their assigned target which was the railway yard and the docks at Nordenham, Germany. He leaned back into his seat and looked at how well the squadron had maintained the combat box and devastated the target. He was happy as well as proud of the progress the squadron had made the past few months. He mentally fumbled for today's date, then remembered it was the first of March, his birthday. *This mission was a great birthday present*, he thought.

"Looks like Viceroy 22 was damaged more than reported as their bombs hit closer to 2nd Air Division's target than ours. Everyone else did great despite the flak," came the voice of the tail gunner who was getting ready for the returning German fighters.

"Think Viceroy 22 can make it home?" Coltrane asked.

"I doubt it, Colonel." "He's badly hit by flak and the fighters also did him a job on the way in. He's lost his both inboard engines and is sinking below the box," was the sadly spoken report.

"Keep an eye on him. I can see the Me-109s starting down on us," Coltrane said. "So far we've only lost three of the 55 that we started with. It would be great if that was all that we lost on this first mission over Germany. I hope our fighters get here soon."

"I've got two Me's on the port headed straight for us," said the left waist gunner.

"Roger, turrets take a crack at them," ordered Coltrane. The vibrations from the three sets of fifty caliber machine guns were suddenly offset by hits from the German fighters. "Give me a damage report!"

The engineer reported back quickly. "They got Segar in the leg, but he'll make it. Not much damage. It'll keep the metal shop boys up late tonight, but that's all."

The wounded gunner came up on the intercom. "Eat your heart out! I got my ticket back home. This will get me sent home for sure," he said as the engineer placed a tourniquet on Segar's wounded leg. Segar was smiling, knowing he was homeward bound. The injection of morphine given by the engineer added to his euphoric attitude.

"Bandits, 12 o'clock," came the cry of the top turret. "No, wait, those are our Little Friends," "Go get them nasty Huns!"

Coltrane relaxed and signaled for the co-pilot to take over the flying duties. The strike force of B-17 bombers was headed back to their home bases. "Not a bad first strike into Germany," Coltrane thought.

Silence came over the B-17 as the four engines were turned off. Coltrane remained in his seat and reflected on his many combat missions. For him, combat was to only be a memory. He was now headed for staff positions for the rest of the war. He finally got up and climbed out of the access door to a waiting Sargent Major Royston.

"Sir, hop in the jeep. You have a meeting at 1700 hours at General Eisenhower's new headquarters at Bushey Park in Teddington. You need to sign over command to Colonel Capeheart who is waiting in your office. I am to pass on to you that Major Beddows will meet you at Bushey Park."

"What the fuck is going on?" Coltrane said.

"They have moved your schedule up a few weeks, you are about to become a one star." "Sir," Royston said, then added, "Sir, if you can get me transferred to your staff, I would really appreciate it. I'd sure hate to go through this damned war with anyone else but you."

"Pack your bags. I'll fix it at headquarters. Find a good replacement so Capeheart isn't left in a lurch."

"Already done sir! I have your dress uniform ready as requested. Your bags are packed, and I'll have you there with time to spare," a happy Royston said. Bart wasn't quite as joyous as he was afraid of the unknown in this plan.

* * *

Bart was standing in the main salon of the huge house that was being renovated in prelude to it becoming the headquarters in the fall for General Dwight David Eisenhower for his as-yet unannounced selection as the Supreme Commander of Allied Forces Europe. Annabel came in with Sir Hugh Dalton, Curt Lemay and two other general officers. Only moments later came General Eisenhower and his entourage. Also, with him was Air Marshal Leigh-Mallory, the Commander of all Allied Air Forces Europe and Major General Ray Baker.

Coltrane came to attention and saluted as Ike came up to him. After returning his salute, Ike said "I have wanted to meet you for some time. I am impressed with your development of the Black Bart operation and other impressive achievements. President Roosevelt asked me to personally conduct this ceremony." He nodded to a Lieutenant Colonel who came to attention and commanded, "ATTENTION TO ORDERS!" At those words all present came to attention as the adjutant read the first of two general orders. He was awarded the Distinguished Flying Cross with two oak leaf clusters, two Silver Stars and a Bronze Star with V and with two oak leaf clusters for his numerous missions behind enemy lines.

Then the second order was read, “By order of the President of the United States with concurrence of the United States Senate, Samuel Barton Coltrane is promoted to Brigadier General, United States Army.”

“Congratulations, Bart,” Ike said after he pinned the stars on his uniform. “I was wondering if you could spend a couple of days with a study group that Lieutenant General Frederick Morgan and Major General Ray Barker are heading up. Your experience and observations would be of great assistance to them.”

“Yes sir, I’d be honored to help them if I can,” Coltrane responded.

“Excellent, General Baker’s office will contact you tomorrow to make all the arrangements,” Ike said as he again shook Coltrane’s hand and left at a fast pace.

The group became active again and congratulations given before departing as well.

Lemay came up to him. Before he could say anything, Coltrane quietly whispered into his ear. “What’s the deal with Morgan and Baker?”

Lemay got closer and replied, “OVERLORD! They are designing the invasion of Europe. They have a very long list of questions that you can best answer for them. Your experience will be incredibly important to them and their plan. After that, it’s off to 1st Air Bombardment Division Headquarters with you. We’ll miss you in the group, but you can do a lot of good in the ops job there. I’m still looking at September for your transfer to the other job that Hap mentioned. Things are starting to really heat up in the areas that your help is needed. I still can’t tell you any more than that,” he concluded. He saw Annabel and motioned her over. “I won’t be able to be at your wedding, but all the best,” he said. “If Hap doesn’t have a heart attack, he will be with you then. He is actually looking forward to it. Annabel, until we meet again, good luck.” Then Lemay gave Annabel a kiss on the cheek and departed. He turned while walking away and said, “Happy Birthday!”

A very happy Bart Coltrane asked, “Where are we going for supper?”

“Love, we are meeting Elizabeth and Philip at the Ritz. It’s time for you to get involved in the wedding plans,” she said as they left the salon.

Chapter Thirty-One

It was half past midnight when Annabel and Bart entered Annabel's London home. It was typical of the other expensive homes on Bruton Street in London's very stylish Mayfair area. It was the address of wealth and political prominence. The American Embassy was just a stone's throw from the four-floor residence. They went into the library and stood before the fireplace warming themselves after a cold walk from supper at the Claridge Hotel. Bart went over to an antique serving table and poured a fine Napoleon cognac into two brandy snifters. He handed one to Annabel as he put his arm around her. Neither said anything at first, and then she asked, "I assume that the 2nd of June is acceptable."

"It certainly is as long as you show up," he said as he hugged her with his arm. "What kind of wedding do you want, a big or small wedding? Here, or up country?" he asked.

"I am expected to have a highly visible wedding. However, given the hardships made by the war, we might be able to keep it a little smaller than usual. Perhaps we could use the Church at Temple Mount instead of Westminster Abby. We could keep it to 200 to 250 people, maybe," Annabel said in a matter-of-fact tone.

Bart was shocked, but came back with a question, "If we used Westminster, how many would attend?"

'Oh," she said lifting her head and eyes upward to the ceiling, 'at least 500 or so, and the archbishop will insist on conducting the ceremony. He is an old family friend and helps me with the charities. Besides my social obligation, you will be a Brigadier General and that requires a little pomp and circumstance as well.

Bart turned his head slightly and rolled his eyes. *So much for a quiet wedding at a small English countryside church*, he thought.

She thought for a moment then said, "Let me talk with a few people on what is required and appropriate. I definitely want Elizabeth and her boyfriend Philip Mountbatten involved. As he told you tonight Philip is in the Royal Navy doing has part for the war effort and a really nice guy. Elizabeth writes to him every day. She intends to marry him even if her parents continue to object. Her father calls him 'The Hun.' He is really a great chap and is totally in love with Elizabeth. Elizabeth always helps me with my charity work. That's unusual for most 17-year-old girls," she continued.

Bart was listening closely to Annabel's description of her friends and things that she wanted to have at the wedding. He looked at her and decided to show interest by asking her a question. "I was going to ask Elizabeth where she went to school but you girls never gave me or Philip a chance to get into the conversation."

"Philip is in the Navy but is assigned currently to a posting at Whitehall. So, he has a lot of flexibility to court Elizabeth." As far as her education, she was home-schooled because Elizabeth's father is King George the Sixth. This has got to be somewhat overpowering to you. Don't worry, dear, it will all work out. I'm sorry, but I am obligated to certain formalities. Please be patient and don't worry about a thing."

Bart smiled sheepishly, "I should have known that you would be involved with the Royal Families in England. We will do everything proper. I am ready for anything that you want to do. Just tell me where and when I am to be at any function. This could be fun," he said in a happy tone as his hand slid down her back to her butt. She jumped when he pinched it.

Bart went over to the overstuffed leather sofa and sat down. "We need to talk about what we're going to do after the war. I only have nine more years in the service to qualify for my retirement. Lemay and Arnold are looking to me to help them with the post war Army Air Corps reorganization."

"Can you get out after the war?" she asked.

"Sure but flying is all that I know. I have to make a living for us," he responded. "But I am open to new ideas."

"Is there any type of civilian flying or business that you would like to pursue?"

Bart became quiet and thoughtful. "Well, there is going to be a great demand for air freight after the war. Here, Europe, Africa and in the India-Southeast Asia area. But that takes a lot of money. But it's something that we could do together," he said.

She smiled. "Yes, it would be wonderful to do something like that together. How much money would it take to start and operate the air freight company?"

Coltrane thought for minute and took his finger and wrote some imaginary numbers on the top of the coffee table. He mentally came up with his answer, then turned to Annabel and said, "If we bought Douglas DC-4s and DC-3s that are not going to the military or will be excess at the end of the war, we could probably cover all of the good markets for about $3,500,000 US dollars. Do we finance this at a bank, or do you want to finance it yourself?"

Annabel smiled and got up and went over to Bart and extended her hand and said, "We have a deal, partner. We will pay cash."

Coltrane smiled "I am glad you think that way. This will work for us, and it will be fun. Now why don't we go upstairs and discuss the matter in bed."

* * *

"Mr. President, Admiral Leahy and Colonel Donovan are here as requested." Missy said in a cheerful voice.

"Send them in, please." responded the President. "Take seats gentlemen. I want to discuss this plan you two have submitted concerning clandestine operations in Europe. I like it! I want Donovan and his crew to become the primary intelligence source overseas for the United States. It will be done under great secrecy under the name of Office of the Coordinator of Information. Your mission as the Director of the Office of the Coordinator of Information will be to conduct multiple espionage activities and missions, including collecting intelligence by spying, performing acts of sabotage, waging propaganda war, organizing and coordinating Resistance groups in Europe, Burma, and the Pacific theater. Did I leave out anything? You will also provide military training for guerrilla movements in Europe and Asia. You will need to work with the British Special Operations Executive, General Chenault and Vinegar Joe Stillwell in Burma and any other organizations engaged in defeating the Axis Powers that you may elect to use. Your old buddy Sir Hugh Dalton is anxious for your arrival in London. Are there any questions Bill?"

"Mr. President I am delighted to undertake this operation for you. It would appear that I will need to recruit a Penguin for Antarctica, but we will work that out, sir. You do know that the spying and espionage business is usually ugly and not for the faint of heart. It's a nasty business and I undertake the job with your understanding of the mission and the repugnant aspects of it." Donovan said in a strong commanding voice.

The President responded equally as strong and said, "I wouldn't have it any other way! Now having taken care of that matter, Colonel, you may go and do your Cloak and Dagger thing while the good Admiral figures out a strategy for the Pacific Theater."

Donovan, now on active duty, came to attention with a big smile on his face and said, "By your leave, sir."

Chapter Thirty-Two

It was over two hours before the wedding was to start, but Bart was to arrive early to meet with the archbishop and other church officials concerning every aspect of the ceremony. Bart really didn't have a clue how popular his bride to be was in England. Her charity events for children and the war veterans were known and respected throughout the British Empire. Her wealth was enormous. She was one of the wealthiest members of the empire, but you would never know it to look at her dress, car, and casual day-to-day activities. *She may be a 'Blue Blood,'* Coltrane thought, *but she is as common in life as the people of England and West Texas*. Bart heard a call from a man in a poorly fitting suit who called out him, "General, I am Harbone from the Times of London. Could you spare a bit of time with me?" he asked.

Coltrane did not trust the press, but for some reason took a liking to this one. "Sure," he said smiling. "What can I do for you?"

"Looks like your wedding is going to be a bloody circus out there," he said jokingly.

"My sentiments exactly," Coltrane replied as the two laughed together.

"How does it feel to be marrying one of England's finest flowers?"

"For an old West Texas crop duster, it is a dream come true. She gives me a warmth inside that could melt the Arctic ice cap. She's intelligent and a real partner in every aspect," Coltrane said.

"That's quite a mouthful, mate," the reporter said, then asked "What is a crop duster?"

Bart smiled and replied, “Out in West Texas where I come from, we grow miles and miles of cotton. The cotton fields go as far as the eye can see. Cotton has a natural enemy called the Boll Weevil, which must be killed, or you lose the crop. Given the vast area, we use aircraft to spray the insecticide on the cotton. We fly about five feet off the ground and spray a couple of thousand acres per day. I used to be one of those crop dusters. Not a glamorous job, but I did get to fly, and it paid fairly well.”

“Fascinating,” he said as he wrote down his remarks. “Will you and the Duchess be relocating to West Texas after the war?”

“No, we’ll be staying here in London. I love it here and she intends to continue her charity work.”

“Since you are an American General, I assumed that you would be relocating.”

“Our home will be in London, and I will go where the Army sends me until I retire in a couple of years. There is still a war on,” Coltrane said.

The reporter looked at the General for a moment then continued, “It’s impressive to have Princess Elizabeth as the Maid of Honor. There are rumors that the King was not to be present to give away the bride because of his distaste of young Mountbatten.”

Coltrane saw the trap and responded, “If you would read your own paper, you would know his majesty has been down with the flu for over a week. As far as any problem between them, I haven’t been told of any. I do believe that the story is substantially blown out of proportion. I didn’t expect the King to come to the wedding of a commoner like me.”

The reporter almost broke out in laughter. “Commoner, you say. Brigadier General Black Bart Coltrane. You came to the aid of Great Britain in our darkest hour before the US entered the war and flew over 200 missions over enemy territory. I seriously doubt the British people would even consider you a simple commoner. A British hero maybe but never a commoner. Thanks for your time, General, and all the best in your marriage. Cheerio.”

Bart went inside the Abby and was struck speechless by the beauty and majesty of this incredible church. The ornate detail on the high columns and walls were almost overshadowed by the woodwork, flags and stained-glass windows. He felt very humbled by this magnificent structure. A young priest saw Coltrane and offered to take him to the archbishop, who was waiting for him. The head of the Church of England talked with Coltrane and discussed the procedure again with him. He took him to the cathedral and pointed out aspects of the formal wedding as it would happen and what he would do. Then they returned to the office. Bart was ushered to a nicely appointed waiting and dressing room to wait for the ceremony to start. Fifteen minutes before the service, General Arnold arrived. He was very tired and did not look well. Bart thanked him for doing him the honor but would not be offended if he wanted to go rest instead. The General said "no" with a decisive voice. "This is important," he said. "It's important for you individually, as well as the United States. This is an important event for both countries."

Bart had not considered the political impact of his wedding, but quickly understood the situation. He could hear the massive pipes of the organ begin to play. The young priest returned and escorted them to the rear of the cathedral and placed them into the proper place in the procession. "It was time," Bart thought. He was about to marry a woman that absolutely warmed his heart and made his knees like Jell-O. He truly loved Annabel and looked forward to the rest of his life with her.

The trumpeters sounded the opening notes to 'Trumpet Voluntary' followed by the magnificent pipe organ as the wedding procession started down the aisle. Bart suddenly had weak knees and butterflies in his stomach. *Combat wasn't as bad as this*, he thought.

Chapter Thirty-Three

President Roosevelt sat in his wheelchair in the Old Cabinet Room at The White House. A screening of 16-millimeter film footage of the construction of the related airfields in China was in progress, hundreds of coolies were seen carrying stones, carefully placing, and packing the stones into a hard surface. A giant roller was seen being pulled by at least a hundred coolies. The President asked, "... And which base is this, Hap?"

General Arnold answered "Pengshan. It's the last of the four B-29 bases under construction in the Chengdu area."

President Roosevelt looked over at General Arnold and General George Marshall ... he saw both watching the film intently. President Roosevelt took his cigarette holder out of his mouth and pointed to the screen. "All built by hand! Why ... it's almost like watching the building of the pyramids."

General Marshall responded, "Certainly as primitive!"

President Roosevelt asked, "When will they be in service, Hap?"

"Within the month, Mr. President," General Arnold replied.

The film concluded and the screen went to black. The room lights came up as General Arnold rose and walked to a wall map featuring East Asia and temporarily fastened to the wall for this conference. He pointed to the related areas on the map. "All four groups of the 58th Bomb Wing are on location in the Calcutta area now. They'll stockpile gasoline in the four forward staging areas around Chengdu; Pengshan, Kuinglai, Kwanghan, and Hsinching," He then continued "That uh .... that effort's been delayed due to overheating problems with the R3350 engines."

President Roosevelt asked, “Engine problems? But I thought we had all of that resolved, Hap!” General Arnold said “We’re working on it, Mr. President. General Wolfe’s assured me that he’ll start hauling gasoline and supplies over the hump well before the end of the month.”

President Roosevelt turned to Marshall and asked, “The language for the Twentieth Air Force Charter, has it all been worked out, General Marshall?”

General Marshall replied, “Yes, Mr. President,” The Twentieth Strategic Air Force has been created and officially placed under the authority of the Joint Chiefs themselves, with General Arnold as its Executive Agent. General Hansell will act as his Chief of Staff. Admiral King provided the final definitive language to the JSSC people that established Hap in that position.”

President Roosevelt seemed astonished, “Ernie agreed?” His grin broadening as he remarked, “Remarkable. Who would ever believe the Navy was supporting the creation of the Air Force! Your arguments for the independence of the Twentieth Air Force have apparently been more persuasive than any of us thought, Hap.”

General Arnold responded while grinning, “I’ve tried, Mr. President.”

President Roosevelt turned serious and said “We’re all aware of the economic, logistical and operational problems inherent in the Matterhorn plan, Hap. Of course, the objective justifies the risk … getting our B-29s within striking range of the Japanese home islands. But … I want every B-29 in the 58th Bombardment Wing over the Japanese home islands the day Nimitz begins the Marianas Invasion,” the President said, glancing at Marshall questioningly.

General Marshall nodded and replied, “June 15th.”

President Roosevelt said with a firm voice “That’s just two months off, Hap. I … I’m not going to tolerate any excuses on this one. You WILL have our boys flying over Japan on June 15th!”

General Marshall got up and crossed to stand at the map with General Arnold and pointing appropriately to the related areas on the map. General Marshall looked at Arnold, then turned to the President and said, "With the Japanese amassing supplies and equipment up here in the Bend of the Yellow River, it's pretty obvious they're getting ready to advance against Chennault's bases down here at Kweilin and Linchow. All of the Hump tonnage the Air Transport Command can manage will be required to reinforce Stillwell's Army … and Chennault's 14th Air Force. They've got to hold East China at any cost! Your boys are gonna be on their own. They'll simply have to supply their forward base there in the Chengdu area for their early missions against the home islands."

General Arnold was nodding his understanding and replied, "Of course, sir! General Stratemeyer has already apprised us of the Air Transport Command limitations, General Marshall."

President Roosevelt became serious again, "There are several strategic and political advantages to be gained in staging a successful B-29 mission against the home islands on the exact date of the Marianas invasion … not the least of which is making the Japanese aware they're *already* vulnerable to Twentieth Air Force strategic bombardment with our B-29s operating out of India, even without the Marianas! Otherwise, they might increase their commitment of forces to defend the Marianas Chain to prevent the building of our B-29 bases there."

"I understand all of that, Mr. President," said Arnold.

President Roosevelt continued, "And … another thing. Operation Overlord … the long-awaited invasion of Europe … it's currently scheduled for early June. A significant B-29 effort against Japan on that date would be highly desirable. The reasons are obvious."

General Arnold again responded, "I understand, Mr. President."

President Roosevelt looked at the two Generals and said, "I … uh … think it is best to keep the Twentieth Air Force … and the unique nature of its command system … that all ought to be kept under wraps until the June 15th Mission over Japan. Chiang Kai-shek's going to be damned unhappy that the B-29s weren't put under Chennault's command!"

General Marshall responded, "Of course, that would have been a disaster, Mr. President. Chennault and the Generalissimo are totally committed to a 'China First' policy."

President Roosevelt wearily said, "I know, General Marshall … I know. It's been the same with Douglas MacArthur and the Philippines. The rest of the global war can go to hell until the Philippines have been retaken!"

"I understand, Mr. President. I have General Coltrane standing by outside should you have any specific questions. He has been in India and knows firsthand what the situation and problems are," General Arnold said.

"Bring him in. I have always wanted to meet him. He has had one hell of a career. I value his opinion," the President ordered.

Coltrane marched in and rendered a salute.

Roosevelt nodded extended his hand to meet him. "A real pleasure to meet you after all these years, Black Bart," the President said in admiration. "Now take a seat and give me some short and hopefully sweet answers to tough questions."

"Yes, Sir," he said as he sat in a straight back chair almost in front of the President.

"I have to leave, Mr. President, if I may?" said General Marshall.

"Of course, George. We'll talk some more later."

As General Marshall left, the President asked Coltrane, "What do you see as the biggest problem that we have in our India operation?" Roosevelt asked.

"Short term will be logistics and fuel to forward bases," General Coltrane smiled as he responded.

The President said, "Now, tell me about the other supply and fuel problems."

Coltrane resumed his briefing, "The other supply problems will resolve themselves in time. The fuel over the Hump is something that can only be done by air for now. I think that greater aviation assets other than B-29s should be added to relieve the situation to some degree. As long as we must fly out of China, we will have this problem, Sir."

"The supply chain has no flexibility due to the standing operating procedures set forth by General Wolf's headquarters. It's not a matter of quantity, but its priority and distribution. Critical engine parts arrive at the port, but they are handled essentially the same as the general supplies. That adds a week to ten days to the delivery of the critical parts and equipment."

The President interjected," Do you have a solution, General?" Arnold looked shocked at the response.

"Yes, sir! I would suggest that the critical parts be identified at port and flown directly to the destination airfield by civilian contract air freight, Sir." Coltrane said and awaited questions.

Arnold thought quietly then said, "That would be an excellent way to resolve the problem."

The President then asked, "Are there any air freight companies over there that can do the job?"

"Yes, sir. There is one in the area that can do the job but it's about to go out of business. I can get the company a bridge loan out of London to turn it around so it can do the job, if the President directs, Sir," Bart said with confidence.

"Who would make that kind of financial risk in that part of the world during war time?" asked the President.

"One of my wife's companies will undertake the risk, Sir, but it constitutes some conflict of interest on my part, and you must approve such conflict, Sir. But the bottom line is that it can start direct shipments within thirty days if you and General Arnold approve the plan, warts, and all," Coltrane finished in a softer tone.

"Conflict of interest, hell, Bart, if we maintained a strict ruling on conflicts the war industry would stop by sundown. Yours is negligible at the most. You are hereby directed to proceed to India via London and establish the new air supply system immediately. Hap, you send General Wolf the appropriate directives implementing

Coltrane's plan," the President said in his formal authoritative voice before smiling.

"Maintenance and ongoing B-29 modifications will continue for a long time. That can't be quickly changed. Weather over Japan will always be a problem for high altitude bombing. Especially with the very high jet stream winds we have to deal with. Another significant problem will be the chain of command. Everyone wants control or at least priority over the B-29 strike capability. The sooner we can base out of the Mariana Islands, the better performance will become, Sir," Coltrane said with conviction.

The President looked at Arnold. "He sure doesn't pull any punches. Bart, I understand that you sneaked out on a reconnaissance flight over Japan. Is that true?"

"Yes, Sir, I needed to get a first-hand feel for what the situation is and what problems our bombers will encounter. I couldn't find out behind a desk," Bart said.

"So, your points were based upon actual experience?" Roosevelt asked.

"Yes, Sir," Coltrane replied.

"You will consider this a direct order from the Commander-in-Chief. Stay out of any and all aircraft going into combat! Your experience and judgment are far too valuable to lose in combat. Do you and General Arnold understand?" the President directed.

Both men nodded and said, "Yes, Sir" together.

"Do you think that bombardment will eventually do enough destruction to get the Japs to surrender?" Roosevelt asked.

"Sir, air power is the only way that we can reduce the Japanese capability to wage war, reduce their will to fight, and avoid an invasion of the homeland. The invasion will cost millions of US and Japanese lives. Air bombardment is the key, Sir," Coltrane said with an air of conviction.

"Very well put, Bart, and you are right," said the President. "Will the B-29 do the job for us?"

"Yes, sir. It's the best that we have today."

"Today," said the President. "I interpret that to mean that you are looking ahead to the replacement aircraft. I have been told that you have been spending some time with Ted Hall at Convair. So, what do you think of the B-36?"

"Sir, my read is that it is an essential weapon that can deter any Russian strategic or global conflicts. It has great range and altitude capability as well as the ability to drop up to 72,000 pounds of ordinance. However, it is slow, and it can't refuel in the air and the potential fuel and hydraulic leaks are even more of a limitation to its capability. Plus, there are a series of design problems that must be resolved before we start construction," Coltrane said looking at Arnold to see if he had said too much or was too frank. Arnold smiled and nodded.

"So, you see the Russians as a post-war problem for global security?"

"Yes, Sir," Bart replied.

"So, do I, General. Now what are your thoughts on Boeing's Model 424?" the President said as he watched Coltrane's reaction. "Yes, Bart, I know that you have been talking with George Schairer at Boeing. I have my own spies out there as well," he said smiling very broadly.

"Sir, that is the future and the answer," Coltrane said sheepishly. "What they are working on is an all-jet intercontinental bombing platform that will keep the global peace. If they can conquer some design problems, the aircraft will fly higher, faster, and longer than the B-36. It can be the next generation platform for 'Silver Plate' and that nuclear capability is what is needed to deter the Russians. If it is developed and placed into a special mission bomb wing whose mission is to be on constant alert for enemy attack, we can keep the peace, Sir."

"'We" means in a new separate Air Force, I presume?" he said.

"Yes, Sir," Coltrane replied.

"You make an exceptionally good case for service separation and strategic bombing capability. You seem to know an awful lot about everything we are doing today and tomorrow. For the sake of the country, stay out of combat. You know too much classified information to be killed – or worse – captured."

Then the President looked at Arnold and continued. "Hap, I see why you brought him to this meeting. He's a good and convincing proponent for air power. He's also insightful into our problems in the Pacific. Keep up the good work, Bart."

The President looked tired and weak. He motioned to the aide to come over to wheel him out of the room. Then he turned to Arnold and Coltrane. "Gentlemen, you'll have to excuse me, I am not up to snuff right now. Good day."

The two Generals left the room. As they exited the oval office, Arnold held Bart by the arm. "That was excellent! You did good on every subject. You've made my job to sell air power a lot easier." He paused, and then continued, "So you don't think much of the B-36?"

"It's going to only be a stop gap answer to our long-range objective, sir. But it will give us the platform we need to get to the all-jet Boeing 424. There is our future," Coltrane said.

"You have obviously done a lot of study into the two aircraft. More than I have seen before. Now let's find ways to end the war in the Pacific before the body count gets too high," Arnold said as he walked away.

Chapter Thirty-Four

At the Berghof, Obersalzberg, Germany on July 23, 1944, Herman Goering's voice was heard as he talked with Albert Speer. "You must not go through with this madness, Speer."

In the group were War Production Minister Speer, Reichmarschall Goering, Generalfeldmarshall Keitel and General Lieutenant Adolf Galland. Four German industrialists stood nearby in a separate grouping. Several high-ranking German officers came and went around the entrance as Goering and the others talked. Goering was angrily admonishing Speer, "The Fuhrer … his burden is already great enough without this!"

Speer quietly and resolutely replied, "It is time he knows the unvarnished truth, Herr Goering. The Luftwaffe is finished … and … so are we. It is simply a matter of time. The end is inevitable! Already Berlin is a mass of rubble. And now to the oil refineries."

Goering looked at Speer, "That's treason, Minister Speer!"

Speer nodded, and unperturbed said "It is fact, Herr Reichmarschall."

A frustrated Goering was eyeing General Adolf Galland ominously, "This is your doing, Galland. You are the one who told me enemy long-range fighters were shot down over Aachen, hundreds of miles further than they can penetrate!"

General Galland responded, "But sir … I asked you to go see for yourself."

Goering said "Why go? I knew they weren't there! You've betrayed me, Galland. The Commanding General of the Luftwaffe fighter forces! And you've betrayed ME!"

General Galland stated "I have betrayed no one, Herr Reichmarschall … least of all you! I have cut training flights to one hour per week to conserve on precious petroleum. I have held our fighters down except where our most vital war production was under attack. Held them down to keep those from being destroyed by the 8th Air Forces long range B-47s, P-51s and the damnable P-38 forked tail lighting! But I cannot perform the impossible, Herr Reichmarschall! We have suffered grievous losses. We are unable to prevent the daylight bombing of our industries any longer."

A German general and his aide emerged from the Salon, walking by the Speer group to exit the Berghof. The aide announced, "Gentlemen … the Fuhrer will see you now." Goering said to Speer in one last desperate attempt, "You must not do this!"

The group and the German businessmen entered the salon, Speer entering last. The German businessmen entered the Salon, remaining near the door as Speer, Goering, Keitel, and Galland greeted the Fuhrer.

Adolph Hitler rose from the small, ornate table where he had been working to shake hands with Speer who then nodded to the businessmen. The group came over into Hitler's presence as Speer refreshed the Fuhrer's memory as to their identity.

Speer said "Mein Fuhrer … Herr Krauch, the Director of our Chemical Industry."

Hitler, in a pleasant and informal voice, said "Herr Krauch …"

Speer said, "Herr Pleiger, Reich Commissioner for coal and our synthetic fuel plants"

Hitler nodded and uttered a polite "Herr Pleiger …"

Speer then introduced "Herr Buetefisch, the head of the Leuna Works."

Hitler looked cautiously at the man. "Herr Buetefisch, I understand the Leuna Works were heavily damaged in the May twelve bombing."

Buetefisch responded, "Yes, Mein Fuhrer … Our plant is out of operation. It will take some time to repair it."

Hitler softly spoke, "That is too bad. Our tanks benefit greatly from your plant's synthetic fuel output!" Buetefisch said apologetically, "I'm sorry, Mein Fuhrer."

Lastly, Speer introduced, "Herr Fischer, Mein Fuhrer, the Chairman of the Board of I. G. Farben."

Hitler, in an upbeat voice said, "Ah, yes, it is good to see you again Herr Fischer."

Hitler paced a few steps, his hands behind his back, and then turned to the group.

"Gentlemen … I have asked you here along with Reichmarschall Goering, Generalfeldmarshall Keitel, and General Galland, hoping we might reach some understanding as to where we really stand in terms of synthetic Petroleum production."

Goering quickly added, "Mein Fuhrer … we have nearly eighteen months of reserves on hand!"

Hitler momentarily ignored the Reichmarschall, "Herr Speer …?"

Speer looked at Hitler and responded, in a confident tone, "Our immediate sources of supply have been interrupted – production temporarily cut by at least thirty percent, Mein Fuhrer. Two or three more raids of the May 12th magnitude against our fuel refineries could drastically restrict our source of supply. Such damage would require months to repair."

"Herr Fischer, do you agree with Minister Speer?" Hitler asked. "Most certainly, Mein Fuhrer," Fischer replied. "The I.G. Farben synthetic fuel facilities were heavily damaged May 12th. Production has been interrupted severely. It is a most difficult situation, Mein Fuhrer!"

Hitler reassuringly said to Fischer, "You'll manage somehow."

Herr Pleiger then reported, "Our coal pressurization facility has been shut down for extensive repairs, Mein Fuhrer! Without our process, there is no synthetic fuel production!"

Generalfeldmarshall Keitel anxiously placated Hitler, "We've been through worse crises. We were foolish in building our synthetic production plants so closely together in the Ruhr. Now, with South

Africa and the Ploesti fields in Romania cut off, our only source of petroleum supply is our synthetic plants here in our own Ruhr."

Hitler paused, then posed the hypothetical question, "If the 8th Air Force Bombers were diverted to other objectives ... the interdiction of an invasion site for instance. Would you have enough time to relocate some elements of our fuel production?"

"Perhaps," Speer said. "It would depend on how long that time might be."

Hitler tossed his hair to the side as he said, "Two or three months?"

Speer lowered his head slightly and replied, "I do not think so, Mein Fuhrer."

Reichmarschall Goering said in a false air of confidence, "Perhaps it *could* be done!"

Keitel said in an attempt to satisfy the Fuhrer, "We shall be able to bridge the gap with our reserves. How many difficult situations have we already survived, Mein Fuhrer? We shall survive this one, too."

Hitler, was unimpressed with Goering's and Keitel's observations, "In my view, the fuel, Buna rubber, and nitrogen plants represent a particularly sensitive point for the conduct of the war, since a great magnitude of vital materials for armaments are being manufactured in such a small number of plants. Our only hope lies in the chance that the Allied Air Force command is as scatterbrained as our own ... and their bombers will be diverted to other targets before they destroy our plants altogether. Otherwise ... we ... we may be faced with a particularly grim set of options." Hitler crossed back to his desk, oblivious to the presence of the others who now begin to exit quietly before Hitler's temper flared.

Chapter Thirty-Five

Sargent Major Royston drove the jeep slowly over the rain rutted dirt road leading to a small airstrip near the Village of Barakpur some 16 miles north of the Calcutta dock area. After a particularly hard bump, Royston muttered something under his breath.

Brigadier General Coltrane was riding in the passenger seat and Coltrane's aide-de-camp in the rear seat. The bumps kept the aide airborne more than seated. Coltrane looked over to Yank Royston and said, "I take it that you are not impressed with the Indian road infrastructure."

"Sir, we are a small jeep that can deal with these monster ruts and bumps, but a loaded deuce and a half truck will break an axle for sure," Royston said as he held onto the steering wheel as his ass left the seat.

"I am sure we can get a road crew and rock brought in if we need to work out of here," Coltrane said as he grabbed the seat to keep from being launched out of the vehicle.

Suddenly, the jeep came out of the heavy forest and into the wide-open area of the Barakpur Airfield. Bart saw several small buildings scattered on either side of the rock and gravel runway. There was one larger building that resembled a hangar. He pointed to it and Royston turned towards it. The road was partially rock and somewhat smoother. They pulled to the near side of the hangar opening. Inside there was an old German Junkers JU-52/3m with its three engine cowlings off being serviced behind what was an American Douglas DC-2 which was a vintage transport from the mid 1930's. It had been replaced in the US Army Aviation fleet with the larger and more powerful C-47, the military version of the DC-3. He got out of the jeep and looked around and saw another DC-2 and JU-52 parked close by. There was an assortment of other foreign aircraft parked around the airfield. From what Bart could see, most were one step from being abandoned. Some were missing propellers or engines, even wings. Quite a state of disrepair. He could see the effects of the war on private enterprise.

The aide stopped a passing mechanic and asked where the office was. The Indian mechanic looked at the US Lieutenant with some skepticism but pointed to a door on the far side of the hanger. The group walked over to the office carefully noting as much as possible about the facilities and runway.

Bart knocked twice on the door jamb part of the open door to the office and called out, "Mr. Majumder?"

"Yes?" called out a voice from a room off the office. Then a man in a World War I flight suit came out of the room and into the light. He was a remarkably fit man for his apparent age. His almost snow-white hair and leathery face made him look older than he probably was.

"I am Majumder," he said with authority. "You must be the yank General the government office called me about," the man said in a perfect British accented English.

Bart extended his hand, "I'm Brigadier General Bart Coltrane, Mr. Majumder. I'd like to talk to you for a few minutes if you can spare the time." Majumder looked cautiously at Coltrane then asked, "When I was last in London back in 1940, there was a yank pilot flying for the RAF behind the lines operations. As I recall, they called the bloody bloke Black Bart. Any connection, General?" Coltrane was somewhat taken back and embarrassed by the obvious question. "Sir, this is Sargent Major Yank Royston. He and I flew those missions. I guess that you could say that I am Black Bart."

The heretofore dignified Indian pilot became quite animated, "Black Bart! He cried out as he grabbed Coltrane by the shoulders and gave him a bear hug. Then he turned to Royston and shook his hand so hard that Royston thought the hand would be crushed.

Not the grip of an old man, thought Royston.

"Please come with me, gentlemen," said the Indian pilot. He took them into a back office behind his more austere and disheveled office he normally worked out of. The back room was paneled and decorated in the traditional British style. There was a fine cherry wood conference table and chairs in the center of the room. On the far wall was a full bar complete with mirrors and three dozen bottles of liquor. It could have been any bar near Piccadilly Square. The bar stools were padded armchairs with heavy wood legs. They were unique in that each bar stool had its own set of aircraft safety belts as ornaments.

"What can I get for you chaps?" asked Majumder. "Surely it isn't too early for you blokes?" Royston and the aide got quiet and looked away for a moment. Bart looked at his watch and said, "Well it's after 1700 hours in Washington, and I am here on their business. So, scotch for me," Then Coltrane looked at the other two, "What's your pleasure?"

A very happy Majumder filled the order and walked to the table with the drinks on a silver serving tray. He motioned for everyone to take a seat. He lifted his glass in toast and said, "To the King!" The others raised their glasses and toasted as well.

Royston here was born in England," Coltrane said. He came over to the states as a kid and later joined the US forces. I can't help but ask your background. You're Indian, but you have a hard-British accent and have this British style bar in deepest India. Do you mind explaining to a curious yank?"

"Bloody well, right, old chap," said Majumder. "I was born near Bangalore to parents who had a great deal of wealth and were politically popular here and in London. I went to school near London and later was selected to attend Sandhurst. I flew Sop's in the Great War over France. I got shot down but was rescued before the bloody Bosch could get me. I loved England and its culture, but my dying dad told me my fame and fortune were in India. He bloody well was right, you know. I couldn't live in London, so I brought London to

India. This is part of an actual bar that was destroyed by a Zeppelin bomb. I packed it up and sent it here. It's my part of Heaven on Earth. I got back and started the air freight business and was doing well until the bloody Japs went into China. They bloody well made a cock up of my routes into China. That was most of my business. So, I am closing, and moving back to London. I still have my inheritance and property near Bangalore and in Sussex as well. I don't need the grief or the financial loss over time. But that's me. What can I do for you?" Majumder asked as he poured another round.

"Did I hear you say that you were flying those old planes into China?" asked Coltrane.

"Certainly, old chap. I went into the western area every week with one to three flights," he said in a matter-of-fact tone.

"Didn't the Japs attack you?" Bart asked.

"No, they didn't want any political problems with shooting down unarmed Indian cargo planes carrying civilian cargo and not war supplies. Besides, they fly much higher than we do. We can't fly very high with a full load of cargo in these old crates. We fly from here or wherever the cargo is picked up at and fly to Doom-Dooma in the Far East near the mountains. We refuel there and snake through the mountains into China. We can go as far as Chengdu, Chaklai, or Kunming. If we run short on fuel, we stop at this out of the way point near Zhongdian, run by a bunch of Chinese traders, or some say, bandits. They will sell fuel to anyone, even the Japs if they have cash. Nowadays, I think that they would just kill the Japs and take their plane and money. They have hurt their trade a lot."

"You spoke about a financial loss if you continued. Is it solely because of the loss of business or are there other reasons?" asked Coltrane.

The Indian thought for a moment, then sipped his drink before answering. "It's the loss of the China market to be sure, but you add to that the high maintenance and fuel costs of those four birds out there that have a financial foot to my groin. I have one DC-2 and one Junker that will fly. The other two are parts birds for the flying aircraft. I need money for repair parts, fuel, to pay crews, and the like. With fewer contracts, the funds just are not there to justify staying in business. I would love to have a contract or two with your government hauling cargo, but you have your own support aircraft. So bottom line, as you Yanks put it, we close and sell off the assets." The Indian pilot said as he quickly finished off the scotch in his glass. "Besides, I want to retire."

Bart said with a soft tone, "I am sorry." He waited a moment then asked, "How much money would it take to turn this around and get all four birds flying? How much do you want to sell the whole operation?"

The Indian knew a loaded question when he heard it. He thought for a moment then replied. "General, those aircraft may be old and junk, but they are worth something. So is the business itself. I wouldn't take less than 280,000 pounds sterling. As far as putting it all back in the air, I'd say 40,000 pounds sterling for parts and another 40 to 50,000 for operating funds."

Coltrane leaned back in his chair and took a big gulp of scotch and motioned with his finger for more. Majumder was more than glad to accommodate the request.

"What about the pilots, crews and other personnel; will they stay on for a new owner," Coltrane asked?

Majumder could see where Coltrane was going. He would make a great deal. It was a deal of a lifetime for him with the US government funding it. "Of course, they would stay. Good jobs are hard to find these days with the bloody war going on."

Coltrane looked at him for a moment then turned to Royston and his aide, "Would you give us a couple of minutes alone? Royston, go look at the maintenance operation."

"Yes, sir," they said in unison and departed.

Bart looked at the crafty Indian and smiled, "I could see dollar marks in your eyes a few moments ago. You know what I am wanting in general," he said pausing. "Let's get down to making a deal. The

US government is NOT involved. It has sanctioned a private British concern to enter into an agreement with you, however."

Majumder was suddenly confused. Had he misread the American?

"Here is the proposition," Coltrane said in a measured business tone. "You will be given a non-recourse loan from a British company for one hundred thousand pounds for repairs and operational cost. The lender will pay you 300,000 pounds for an option to buy your entire company and its operations two days after the Japanese surrender for ten pounds sterling. You agree to continue management of the company and will retain all profits during the period prior to the British company exercising its option to buy for the ten pounds. The US Army Air Force will enter a commercial air freight contract with you to carry priority cargo to its bases in India and China. You will only charge the Army the standard rate that you are currently charging local clients. You will not disclose to anyone what the cargo is and where it goes. That one item will get your contract canceled on the spot. When the aircraft takes off with our cargo, there will be two Army Air Force Guards on board who know the general route to China. If your pilots, try to divert for any reason the guards will shoot and kill the pilot. I assume the co-pilot will remember the correct course. The Army will make Avgas available to you at commercial rates should you not be able to get it from the civilian source. Needless to say, you will lose some money buying from the Army, so keep your fuel supplier happy. When you are called for a shipment, you will immediately do whatever it takes to get that cargo to its destination. Army cargo has absolute priority. That's the deal. Are you interested?" Coltrane said as he picked up his glass and finished the scotch.

The Indian air freight company owner sat there in silence remembering all of the terms and conditions. *Where is the trap or the hook?* he thought. "That's a very nice offer, General. I can't find fault with it."

"You won't," Coltrane said. "It is designed to give you what you want and what the buyers want, plus encourage you to stay on and run it until after the war. All you have to do is deliver the cargo and keep the operation and cargo a secret. Do you accept the offer?"

The Indian pilot looked at Coltrane and said, "Care for another scotch … partner?"

"Very good, but I am not a partner only a facilitator," Coltrane replied smiling. "Let me have your bank information and I will have the 100,000 pounds wired to your account tomorrow. The option agreement will be ready in two or three days, then you will get the 300,000 pounds option money. And there is one other condition," Bart said.

Majumder stiffened in anticipation of a killer deal term. "You will agree to fix that damned road coming in here," Bart said almost laughing.

"I'll personally get my shovel and get to work," Majumder said as he poured yet another scotch for the two of them.

Chapter Thirty-Six

It was a beautiful July day in Washington. There was an informal gathering of senior War Department personnel in the office of General Arnold. He was honoring General Lemay for his successes in Europe by pinning a Distinguished Flying Cross on an olive drab tunic already festooned with several rows of colorful service ribbons. General Hansell and other USAAF officers are smiling and shaking Lemay's hand with pride and admiration.

General Arnold stepped back in next to Lemay and said "Congratulations, Curt." The others excused themselves and left Arnold and Lemay alone.

"Thank you," said Lemay. General Arnold walked towards his clerk then turned to face Lemay, his hands behind his back. "Curt, I'm gonna give it to you short and sweet. Our B-29 program has been a debacle so far. It's dangerously close to collapse. And it isn't just the problems with the airplanes themselves, either. Chang Kai-shek, Chennault, Stillwell, even Mountbatten, they're all escalating the problems we're having. Add to that is the air logistics problem. Thank God, Bart Coltrane was directed by the President to get there and organize an air logistics operation to support the critical parts issue. It could be the bridge from our Standard Support System to the individual units." Arnold paced, his hands still behind his back, and then said "That should help some. But we need more."

General Arnold looked at Lemay and in a serious tone announced, "I've relieved Kenneth Wolfe of the command out there and promoted him, in fact, and brought him back to Material Command here in the States. That's really his field anyway. We need a professional bombardment man running the Twentieth Strategic Air Force … a man with combat experience. "It's time to move you into that job as we have planned," Arnold was now leaning back against his desk, "Curt, if we can unleash the full B-29 potential against the Japanese home islands in time, we may be able to avoid an invasion. Even the most conservative estimate places Allied losses at least a half million lives … troops … not counting Japanese civilian losses, which would be even greater. There are other considerations, too," Arnold said, looking at Lemay with the serious gravity of the situation. "The future of the United States Air Force … it's growth and peacekeeping role in the troubled aftermath of the war … all of that, Curt, will be affected by the success … or failure … of the B-29. You'll be on your own … answering to this office ONLY. Even your target list and priorities will be prepared and authorized by the Joint Chiefs and issued through this office."

Lemay interrupted, "What about missions, General? I'll obviously need to fly quite a few of them."

General Arnold smiled and continued, "I'd anticipated your desires along those lines, Curt," he said, holding up one finger. "We … we're authorizing one … just ONE!"

Lemay argued, "A field commander ought to lead missions – especially those that involve the initiation of previous untried procedures."

General Arnold, in a raised voice said, "ONE, Curt. That's final! Now unless there is something else, I have Bart Coltrane waiting outside. He's doing a great job, even better than we hoped. I have to tell him about Zak Middleton. He got shot down and was badly injured.

General Arnold hit the button on his intercom system, "Send in General Coltrane," he said with authority. Seconds passed, then the door to General Arnold's office opened and Brigadier General Bart Coltrane marched into the office and formally reported to General Arnold. Arnold returns his salute and extends his hand. "Welcome back to the States, Bart. Take a seat, Curt has a logistics problem that he needs your help with. Basically, he needs some short haul air delivery system for fuel, parts and personnel in India and China. You two can go over the details later. But first I wanted to let you know about Zak Middleton," he said as he saw the sudden expression on Bart's face.

"Zak was on a Black Bart mission over eastern France when two Me-109s caught him in a crossfire. He was able to fight them off with one kill and one probable before he went down. An American unit cut him out of his plane. The others were killed. He was badly wounded but is alive and doing well in England. He will probably be out for the rest of the war. They're going to retire him with full pay. He should recover enough to fly, but not for the military. He turned down a desk job, so SOE decided to pin a medal on his ass and put him out to pasture. You may want to stop by and see him on your way to India and China.

"Wow," said Bart. "Retirement. That's not going to set well with him. He's all action and sitting on the sideline will kill him."

"Well, perhaps he can land a civilian pilot job in a few months," Arnold said in a positive tone then changing the subject. "Bart, on your next trip to China would you look into why we are not getting our downed pilots and crews back from the Vietnam area. We know they get on the ground safely but that's all. The local Minh agreed to get them to China in exchange for some military support," stated with a wrinkled sorrowful face. "Now you two go figure out how to cure Lemay's problem." Both generals got up and saluted General Arnold and left the room.

* * *

Lemay looked at Bart and asked, "Hungry? We can grab a bite downstairs in the Flag Officer's Mess before we head out."

"Sure, I've never eaten there," Bart responded. As they entered, the facility was busy and crowded.

They were looking for a couple of open chairs when a voice said, "General, these two seats are not taken."

Lemay turned to see where the voice came from. It was an older man in civilian clothes wearing round glasses. They immediately sat down. Lemay was quick to thank the gentleman. "We appreciate your generosity, sir. I don't think we have had the pleasure. I'm Curtis Lemay and this is Bart Coltrane," he said in a congenial tone as he extended his hand.

"Good to meet you, fellas. I'm Harry Truman," he said in a Midwest country accent.

"Senator Truman?" asked Bart.

"That's what they tell me, but I've asked for a recount since I got here," Truman said in a funny tone. "You two are not unfamiliar to me. Lemay, you're bombing the Germans back to the Stone Age and young Coltrane was flying behind the lines before the war started," Truman said as he looked at each man as he spoke.

"Actually, Senator, I'm operating B-29s out of India and China now," Lemay corrected.

"Well, there you have it. It just proves what is going on in this damned war that we in the Congress don't always hear about," Truman said in frustration. "How about you two bring me up to speed on the situation while we eat?"

Lemay saw a chance to get another true believer in strategic bombing and he took it. Between bites, he and Coltrane gave the Senator a thumbnail history of bombardment in Germany and Japan.

After almost an hour, Truman looked at his watch. "Gentlemen, this has been wonderful. I never knew one-tenth of what you told me. I can see your point about the need for a separate aviation branch. It would be difficult to make such a drastic reorganization during the war, but afterwards would be a good time. When we scale down to a peacetime posture would be an excellent time. I'll chat with my cohorts in the Senate about it. I do ask a favor of you two. Each time you come through Washington, stop by my office, and keep me updated. It helps to know all the facts when you're voting on important issues," said the Senator as he stood up and extended his hand. "Best of luck to both of you! I appreciate the job that you are doing," then he walked out of the room at a brisk stride.

Chapter Thirty-Seven

It was late in the afternoon and as usual, it was hot as Coltrane, his aide-de-camp Lieutenant Ford and Sargent Major Royston entered the old hospital. The Sergeant behind the desk quickly stood to attention as the American General approached.

"Afternoon, Sergeant. Could you direct me to Lieutenant Colonel Zak Middleton's room?" Coltrane asked.

"This way, sir," he responded and marched to the far-left wing where Zak was seated in a wheelchair looking out the window seeing nothing, but in a full stare out into the trees. The Sergeant knocked on the open door and reported, "Sir, you have visitors!"

"Very well, who are they?" responded a very dejected man.

In a loud booming voice, Bart said, "The son of a bitch that is going to kick your ass out of that wheelchair!"

At the first sound of Bart's voice Middleton's attitude and facial expression made a sudden, positive change. "Bart!" he called out as he spun the wheelchair around to see Coltrane and Yank Royston. He tried to get up, but just quite couldn't muster the muscle control to do it.

"Sit down, you bum!" Bart cried out. "Save your energy for the nurses."

Zak lowered his head slightly and said in a low tone, "Nurses here look like gorillas and were trained by the Gestapo. Be careful when you leave. They're known to roll soldiers for beer money. Yank, so good of you to come, too," he said reaching out to shake his hand. "Your mere presence has shortened my recovery time."

"Good to see you, sir. You look a lot better than I expected for someone who went through what you did," Yank said.

"So good of you to say so, old boy. I appreciate that. Sometimes I think that I'm all washed up and life is nothing more than playing checkers in Hyde Park. But the fact is, I'll have a full recovery. It'll just take some time. The sawbones told me that I could fly again, in time. Now that was good news. The bad news is they're promoting me to full Colonel and putting me on the retirement list. I haven't a clue what I will do with myself after I get well. Ghastly thought being retired," Zak said in mock sadness.

"I need to talk to you for a moment in private. Before they go, could you tell us how the buggers got you?" Bart asked.

"Actually, it's quite simple. I had my head up my ass. We had just made the drop to the French Resistance, and I started a turn back towards home. I let myself get too high and the bloody ack-ack hit me with a couple of rounds in the aft section. I pushed the nose down to get in the trees when a line of tracers came from the right. I knew it had to be a Me-109. I chopped power and turned directly into him and hit him with a long burst of .50 cal as he flew by. That was all of Mr. Jerry. Then I started taking hits from the high left. Another Me-109! I had problems with my right engine, but it held for a while. I saw the second Jerry coming down from my 10 o'clock high position maybe a mile away. I could see he was extremely fast and heading down to get me on the inbound pass. So, I pulled one of your tricks and chopped power again and turned into him in a climb. As I passed upward, I hit him with a full stream of fire. I obviously hit the bloody bastard, but he got away smoking. I started looking around to see what condition I was in and the aircraft status. Everyone was dead. I had been hit twice, but for some reason, I didn't feel any pain until then. The right engine crapped out and I could feel the plane shake and break up. So, I made a crash landing in the cow pasture in front of me. I hit a drainage ditch which took everything behind the cockpit off. The nose section with me in it bounced twice before hitting a hedge row head on. The next thing that I knew, I was here.

I had been out for three days. The quacks here have done a marvelous job fixing me up. Full recovery is their prognosis," Zak finished with a flare in his voice.

"Unbelievable!" Yank said. "It's beyond a miracle that you made it at all."

"Yes, yes, Royston my good man, but remember, the one confirmed and one probable as well," Zak said and everyone broke out laughing.

"Okay guys, please give me a minute or two with this *old war hero*," Bart said with emphasis.

"See you, Colonel," Royston said as he and the aide de camp left.

"Now," Bart said with clear intent. "What I am about to tell you is only known by me, Annabel and our attorneys and accountants, so keep a tight lid on this or some very nice people will get their feelings hurt and my ass in big time trouble. Can I have your word as to secrecy?"

"You know that you do, Bart," Zak said, emotion welling up in him.

"I'm leaving the service at the end of the war. I'm not following Hap and Lemay in their post war effort to get a separate branch for aviation. What they need from me will be done before I leave. I won't leave them hanging out to dry on this. Enough said. Annabel and I are going to start an air freight service out of Heathrow before Christmas 1945. I plan a second hub in Genoa shortly after that. It's in Allied hands and secure now. Third hub will be in Hong Kong with a fourth in Manila. We have contracts for six C-54 and twenty-five C-47s. Half are ready or will be ready for pickup on 1 November. The war production board has agreed to the civilian release since the U.S. and British governments will obviously be our main clients in a post-war economy. The war here as you could see will be over in less than a year maybe sooner," Coltrane paused slightly to see the reaction on Zak's face then continued. "We can expand as fast as the market allows us. Annabel is financing, so we have plenty of available funds. Annabel and I want you to join us when you get out of here."

"Bart, thanks, but I don't need your pity," Zak said sourly.

Bart suddenly moved his face to within eight inches of Zak's and said in a very harsh but quiet voice, "and I don't need a Chief Pilot and General Manager with a bad fucking attitude! The offer is real, and I don't want to hear a negative reply. The doctors told me that you would be on your feet and out of here in a month. You will need another month to fully recover. At that point, you are no longer limited including flying. I want you to get with Annabel when you are up to it and start putting the pieces together for me. I will meet with Sharp and Royston tonight and tell them of my plans. They will be offered jobs as well. Sharp will be your operations manager. Royston will be in charge of maintenance. Accounting and legal is covered by Annabel's people. I am stealing a cargo sales hot shot named Tommy Adkins and the best cargo manager in the business from BOAC. With the defeat of Germany within distance sight, I can get early releases from Washington on any combat pilot, mechanic or otherwise that have been over here in combat for over six months. I think we can even get a few Brits to join the colonist venture. Do you get the picture?"

Zak was awestruck. He could only nod.

"I'm leaving for India and China tomorrow to find a solution for Lemay involving his aviation support. I'll be gone two, maybe three months. When I get back, I expect you and Annabel to have everything ready to go. On 1 December 1945 I want to have a meeting with everyone that you have. I expect to be flying cargo here in the UK by Christmas and out of Manila by the first of March 1946 or sooner. Now, can poor pitiful you get the job done, or do I have to find someone else?" Coltrane finished in a slightly softer tone than he started.

Zak looked at Bart for a moment then said, "Go eat fish heads and rice. We'll be ready for you when you get back."

Chapter Thirty-Eight

Bart Coltrane was starting to sweat in the hot and humid atmosphere at Barakpur, India Airfield. He opened the side cockpit window of the C-47 as he shut down the two engines. After shutting off the master power switch, he got up and went to the rear cargo door. The crew chief had already opened the big door and put the metal steps in place. As he climbed down, he heard the voice of Colin Majumder say, "My God, a General doesn't have his own pilot? Did you get in trouble and have your pilot taken away from you?"

Coltrane started laughing even before he finished getting down. "Yeah, I must have pissed Vinegar Joe off really bad." He shook the Indian pilot's hand warmly. "Great to see you again, Colin. You've been doing a great job, far beyond my expectations."

"Thanks, General. The money is a great incentive." Majumder then pointed his thumb at the Indian pilot standing next to him, "This is Shashi, one of the best pilots that I have ever flown with."

Bart looked the man in the eyes as he shook his hand. "My thanks for keeping this operation going in spite of Colin."

The humor caught Shashi off guard, and he fumbled his verbal reply, then he got his wits back and said, "The honor is all mine. Your combat reputation has proceeds you, sir. I'm honored to fly with your operation here at Acacia."

Bart looked back at Colin and asked, "Where are you off to today?"

Shashi and I are going to make a supply run to Kunming with these two new C-47s you got us. What are you doing over here? I thought you were in Washington."

"Actually, General Lemay asked me to look into the downed pilot situation in Indochina. We're not getting our downed aircrews out of Vietnam.

We see them go down with good chutes, but they just don't get out. Either the Japs are getting them, or the Viet Minh are not following through with the agreement they made with us a couple years back in exchange for arms."

Majumder looked at Shashi then back to Coltrane. "I could give you my opinion, but I'm too far removed to be of any significant value to you." He looked up into a clear sky then into Coltrane's eyes. "If I know you, you'll want the hard, cold facts. Can you spare three or four days to get the truth?"

Bart quickly replied, "A week if it's necessary to get an accurate understanding of the situation."

Very bloody well then … you fly the other C-47 instead of Shashi to Kunming. From there we'll go and see some friends of mine that are really doing some damage to the Japs in Vietnam," said Colin with conviction. "You can find out for yourself the answers. We'll fly the supplies to Kunming, then we'll fly some supplies to a place just north of Vietnam and you can talk to my friends. They're the best people to tell you the facts."

Coltrane looked puzzled, "Who are you taking me to meet?"

"My friend is Nguyen Sinh Cung. You'll also meet a couple of his friends, Giap and Dong. They'll give you the answers that you seek," replied Majumder.

"What kind of supplies are we delivering to them?" Coltrane asked.

"Mainly rice with some medical supplies and ammunition," he said softly. "They send me whatever money they have available, and I get them what supplies I can buy for them. I personally pay for the flight time and gas. I respect the job that they're doing against the Japs with almost no money and bloody little outside support. That's all that I'm going to tell you. The rest will become very apparent once you get there."

Coltrane saw a deep respect and admiration in the words Majumder spoke. "Good! Now when do we leave for Kunming?"

"Now! We fly there and offload the stuff for the Army and load up the Viet Minh supplies before sunset. We lift off from Kunming at 0330 hours. That puts us there at dawn before the Jap air patrols start flying. "Think you can keep up with me flying through the mountains?" Colin asked in a joking tone.

"I'll try," Coltrane said as he slapped Majumder on his shoulder. "Let's go. I want to see how you get through the Himalaya Mountains."

The first beams of sunlight were starting to appear in the Eastern sky as the two-cargo aircraft started to circle around a dirt road in a Chinese valley. Bart was following behind Majumder and listening to his narrative about the landing field which was nothing more than a road.

"You can see the road is clear of any obstacles and is quite smooth. They keep it well maintained just for our deliveries. It's a remote area of China some twenty miles north of the Vietnam border. They're safe here from Japs and patrols, but they do have two Jap air patrols a day. They're very predictable. One after breakfast and one after lunch. The Japs aren't too aggressive in the area. They're constantly looking for the Viet Minh Resistance fighters. The Viet Minh are taking a heavy toll of the Japs near Hanoi and much further south." Majumder paused as he focused his attention to the power and propeller settings as he leveled out at 1,500 feet above the ground below. Then he continued. "We'll land to the north on the road. Set down as soon as you can as you only have 4,700 feet before the hills at the end. That should be more than enough room for a pilot flying a desk," he said poking fun at Coltrane. "When you get to the end, just follow the people on the ground. They'll help you go between those hills into the protected area."

Bart could see what he was talking about. He noticed a canyon area at the north end of the road. It was about 3,000 feet by 2,500 feet in area with jungle surrounding the open area. Coltrane followed

Majumder, a mile behind. The landing was smooth. Coltrane seized the opportunity to take a jab at Colin Majumder. "Don't you wish Barakpur was this well maintained?" There was no reply.

As Bart taxied the C-47 to the end of the road, he saw the other C-47 literally disappear into the jungle. A man in black pajamas started to direct Coltrane to a specific part of the road that went between two hills covered in trees and vines. He only had a few feet of clearance one either side of the 44-foot wing tips. Slowly he moved forward in the direction of the man in black with an old rifle slung over his shoulder. Suddenly, he was in the open area of the valley. He was directed to an area where the jungle reached out over the top of the cargo plane. It would be almost impossible to be seen from the air. He shut down the two engines and went to the rear. His crew chief, a young Indian lad of no more than twenty years old, already had the aluminum steps in place so Bart could get down.

There were at least thirty armed Viet Minh surrounding the aircraft when he got down. He stretched the stiffness out of his body while he waited for Colin to come to his rescue. Bart could see that most of the attention was on what was in the aircraft and not on him. That was a relief.

Colin gently worked his way through the crowd along with three other men who were older and obviously in charge.

Colin stood between Coltrane and the three gentlemen and started the introductions. "Brigadier General Bart Coltrane, may I introduce my good friends, Nguyen Sinh Cung, Vo Nguyen Giap and Pham Van Dong of the League for the Independence of Vietnam, which is also known as the Viet Minh."

Coltrane stood at attention and with a very slight polite bow, extended his hand and said, "It's my honor to meet such distinguished warriors for freedom. Your efforts against the Japanese are commendable."

The three men did not immediately react or reply to Coltrane's comments. Then the short, younger man asked, "General, why are you here?"

Stunned by the direct question, Coltrane knew he was speaking to a front-line soldier who had no time for platitudes. "I'm here to find out what has happened to our downed flight crews," Coltrane stated bluntly.

The older man with the slightly graying mustache and goatee responded, "Some are here awaiting transport out. We've no way to transport them to friendly Chinese bases. We had an arrangement with the OSS to send them back on supply planes. There hasn't been a supply plane from the Americans in almost a year. The last plane had two thousand rounds of ammunition to go with the old-pre-World War I surplus rifles. Junk at best! No food, medicine, radios, and enough modern rifles and machine guns to fight the enemy. Can you explain why the delay and why we're given these old obsolete guns and a handful of ammunition?"

Coltrane looked the leader in the eye and replied, "I'm at a loss for an explanation, Sir. I'm not aware of the details of your arrangement with the OSS. I do not represent them. I represent the United States Army Air Force and General Curtis Lemay, Commander of the XX Air Force. It's obvious that your efforts and needs have not been made known to the Army Air Force and General Lemay. Perhaps, this would be a good time for you to tell me exactly what your objectives and critical needs are. I'll do what I can to resolve the impasse and get what you need."

Nguyen Sinh Cung smiled and said, "It is said that a picture is worth a thousand words. Walk with me and see for yourself, General." The man started for the tree line followed by the others. As he walked, he motioned to the men standing around who immediately went to the two aircraft to unload them.

Coltrane looked at the leader and the other two and asked, "What association do you have with the Resistance leader known as Ho Chi Minh?"

Nguyen Sinh Cung, the man with the goatee, smiled and said, "I'm Ho Chi Minh. I took the name for protection while I was exiled to France. I'm the one your OSS called Agent 19."

Coltrane saw something in the man's eyes that spoke of integrity and intelligence. He had come to the right man to get a clear picture of the war in Indochina.

"General, we're a people that have endured countless attempts by outsiders to conquer this land. The latest invader is the Japanese. They too will be repelled as all others have been in the past and will be in the future."

It may take time and blood, but in the end, we shall endure until victory is achieved. Your western world, Europe and the Japanese think in months and years. We don't think in these terms. We look at the long term no matter how long it takes. This is our home and we're prepared to fight to the death, no matter how long it takes. This is a large country with a diversity of climate and terrain. It's home to us. For you, it's a mountainous jungle with endless rice paddies and oppressive heat. Vietnam is a very difficult area to fight in for outsiders. We employ a completely different form of combat. We use the land and millions of people to our advantage. We choose to use the unconventional form of warfare. The peaceful rice farmer you see tending his rice fields by day is a warrior by night that ambushes your patrols and bombs your bases. The aggressor doesn't know who the enemy is and can't arbitrarily kill everyone they see. Your own morals and world opinion would never allow such slaughter. We've tens of thousands watching the enemy's every move and reporting it to us within a few hours or less. We've agents working for the Japanese in all of their offices and facilities, so we know everything that they're planning. Our intelligence gathering capability is very extensive. So, you're in a quandary as to how to fight us." He looked at the intensely interested Coltrane. "Please don't be offended by my use of the term 'you.' It's meant to reflect all outsiders, not you or your country individually."

Coltrane nodded and continued to walk by this astute leader known as Ho Chi Minh. Ho could see that he had Coltrane's interest and attention. He would not lose this opportunity to educate this American general.

"This area inside the protective hills is our training and supply base. We call it Happy Valley," Ho continued. "We're outside the normal Japanese areas of military influence and domination. We see air patrols a couple of times a day. Our primitive communication system alerts us when they take off from Hanoi and what direction they're headed. We're able to hide until they're gone. The valley is perfect for us. It's only twenty miles to the border. We can be safe from the Japanese here. The surrounding mountains cannot be scaled by a significant military force. We've automatic weapons on top to fight off any attempts. We've a nice stream going through Happy Valley for water and fish.

"It's an excellent headquarters for planning and training. We train over a thousand Viet Minh every month. They're then deployed to various parts of the country to establish individual cells of four to eight men. Each cell is trained by those who are trained here on political philosophy, community development and guerrilla warfare. The military planning and execution are directed by Vo Nguyen Giap here," he said pointing to the short man walking next to Majumder. "On any given day or night, he executes anywhere from four to ten attacks on the Japanese or French."

Coltrane reacted to the mention of the French. "But the French are on our side."

"They're ruthless colonists. They take and take and give back nothing," said Dong.

"So true," Ho said. "The French are only a friend until we eliminate the Japs then they'll resume their conquest for all of our resources. The French cannot be trusted."

They had walked well into the trees. They had come upon what appeared to be a dispensary or makeshift hospital. There were twenty or thirty men lying on mats with serious wounds. Medical personnel were applying crude medical treatments to the suffering soldiers. Coltrane was horrified.

Ho pointed to the men and their individual maladies. "This man has gangrene and we've no medicine to treat him with. We'll give him a natural painkiller to make him comfortable until he dies. This man needs surgery to be saved. We've so little for our people. The medicine that you and this black-market thief brought in today will be of enormous help, but it will only go so far. We need more." Ho had affectionately put his arm around Majumder's neck. "If it wasn't for this wartime profiteer, we would be in real trouble. He takes the very few dollars that we can get and supplies us with what he can. Our hearts and loyalty to Colin is without limit. He's our only outside help. Your promised support has been almost non-existent," Ho said in despair. They walked over to a group of soldiers squatting around a small fire cooking rice. Ho reached down and picked up one of the weapons and handed it to Coltrane. "Do you recognize this weapon?"

Coltrane took the weapon and looked at it then answered, "Yes, it's a British Enfield musket from 1857." Then he pointed to a small stack of British Enfield rifles that predate World War I. "I recognize that old Enfield No. 4 rifle as well. Don't tell me this is what you're fighting the Japs with?"

"Unfortunately, these are our main weapons. Most of them were supplied by your OSS. We also have twenty or so Lewis machine guns from World War I as well. We take the more modern weapons from the Japanese we kill, but that's not enough. We need a large volume of modern weapons and lots of ammunition if we're to be effective against our mutual enemy," Ho said as he watched Coltrane's facial reaction. He saw the expression of a man shocked and dismayed at the revelation.

Bart looked at the military mastermind of the Viet Minh, Vo Nguyen Giap and asked, "How do you fight the Japs with these antiques?"

The genial man smiled and said, "We seldom rely on the guns. We watch the enemy and learn his weakness, then attack swiftly and disappear. The habits and standing procedures of an organized army is always its worst enemy. They're predictable in everything they do. That gives our guerrilla force an advantage and we exploit it to the fullest. The Japanese have a rigid chain of command and attack procedures that makes them vulnerable to our type of hit and run attacks."

Coltrane shook his head in amazement, "How many units do you have in the field attacking the Japs?"

Giap looked at Bart and said proudly, "We've over twenty thousand operational cells from here to the southern tip of Vietnam. We hope to have three times that number in the field by the end of 1945. Our nationwide recruiting is going very well. In addition to the trained strike cells, we have over 380,000 trained troops ready to fight. All we need are guns, ammunition and explosives."

Coltrane looked at him and nodded in acknowledgement. Then he turned to Ho Chi Minh, "Sir, you said that there were some downed airmen here. Could I take them back with me?"

"Yes, you brought supplies and you've learned firsthand what we're doing for the war effort. Now you know what we need to defeat the Japanese. Can I assume that you'll make your superiors aware of our situation and efforts?"

"Yes, sir, you can count on my reporting this through my chain of command to the President. You can also count on additional supplies from the U.S. Army Air Force operating out of India and China," Coltrane said with confidence.

Ho pointed to another area of the jungle. As he got closer, they could see U.S. Army aircrews huddled together and laying on mats. They came to attention as Ho approached. Then a Lieutenant Colonel saw Coltrane, with great effort he got up, came to attention, and saluted. "Sir, Lieutenant Colonel Roger K. Danforth reports to the General."

"At ease, gentlemen," Coltrane replied. "Can I give you men a lift back home?"

There was a chorus of cheers from the group.

"How have you been treated?" asked Coltrane.

"Sir, it's been very rough, but we've been treated as well as can be expected. They just don't have anything. They can't take care of their own people, much less our guys. But they do what they can."

Coltrane turned to Ho and Majumder and asked, "Can we take those eight really bad soldiers back to Kunming for medical treatment? I think our medical staff there can save them and get them back to you ready to carry on the fight for your homeland."

There was no immediate answer from Ho. He stared into Coltrane's eyes for a few seconds. Then he reached out and grabbed Bart by his shoulders and said, "We have a new friend and ally."

Bart turned to the Army Lieutenant Colonel and instructed him to put his sick and wounded on board the aircraft then put the Viet Minh casualties on board as well.

"Sir, this has been a real eye opener. I'm sure that President Roosevelt and General Lemay will ensure that additional supplies of weapons, food, ammunition, medicine and other useful equipment will be forthcoming," Coltrane said with authority. Ho looked at Coltrane and extended his hand and said, "Thank you, General, I shall count on your support. Have a safe flight back."

Just after the two C-47 took off, Coltrane looked at the very rough terrain and made a radio call to Majumder. "You know Colin, I'd hate to be in a war against those three. I don't think that we could win a war in these conditions against them."

Majumder replied, "Strange, Giap said that he would hate to be in a war against you and others like you."

There was silence as they flew to Kunming.

Chapter Thirty-Nine

Bart Coltrane gently touched the big B-29 down on the island of Guam, the home of the XXI Bomber Command. He was flying one of four new replacement aircraft joining the air war against Japan.

As he got out of the aircraft, the Commanding General's staff car drove up. The young Army Captain riding in the back got out and came up to Bart. "Sir, General Lemay sends his compliments and requests that you join him at the headquarters."

"Very well," Bart said and looked at his aide-de-camp Lieutenant Ford and Sargent Major Royston. "Grab my gear and take it to the BOQ then meet me at General Lemay's office. Sergeant Major, get a drink or two and meet me at General Lemay's office at 0800 hours tomorrow." Then he got into the car.

"Bart!" Lemay said in a tone that was almost a yell. "How did you get in the pilot seat of a B-29?"

"They were short a Command Pilot for the ferry mission here. I got a B-29 check out in Wichita and I took advantage of the situation."

"Good for you. The Chief of Staff would call the MP's on me if I even got close to one. Come in here and let's talk." Lemay looked at a Master Sergeant standing by the door to his office. "Nobody disturbs us. You understand?"

"Yes sir, nobody disturbs you," he replied as he closed the door.

"Sit down, Bart. You came at a bad time. I'm falling on my face out here. Our results are dismal at best. I am not hurting the Japs and the Navy is pointing out our ongoing failures to anyone who will listen. Strategic bombardment is looking really weak just when we need a strong second act after Europe. I am searching for an answer and not finding a damned thing."

Bart remained silent and listened as Lemay recounted his problems from the high winds, equipment maintenance, ongoing engine problems and no concentrated bomb strikes on the critical war plants in Japan. Then he sat down and looked at Bart. "I'm surprised they leave me in command."

"What am I overlooking or missing, Bart?" he asked.

"Well, I have been reading the reports going to Hap Arnold office and I may have a possible solution. But it may be quite risky. It sure will not be favorably looked upon by the world community and the hand wringing liberals in Washington." He said pausing to get Lemay's reaction, and then continued. "Curt, you're trying to pinpoint bomb the main industrial plants that do little more than assemble a final product. You need to go to the source of the parts. Hit the civilian buildings that surround the plants. There is the source of the parts and the backbone of the Japanese industrial capability. Let me ask you a question. What is the main composition of the structures around the plant and for that matter all of Japan?" he said as he got up and walked to the wall map.

Lemay looked puzzled at first then replied, "I know, wood, paper and other non-metal materials."

"Right, flammable structures!" Bart said in a strong voice.

"Look at this," Bart said. "If you flew at low altitude at night and used incendiary bombs you could destroy large areas around the plants which will halt production and terrorize the population. It will break their will to continue the war. Use the wind to spread the fire across your target. You don't have to be in formation to be effective. Just set up your flights where they drop their loads in a solid five-mile line a mile upwind of your target area. The wind will carry the fire and destruction across your target. Just like you did in Germany only on a bigger scale.

"Yes, I know, and I thought of that and even designed a plan to do just that, but I've been reluctant to submit to headquarters. We tried this in China, and it worked but we came under global condemnation. Washington would go rat shit crazy, and the flight crews will think I'm insane. The problem in the public eyes would be that the raids will kill thousands of men, women and children in the resulting firestorm. The world will think me worse than Hitler since we would be focusing our bomb pattern on civilian targets. But you're right, it would do the job," Lemay said as he pondered what he had just been told. "Thanks, I feel better about the plan. The plan may save strategic bombardment, not to mention hundreds of flight crews and reduce the need for a costly invasion of the mainland of Japan. I guess I will have to accept the public scorn for the greater good." Lemay got up looking somewhat relieved and went to Coltrane and put his hand on his shoulder and said, "Thanks again. Now what's the latest on 'The Gadget' and the temperament in Washington?"

Coltrane sat back down and started a detailed report. "Groves is driving everyone nuts as usual. His best guess is that they will be able to test 'The Gadget' in late June or early July. You know the problems from there. Is Tibbets up and operational here yet?"

"Yes, security is still a problem with them," he replied. "Everyone wonders why they're not flying strike missions with the others. It does look suspicious, but it can't be helped. Anything new on separating the Army Air Force from the Army?"

"Sure. Roosevelt is for it, but not until after the war. He sees the need, but the Army and Navy don't see it that way as usual. I think it will work out in time. Personally, I see a threat developing in the post war situation with Russia. Stalin is getting healthy and cocky these days now that Hitler is about gone and we have pumped money, supplies, more money, raw materials and even more money into their economy. I see them as a future threat to our security. We must capitalize on that threat to get Congressional support to develop a strategic air capability to keep Russia at bay," Bart recounted.

"What about the Convair B-36 development?" Lemay asked.

"I spoke to Ted Hall recently. It's going to become a reality for us, but not in time to use against Japan. But it will be a fully intercontinental bomber that is nuclear capable. It will be our vehicle to a separate service to defend the USA against the Russians."

"Very well put, Bart," a smiling Lemay said. Still problems with the bird itself?"

"Yeah! They have a series of design problems involving the hydraulic and fuel tanks that must be fixed, otherwise it's going to be a flying hydraulic leak." It still cannot be refueled in air like we hoped. It is slower than constipation and uses way too much fuel for a 6,000-mile range. If it wasn't for the four jets they added, it would not get off the ground fully combat loaded," he said in despair. "Curt, we must think of it as an interim strike platform. Pray that George Schairer and the Boeing boys can make that model 424 idea fly. We need a pure jet bomber to provide us with the true deterrent that we will need in the future. The jet bomber is the future for the US Strategic Air capability and the new separate Air Force branch."

"Well, Bart, you've said a hell of a lot in the past 35 minutes, and I appreciate it. Are you going to see Hap soon?" Lemay asked.

"Yes sir, he and I are meeting up in Washington early next week. He has to brief the President and he wants input on the same matters that we have discussed and to know how you're going to pull a rabbit out of the hat out here," Coltrane said. "Can I tell him that you're going to use the Germany fire-bombing plan?"

Lemay sat back in his chair and drew in a long breath of concern and replied, "Yes and may God help us!"

"When are you leaving?" Lemay asked.

"Tomorrow or the next day depending on what space is available on an eastbound aircraft," he said.

"Don't worry, I'll get you out of here late tomorrow. Now let's go get a drink and something to eat. I feel like eating for a change," Lemay said as he headed for the door.

Helen tells me that you are going to be a father soon," Lemay said in a warm tone of voice. "Yes, we were surprised to find that out last month. It should be out of the hanger and on the ramp by early August," Bart said proudly.

Chapter Forty

"Damn, it's cold," Bart thought as he got out of the taxi that he and Annabel flagged down in front of the Ritz Hotel for the short ride to the Connaught Hotel in the Mayfair district of London. He helped Annabel out and then walked quickly inside. The hotel general manager was there to greet them and escort the couple to the ballroom where the annual St. Dwynwen's Day gala was to be held. Traditionally, Annabel and her family hosted the charity event to raise money for disabled veterans from World War I. Princess Elizabeth and her boyfriend, Navy Lieutenant Phillip Mountbatten were already there checking out every detail of the services for their friend and event Chairwoman Annabel Beddows Coltrane. The four greeted each other and headed to form the Official Receiving Line. They only had a few minutes before the Master of Ceremony, the Earl of Gloucester, formally directed the two Beefeater Guards to open the doors. The official guests represented the social elite of Great Britain and various officials from Ambassadors to Captains of Industry. This year, the Prime Minister was not leading the dignitaries, due to a virus. Churchill was an institution at this charity gala, so his absence was deeply missed. The line moved quickly as usual until the arrival of Field Marshal Montgomery and General Eisenhower. There was spontaneous applause as they arrived and joined the line of dignitaries. Montgomery led the military delegation. When he was formally introduced to the Chairperson, Duchess Annabel Beddows Coltrane, he made the perfunctory greetings, he turned slightly to the left and gestured to the other military officers and said, "Duchess, I hope that you don't mind my bringing these other chaps that seem to be passing through London enroute to Berlin." There was immediate laughter and polite applause.

"The honor is all mine and welcome, gentlemen," she said with the grace and dignity of a queen. Montgomery then said, "Annabel, dear, this is General Dwight Eisenhower and his Chief of Staff, Major General Bedell Smith. You, of course know my good friend, Sir Hugh Dalton and this is his American colleague, Colonel Bill Donovan."

"Thank you, Monty, I have had the pleasure to meet everyone in your party except Colonel Donovan," she said.

Eisenhower moved just past Annabel with a flowing move to just in front of Bart, "Colonel Donovan is here to have a chat with one of America's finest young Generals," he said with his eyes fixed on Bart's, as he shook his hand. "Bart, the President sends his warmest regards and compliments on the work that you have been doing. According to the President, you have been able to mix oil and water on several sensitive programs. I was very favorably impressed with what he had to say. Besides forbidding me to recruit you for my Senior Staff, he asked me to arrange a private meeting between you and Colonel Donovan tonight if you have time."

"Of course, sir, give me a few minutes to finish the receiving line and I am all yours," Bart said still in shock from the accolades offered by Eisenhower. Then he motioned for the hotel manager who was observing from behind the line. He quietly asked him to find a private room for General Eisenhower and party so they could have a short meeting. He also asked for a bottle of the hotel's best scotch and cognac be made available to them.

It took Coltrane almost ten minutes to complete the formalities and arrive at the private room. When he went in, Eisenhower was just finishing off a snifter of cognac as he headed to the door with Bedell Smith.

Ike shook his hand and said, "I'm leaving you for the mercy of these wolves." Then he departed with a sly smile on his face. Bart knew he was about to become a feast for the two spies.

Bart looked around the room and saw that there was only Dalton, Donovan and another man. It suddenly dawned on him that it was the OSS man that he dropped into Norway. "Mr. X."

Dalton got up and handed Bart a snifter and poured an inch of cognac into the glass. Then he looked at the two OSS agents sitting there smiling like the cat that ate the canary. Then he added another inch. "Bart," Dalton said with some caution in his voice, "I believe that you have met both of these gentlemen in the past," Colonel Donovan needs no introduction, but the other chap ...."

"Yes, Mr. X," Coltrane said as he interrupted Dalton as he approached the man.

Mr. X got up smiling and extended his hand, "My name is Sears. Avery Sears. I'm a Colonel in the Army attached to the OSS. That was some ride you gave me to Norway. I understand that you did over 220 drops like that one ... and you are still alive ... amazing," he said in a warm tone of admiration.

Colonel Donovan leaned back on the overstuffed leather chair and put his hands behind his head while gazing at the crystal chandelier almost above him and softly interjected, "What are your plans for after the war, General? I understand that you're getting out!"

Coltrane was caught off guard by that little-known fact. "Yes, sir, that is correct. I didn't know that had become general knowledge."

Donovan smiled, "Actually, it hadn't. We, or should I say our British counterparts here, came across your plans sort of indirectly. They saw where a newly formed British company named Acacia Air Freight had been formed in the UK. to engage in domestic and international air freight business. The name on the application was Annabel Beddows Coltrane. About the same time, we and the FBI became aware of a rather large purchase of civilian versions of the Douglas C-47 and C-54 transports. Well, as you can imagine it didn't take us long to figure out the plan. Our discrete inquiries on both sides of the Atlantic painted a clearer picture. You will be leaving at some point after the war to take over the expansion of the fledgling business. Initially, your operations will start out of Heathrow, servicing the UK and most of Western Europe. You will also start a smaller operation out of Hong Kong, servicing Kunming, Shanghai, Yokohama and Manila. You plan to expand to regional hubs in Genoa, Italy, Gibraltar and make Manila a hub for the Philippines area. How am I doing so far?" Donovan asked in a patronizing fashion then continued, "You had originally planned to service south and central Africa, India and Southeast Asia before you decided that was too much capital to risk on a startup business," Donovan stared at a motionless and expressionless Coltrane. "You have already recruited a bunch of your old crew and couple of Dalton's boys as well, your wife and her chartered accountants and solicitors have examined every aspect that you presented and found the plan "reasonable," as he started laughing. "Reasonable, in accounting talk means a probable success. Your plan is excellent, General. Your only hang-up is the fact that you really don't want to leave your friends in the service hanging on a limb when you leave. Admirable, but unnecessary. You want to see strategic bombardment become a separate branch of the service and the employment of new weapons and aircraft to deter future aggression on the United States. Both are inevitable whether you are active duty or not. You have been very instrumental in that area. Time will see both of your goals become reality. Your heart is in the right place and so is your civilian future." Donovan said as he watched for Bart to think on that statement and react.

Bart did react as anticipated and asked, "you said that my heart was in the right place as a civilian. What do you mean by that, Colonel?

"You don't have to be in the service and wear a uniform to be of service to the President and the United States of America," Donovan's voice softly said with hard conviction. "The air freight business that you are planning can be of enormous benefit and service to our country as well as our British friends here," he said slapping Dalton on the back as he stood up. "As General Eisenhower said earlier, the plan that Dalton and I are going to propose has the approval of both the President and Sir Winston.

"What the fuck is going on here?" Coltrane said in a burst of anger," My new wife and I came up with a plan where she and I could build a "Mom and Pop" business together. It was to be something that two people in love could do together and have fun doing it. Lord knows we aren't doing it for the money. Her estate and assorted businesses income are many times more than we can ever spend. Money is not a factor, only the ability to do something together. Nothing more! You got into my personal life and want to turn a fun and loving venture into something else."

Dalton raised his hand gesturing for peace and the floor. Coltrane became quiet but totally focused on Dalton. "Bart, you haven't heard the proposal yet so why the anger?" Dalton asked.

Coltrane said nothing but nodded as if to tell them to proceed. Then he went over to the table and freshened his drink before taking a seat at the table. Dalton and Donovan also took seats at the table with drinks in hand.

Donovan continued, "First of all, your wife makes no secret of this venture and everything we know is public information if you look hard enough and we did. You don't buy that many and type of aircraft without the government knowing and being involved. There is still a war on! We do respect your intent and objectives. It is not our plan to change your plan, only to expand it to accommodate a serious intelligence need that both of our countries will have in the future.

Let's take another approach to this if you will permit," Dalton said as he looked for an approving nod from Bart.

"Presently, you are going to hire Zak Middleton to run the company while you are off being an active-duty officer until the end of the war. He will open the main office at Heathrow and sales offices in about ten places in the UK. Sharp and Royston have applications in for release. I'm sure you'll get them approved through your connections in Washington. You'll hire British and American combat pilots as they become available. As the war ends, you'll open sales offices in the larger European cities and start service there as the war ends. You plan to make Genoa and Gibraltar hubs for your 600-mile coverage area. The same can be said for your south Pacific hubs out of Hong Kong and Manila. These plans are economically practical and very viable. You plan to continue your active-duty service until the war is over and you have accomplished some specific objectives that you have promised Hap Arnold and Curt Lemay. So far this is great for everyone. This keeps you on active duty for the end of the war. Then you two love birds will expand and develop the company as the market demands. All of this is fine with me and Donovan. What we want you to do is to add a south and central Africa hub, and India-Burma-Thailand hub and expand your south Pacific hub. Not only with 600-mile feeder routes, but more long-haul routes as well. The OSS or friends of the OSS will enter into a long-term contract with Acacia that will provide an annual retainer equal to your operating budget for the expanded system. Donovan will also get you all the experienced combat pilots and crews that you will need. You or Zak interview them and select the ones you want. You fly all of your normal commercial flights as planned. You will charge your primary client, our two organizations, the standard rate. You can't lose money! The only requirement or string as we say, is that the pilots sent to Eastern Europe, Africa, India and south Pacific hubs are our trained agents … and our missions have priority over other commercial missions. That should seldom be the case, but if a conflict presents itself, our mission goes first. Yes, we are conducting substantial intelligence operations, but it will be done very discretely. That is a must for your operation and ours as well. If our operations and cover are compromised, it defeats our long-term objectives. We'll have a 'contractor's representative' like Avery at each hub to coordinate our needs with your local manager. We're putting our best men in these locations. Avery Sears at your main office at Heathrow, Pete Cyr in Hong Kong, John Webster in India and Mr. Drake and another of our chaps in Africa," Dalton paused to let it all sink in and get a reaction from Bart. Bart remained silent and motionless, so Donavan went on.

"Every effort will be made to help you complete your obligations to Hap and Lemay as fast as possible cutting any post war requirements down smartly. Nobody outside our group can know our arrangement for obvious reasons." He concluded by pouring more cognac into his snifter and looked eye to eye with Coltrane for an answer.

Coltrane said nothing but broke the stare with Dalton. He took a long drink from the snifter and looked back over the room and the occupants. Just then the door opened, and Annabel walked in and went over to the chair next to Bart's and sat down.

"My feet are killing me." Besides standing for so long, I need medical attention on both feet. Monty, may be a great field general, but he can't dance worth a crap." Everyone laughed and sipped the cognac. Everyone was still awaiting an answer from Bart. Annabel quickly saw the situation and broke the silence.

"From the silence I take it Old Iron Ass hasn't agreed yet." That caught Bart's attention. His head snapped toward her.

"You know the proposal then?"

"Yes. Churchill and this mutt Donovan double-teamed on me in Winnie's office yesterday." It sounded like it would fit in with our overall plans and it was an important intelligence operation. I told them that it would be up to you. Besides, it will get you out of the service and its dangers and back into the cockpit with the mistress you love so much. You'll be flying again and that will make you happy. So, I'll put up with your cockpit mistress if you want to take their proposal."

Bart looked over to Sears and asked, "Zak starts opening the office at Heathrow in December. When can you start?"

Chapter Forty-One

It was slightly after 4 pm. on a beautiful April afternoon in Washington when three Secret Service Agents quickly entered the office of the Vice-President. The lead agent said in a strong and urgent tone. “Mr. Vice President, please come with us to the White House. This is a national emergency!” An agent led the way to the waiting limousine with the other two on each arm of the Vice President. There was nothing but silence as they drove a short distance to the White House. They silently took Truman up the elevator to the Presidential Residence. When the door opened, Truman saw Eleanor Roosevelt and Harry Hopkins standing with six or eight military and government officials and the Chief Justice of the Supreme Court.

Eleanor came over to Truman extended her hand and said, “Harry, so good of you to come over so quickly. We have lost Franklin. He died about an hour ago in Warm Springs. It is now up to you to lead our country. What can we do to help you?”

“Eleanor, I am so sorry. What can we do for you?” a shocked Truman said as tears started forming in his eyes.

Harry Hopkins gently grabbed his elbow and led him to the Chief Justice with Eleanor following him and stood next to him. The Chief Justice looked at Truman and asked, “Harry S. Truman, are you prepared to take the Oath of Office for the Presidency of the United States of America?”

Truman responded in a heavy voice, “I am and may God help us all.”

After the formal swearing in and signing of the order assuming the Presidency and Commander-in-Chief of the military, Harry Hopkins pulled him over to a tight gathering of officials and generals. "Mr. President, there is a lot to do and little time. I will collect the cabinet and other resignations and …."

"STOP! Truman commanded. No resignations from anyone. Everyone stays where they are. Nobody gets out of work … and that especially goes for you, Mr. Hopkins."

"Very well, sir. We need to brief you on the situation diplomatically and militarily. The war plans and other domestic issues," Harry Hopkins said as they walked into the Cabinet Room where there were a dozen people standing along the walls with charts in hand.

The President looked at Hopkins and said with a smile, "This is going to take longer than an hour, isn't it, Harry?"

Chapter Forty-Two

August 6, 1945 – three lone B-29s from the 509th Composite Bomb Group took off from Tinian headed towards Hiroshima. A little after 8 o'clock in the morning Colonel Paul A. Tibbets, the Air Mission Commander, and the pilot of the *Enola Gay*, authorized the bombardier Major Thomas Ferebee to release, the 'Special Weapon' or 'Gadget' as it had become known; minutes later sixteen thousand tons of TNT equivalent was released by one bomb. A second Plutonium device was dropped from *Bockscar* on the 9th of August destroying Nagasaki. The devastation was so extensive the Emperor of Japan directed his government to surrender without condition.

World War II was over!

Chapter Forty-Three

General Stillwell peered out the transport window intently. He looked over the vast devastation of the once mighty industrial city. Stillwell turned from the window, pondered the scene below. Yokohama Airport was alive with foreign correspondents and radio newscasters. Many newsmen are on hand for this monumental occasion, some with news reel cameras, handheld and on tripods, atop a specially constructed media stand. The stand was located a long distance from the airplane arrival position. One of the radio broadcasters with microphone in hand was telling people around the world listening, "And … we continue our live broadcast from the Yokohama Airport here where military commanders from all over the Pacific continue arriving to attend the formal signing of the Peace treaty. The ceremony is scheduled to take place on board the *U.S.S. Missouri*, now lying at anchor, in Tokyo Bay itself!"

One of the camera crew directors on the stand above the broadcaster yelled out,

"There's General Lemay!" Lemay departed from his four-engine transport, followed only by his aide. They crossed to a waiting vehicle, a rickety Japanese auto, got in and drove off. Describing the arrival of Lemay, the broadcaster said, "Just alighting from his plane now, Ladies and Gentlemen, is Major General Curtis Emerson Lemay … old 'Iron Pants' himself! Lemay's relentless B-29 forays against the home islands were the overwhelming force that finally brought the Japs to their knees without the long-planned surface invasion of the Japanese homeland itself … an invasion that some say would surely have cost the lives of millions Allied troops and Japanese!"

Stillwell alighted from his airplane.

"The broadcaster continued, "There's Vinegar Joe! It's 'Vinegar' Joe Stillwell. General Stilwell was to command the invasion of Japan, an invasion that will never be.

* * *

Lemay's car pulled up to the Yokohama jetty on September 2, 1945, where a Navy barge was waiting to take Lemay and his aide out to the *Missouri*. Lemay and the aide got out of the car and walked toward the jetty. Suddenly, Lemay stopped before boarding the barge, ostensibly gazing at the fleet anchored in the bay itself.

"That is impressive, Captain," Lemay said to his aide. "Even if it is Navy!" Lemay's features were set darkly, gazed at the fleet, and then walked a few steps away from the jetty.

The aide, sensed Lemay's reluctance to board the barge, attempted to soothe the situation. "You'll only have to be on board for an hour or so, General," the Aide said reassuringly.

"Dammit!" Lemay exclaimed. "It's still a BATTLESHIP, Captain!" Presently, Lemay braced himself and they entered the barge which got under way immediately. Lemay went to be seated and found Bart Coltrane, Colonel Wild Bill Donovan and Sir Hugh Dalton also on board.

"What a pleasant surprise," Lemay said, as he extended his hand to the three gentlemen. "To what do I owe the honor to have Bart Coltrane and the world's top spies on my barge?"

Bart went closer to Lemay and said "Curt, of course we're here for the big surrender, but I wanted to personally tell you of my decision to get out of active duty and go on the Ready Reserves list."

Lemay was stunned but kept his composure. Coltrane continued, "I had a personal talk with the President a couple of weeks ago. He told me that he would agree to a separate Air Force. It may take a year or two to go through the political wars, but it would happen. With that task being a *fait accompli*, I have accomplished the most critical part of the objectives that you and Hap gave me. Now

I plan to become a civilian and join my wife in the development of an international air freight company. It's something that she and I can do together. Granted, we don't need the money, but this is a labor of love. We can have fun building something together. I really do love her, Curt."

Bart started to continue when Donovan interrupted, "Curt, it's not like he is totally out of the picture. Truman has me developing a more modern and extensive intelligence operation out of the existing OSS. He does not want the USA to ever be attacked without warning again. Bart and his lovely bride have agreed to accept a lucrative contract with our group and with Dalton's MI-6 to fly our personnel and cargo under strict secrecy. Truman personally gave this his blessing. It's an important piece of our country's future clandestine intelligence gathering program."

"Bart then continued, "I will always be available to help you and the Air Force, but I will be in a business suit instead."

Lemay sat down without comment. He carefully thought about what he had just been told. Then he smiled and said, "That rag-tag air freight operation in India that you set up was the beginning of your operation, wasn't it?"

"Yes, sir. It's now owned and operated by Acacia Air Freight, Limited of London."

Lemay slapped his knees with both hands as he got up smiling. "I'm proud of what you have done for me, our country and strategic bombardment. You've done more than your share. Now, you're going to continue your service to our great country from a little different approach. Congratulations, you, and Annabel will do fine. I wish you two all the luck in the venture. I especially appreciate the job that you will be doing for these two spies. They deserve a good man like you."

Lemay had just finished as the captain's barge bumped against the *U.S.S. Missouri*, and the group climbed the stairway to the main deck and the surrender ceremony. The Japanese delegation formally signed the surrender documents. Hundreds of military personnel, soldiers, and sailors gathered to witness the event from various vantage points. The *U.S.S. Missouri* band played 'STARS AND STRIPES FOREVER.'

Lemay stood along with Coltrane and Donovan and Dalton amidst the American delegation ostensibly watching the ceremony. When the signing is completed, the distant roar of B-29 engines was heard, attracting everyone's attention. Lemay's aide glanced at the General, who was grinning from ear to ear. Hundreds of B-29s flew overhead in salute. Lemay had his eyes fixed on the mass of B-29s overhead. He thought to himself, "This *makes all the headaches worth it! I hope these tank and anchor lovers understand they are watching the beginning of America's new first line of defense.*"

* * *

Two days later, General Stilwell's four engine transport pulled into park at Lemay's headquarters on Guam. General Stilwell gazed out the window as the aircraft maneuvered to its parking position. Lemay stood at his desk putting personal papers in a briefcase.

Kissner entered, opened the door, peered in ... astonished, he said, "It's General Stilwell, Curt!"

Surprised, Lemay said "Stilwell! You have to be kidding?"

Colonel Kissner opened the door wider and General Stilwell strode into the room, crossed to shake hands with Lemay.

Lemay said with respect, "General Stilwell."

The General simply shook hands, still not speaking. Lemay was disconcerted and gestured to the briefcase, "I ... I was just getting a few things together. Rosie and I, are flying a 29 back to Washington ... non-stop!"

"Yeah, I heard," Stilwell said grinning. "Still bucking for good press!"

Lemay nodded, smiled, indicated a chair, and sat himself down as General Stilwell settled himself into a chair.

Stilwell got to the point, "Lemay … I saw Yokohama. Spent some time there in my youth … remember what it was like. It's been leveled, you know … the entire industrial area … all of it. Your B-29s, they did that."

Lemay said cautiously, "We hit it once or twice alright."

General Stilwell was beginning to grin, "I made a special trip up here on my way home. I made the stop here just to tell you something. I was too damned myopic to understand what you were trying to tell me out there in the Changdu Valley last year … and later here on Guam. Lemay, I've been wrong about strategic bombardment! About the whole concept Billy Mitchell laid out years ago."

Lemay was moved by Stilwell's candor. "Well, you weren't traveling in the military minority, General."

General Stilwell responded quietly, "I know. You people had a helluva rough row to hoe in getting across the concepts you knew would work in this man's war! But … you did. And I guess that's what important … important to the whole damned free world as a matter of fact!" As he searched his tunic pockets, he continued, "I had dinner with some of your big-wigs up there in Tokyo. General Spaatz told us he'd sent a communiqué to Norstad after he had inspected your operation out here. I copied it down in long hand. Ah … here it is."

Stilwell began to read from the crudely scrawled note, "Lemay's Baker Two Nine operation, the best organized and most technically and tactically proficient military organization that the world has seen to date."

Stilwell gazed at Lemay for a moment, and then said, "Guess that just about says it all." Then Stilwell rose, a resigned weariness crept into his tone, "I'm going home. I failed in China you know. Couldn't get along with that Chink Son-of-a-bitch out there! The surface invasion I might have commanded against the Japanese Homeland. Well … your B-29s took care of that! The show's all over for me, Lemay, but … I have a feeling it's just beginning for you airplane folks," he said and extended his hand. "I couldn't be more sincere when I wish you the best of luck, son." Stilwell simply got up, turned and exited, leaving Lemay gazing after him.

Chapter Forty-Four

Monday, December 3, 1945, was an unusually beautiful sunny day in London. Bart Coltrane was at the pilot's controls of a new "War Surplus" Douglas DC-4 going through the pre-take off checklist with his co-pilot. Annabel Beddows Coltrane was strapped into the jump seat just behind the two pilots with their four-month-old son Sam Coltrane. She was smiling from ear to ear and had trouble keeping her excitement from being too obvious - after all, she was a Duchess. Today this Duchess was dressed in a baggy flight suit with several grease stains visible.

Coltrane looked down the Acacia Air Freight ramp at Heathrow airport outside London. He could see the five other DC-4s and fourteen Douglas DC-3s lined up on the ramp going through the takeoff checks. Today was the day Acacia Air Freight would deploy its first aircraft to its new operating bases. The DC-4s were bound to their new homes in Gibraltar, Kinshasa, Shanghai, Hong Kong, Bangkok and Jessore, India. The DC-3s were bound for the same destinations with the addition of Manila and Genoa, Italy. As agreed, two days after the Japanese surrendered, Acacia exercised its option and purchased the entire operation in India, including the old JU52s and DC-2 aircraft relocated to the new and recently modernized operating base at Jessore, India. The dream was coming true for Annabel and Bart.

Bart looked out of the cockpit window at Royston who had driven up the flight line verifying that the aircraft were ready to depart on their individual flights to various destinations. Royston looked up at Bart with a broad smile and gave him a thumbs up and a traditional salute. Bart returned the salute and closed the side window. He depressed the transmit button on the control yoke and said, “Heathrow Tower, Acacia Air Freight, a flight of twenty aircraft is ready for takeoff.”

“Roger Acacia Air, you are cleared to taxi to Runway 27 for immediate take off!”

John R. "Rick" Taylor (OUTLAW 3) is a decorated Vietnam veteran that served in the U.S. Army for ten years. He had overseas assignments in Vietnam, Korea and Germany.

His duty assignments included Aviation, Military Intelligence and Air Defense. His first-hand military experience gives him the background needed to write "The Caves." Today he is an oil and gas executive who has returned to post-war Vietnam to engage in petroleum exploration operations in the Mekong Delta. He has met with many former North Vietnamese combat leaders, including the legendary military architect of the war, General Nguyen Vo Giap. In the early and mid-80s he was an activist for the return and full accountability of POWs and MIAs in the Vietnam War. His job has taken him to central Russia, Chechnya, Turkey, Azerbaijan and Bosnia. He was principal in the early post-war Bosnia war damage assessment and reconstruction planning efforts. Taylor still enjoys his love of flying, as well as sailing and racquetball. He started flying at age 13 and later became an Army Aviator and flew combat missions in Vietnam and Laos. He currently lives in Texas. Rick is the author of A FEW BRAVE MEN, GRUNT AIR, and THE CAVES.

For sales, editorial information, subsidiary rights information
or a catalog, please write or phone or e-mail

iBooks
Manhanset House
Shelter Island Hts., New York 11965-0342
Tel: 212-427-7139
www.ibooksinc.com
email: bricktower@aol.com

www.IngramContent.com

For sales in the UK and Europe please contact our distributor,
Gazelle Book Services
White Cross Mills
Lancaster, LA1 4XS, UK
Tel: (01524) 68765 Fax: (01524) 63232
email: jacky@gazellebooks.co.uk

www.ingramcontent.com/pod-product-compliance
Lightning Source LLC
Chambersburg PA
CBHW060556310726
48982CB00008B/1140/J